VIEWER
DISCRETION
ADVISED

Printed in Australia
Cover and internal design by Shawline Publishing Group Pty Ltd

First Printing: July 2023

Shawline Publishing Group Pty Ltd
www.shawlinepublishing.com.au

Paperback ISBN 978-1-9229-9345-8
eBook ISBN 978-1-9229-9352-6

Distributed by Shawline Distribution and Lightning Source Global

 A catalogue record for this work is available from the National Library of Australia

More great Shawline titles can be found by scanning the QR code below.
New titles also available through Books@Home Pty Ltd.
Subscribe today at www.booksathome.com.au or scan the QR code below.

VIEWER DISCRETION ADVISED

ANGUS STEVENS

To Samantha, Sachin & Edie.

Based on a true story.
Dialogue, certain events and characters have been
created for the purpose of dramatisation.
So, having taken that into account, perhaps
a more accurate statement would be:
Loosely based on a partially true story.

1

FLIGHT RISK

Takeoff isn't until 10:30 but Adam wants to be there early, to leave before everyone wakes up and avoid the hassle of helping Nina get the kids to school, so he doesn't hit 'Snooze' for a third time and instead gets cracking.

Listen to them breathe.

Standing in the hallway looking into their bedrooms, Adam does this ritual hoping to feel connected.

If I can't hear them, do I stay till I can?

Louie is on cusp of teenagerdom, with a body too big for his bed, outgrowing childhood and his dad's jokes; Ella, enjoying being ten, is surrounded by fluffy toys, with Robbie Rose Robinson the world's most adored puppy, tucked in at her feet. Her panda finger puppet is on her bedside table. They have a tradition of him taking it when he goes away. Relieved to have spotted it, Adam pops it in his pocket.

What if I just stick my head into each of their bedrooms, one after the other?

But that defeats the appreciate your whole family sleeping thing.

Well this I'm 'The Rock' angle isn't really cutting it either.

Fuck it.

Downstairs, as he tries leaving without waking the house, Nina calls out, 'Adam?'

Putting down his overnight bag he returns to their bedroom. Nina's a very expansive sleeper. Her limbs take up vast tracts of bed country.

'Heya, little Kinki, what's up?'

'Be safe.'

It strikes him as very un-Nina.

'It's only for two nights.' He kisses her neck. She nuzzles in and loops her arm over him. They hadn't touched all night so he's glad she yelled out.

'Good.'

Her arm feels nice. Then heavy. He drops his head down. It slips off. Released.

In the cab, he decides not to feel bad about how happy he is to be going.

Twenty-eight hours in the air over three days, and maybe he could have arranged things so it didn't have to be him on the road, but he wanted to go. And now, on a glorious mid-November morning, Adam's at the airport bar nearly three hours early, having a gin and tonic for breakfast. He raises his glass.

Fly to San Fran, do the presso, shoot the interviews, fly home. Done.

And it feels good.

The plane trip is perfect. He's got empty seats either side, his new headphones, endless movies, and G&Ts on call.

Drunk at 30,000 feet, he cries watching *Selma* and makes friends with the air steward.

She hands him another G&T, and asks, 'Have you seen *Green Book?*'

The night it won Best Picture, Nina ranted, 'It's a fucking travesty. White men back-slapping over *"aren't we great for not being racist"* bullshit.'

'Yeah.'

'What do you mean, "yeah"?'

'I agree.'

'Adam, you've watched *Old School* fifty times.'

'So what.'

'But you haven't got around to *Moonlight*.'

'I'm waiting for—'

'Or *A Promising Young Woman*.'

'The right time.'

'How many times have you watched *Anchorman*?'

'They're—'

'And *The Waterboy*?'

'Leave Sandler out of it.'

'These directors did *Dumb and Dumber*.'

'*Green Book* is not Sandler's fault.'

'*Something About Mary* and then this...' Nina dripped scorn, 'The Academy's Best Picture.'

'What do you reckon is the worst Best Picture?'

'And he's a flasher.'

'Huh?'

'One of the directors has flashed his dick over five hundred times.'

'Oh, come on...'

'Look it up. He's said so. Including at Cameron Diaz.'

'Okay, Kinki, I—'

'Non-aggressively, apparently. Just as a joke.'

She sipped her wine.

Adam waited. He knew the moment he started speaking she'd talk over him. He hoped that if he waited long enough she'd finish her point, but the moment dragged on, so he thought maybe he'd got it wrong and began with, 'I don't think—'

Nina pounced. 'And now dick flasher's got an Oscar for "*hooray, I'm not a racist.*"'

To the steward's question, Adam replies, 'Not yet.'

*

At San Francisco airport the arrivals line is long. Holding his passport and his overnight bag, Adam is a little hungover, sleep-deprived, but fine. He edges along with the crowd, anonymous.

When he makes it to the scanning device he pops in his passport, gets photographed, takes the printout and moves on. A customs official standing behind a wood-veneer counter compares Adam with the printout and his passport.

But the three don't match up.

'Glasses, sir.'

'Oh, right…'

Adam takes them off.

'Welcome to America.'

The hire car is a huge white Lincoln. Presumably the kid at work who booked it, had his reasons, but to Adam it's bizarre. It reminds him of his last year at uni playing *Cruis'n USA*, and the final race ending on the White House lawn, partying with Bill Clinton and a bunch of pixellated bikini babes.

When racing Louie on the Xbox Adam drew upon this *Cruis'n* experience. Louie seemed impressed until, in their post-race chat, Adam said he just tried to fang it the whole time. This made his son suspicious so he checked their settings.

'Oh my god you're on beginner and you still can't beat me.'

'It's 'cause these controllers are so pissy and fiddly.'

'You're such a bot.'

*

Adam recalibrates his brain for driving on the wrong side of the road and turns onto the freeway. He hasn't been to San Fran since he was a backpacker, and he compares his early twenties self with his present day version. It starts to get ugly and feeling himself heading down a corridor of mirrors he snaps, 'Shut the fuck up.'

Today I'm driving in San Fran and I'm feeling fine. Okay?

Okay.

His Airbnb is in the Castro, the cool, gay part of town. He chose there because it was cool and gay and therefore the most San Fran-ish part of San Fran. The photo that determined which Airbnb he'd stay in showed one side of the house spray-painted with a mural of a young girl with dreadlocks, blowing the seeds off a dandelion.

Following the host's instructions, Adam discovers the key isn't in the letter box. The text he gets from the Airbnb woman says that she isn't sure what's happened but she's just up the street so wait a moment and she'll be there.

When she arrives, Adam's sitting on the front steps, trying not to have the shits about being locked out. Like the house, the Airbnb woman is cool. She has curly brown hair, is wearing a short pink skirt, and has tats along both arms; she's all teeth and friendliness. Her partner stands on the footpath near the front the gate, watching. He's tall, skinny, and tanned, with a shaved head.

Adam gets up, but before he can step past her to give her access to the door, he is blocked in by her crouching down in front of him and picking up each of the little pot plants that line the steps.

Right in front of him kneeling at crotch height, she chats away. 'The cleaner was supposed to leave the key in the lockbox, so I don't know where it's gone, but I keep a spare one around here...'

Adam is towering over her. Jammed in between her and the front door, he feels like he is invading her space, but there's nowhere to move.

'How was your flight?'

'Good, yeah, good.'

As she keeps looking under the pots, Adam glances over at her partner, and smile-nods, but receives nothing in return.

'Success!' She stands up and leans forward. Her arm and chest graze Adam's torso en route to unlocking the door.

She suggests nearby restaurants and bars, but Adam's not listening. The intimacy of standing so close to a stranger and having chit chat while their partner lingers, is too claustrophobic. Wanting to wrap things up, Adam tries to sound San Fran and chill, 'Brilliant, thanks, awesome, yeah…'

For all its authenticity, the Airbnb listing had been tricksy in its depiction. Adam had wanted a San Fran two-storey duplex like in *Mrs Doubtfire*, but instead finds himself in a converted ground-floor apartment. The bedroom is not on the top floor with a gorgeous vista of San Fran but street level with a view of the bins. The black, metal spiral staircase in the living room that once led to the room upstairs is now closed over, leaving the handrails colliding with the roof, while Adam's sense of being stuck in the basement is compounded by the clomp of upstairs' every step.

Plus the walls are covered with paintings, none of them good. They fall into three categories: Mexican-themed blocks of colour housed in heavy, dark wood frames; buxom topless maidens done in a wishy-washy seventies style, with Hawaiian flowers in their hair, and African prints giving the fertility gods some serious respect.

Getting familiar with the place, Adam goes through unlocking, opening and shutting all the doors, windows and wardrobes. In the chest of drawers he finds a mobile phone charger and a red bra. To Adam, who grew up with a brother but no sisters and a mother who kept her thoughts and clothes to herself, the bra had once been a mysterious and wondrous thing. Now faced with this item, functional and lacy, it feels like washing.

He leaves them where he found them, closes the drawer and finds himself thinking of the night before.

Sitting opposite Nina, trying not to stress out about the fact that it wasn't the cheap and cheerful place he'd hoped for, and trying not to resent the fact that the plate-for-two was in fact two bits of fuck all, Adam had been once again struck by the sheer blaze of her. His thoughts bounced between *She's a dogmatic pain in the arse* to admitting *She's kind of magnificent*.

In full flight, Nina was a thing to behold.

She ate without any consideration of etiquette and while cutlery was acknowledged as a sound starting point, if it wasn't doing the job, using fingers was fair enough. She loved making sure that the waiter always thought hers was the best table. If served by a waitress, she didn't care quite as much, but regardless of their gender, at every nice-meal-out, she always had two options that could only ever be resolved by what the waiter thought was preferable. She loved to tip; glorified her time as a waitress and wanted to make sure that she righted the wrongs of all the nights she served tables by tipping an amount Adam found painful. Her favourite kind of waiter would be a gay man within a ten-year age radius of her, who was opinionated and a little bit fabulous.

Adam's favourite waiter was like a note slipped under a door, someone who had all the answers but was barely noticeable.

The restaurant was crowded with dark wooden tables and soft lighting. Among this tasteful setting their date night had an edge.

They hadn't seen each other much lately, so they wanted to make the most of it, especially since Adam would be gone for a few days, but he had brought with him a backlog of resentments while Nina looked like she was hunkered down awaiting his report card.

'Is that Judy Davis?'

Nina shrugged. 'Why aren't you eating the duck?'

'I'm leaving it for you.'

'I picked it 'cause I thought it was something you'd like.'

'Didn't we agree we'd just choose stuff we wanted?'

'Yeah, but you love duck and you're always saying I never consider you, so…' Nina gestured like a gameshow model presenting the prizes, 'I got the duck.'

How can she think ordering the duck makes up for the shit-ton of cooking, washing and bloody everything I've been doing lately?

'Don't you want it?'

'Thank you, it's just—'

'You're stressing out about your trip?'

'No, I just thought—'

'Presenting in the Valley, it's a big deal?'

'Not really.'

She's not even thinking she owes me a thank you.

'You said that it could totally change the business—'

'Yeah but—'

'That it was a really big deal.'

It was true, so much so that Adam was trying not to think about it at all, and instead, whether consciously or not, was focusing all his energies on Nina and the slow squeeze of his domesticated life.

If he had taken the time to consider his assumption that marriage would be an endless stream of mind-blowing moments, Adam may have realised this was based on his sixteen-year-old brain thinking how cool it'd be to be married because every day you'd see a woman naked and you could have sex whenever you wanted, and that this notion having morphed into a vague, ever-deflating sigh of, 'Is this it?' still held a disproportionately large cache in his head.

But Adam didn't get that far. He stopped at, *What's the point of eating out if we're just going to get the shits with each other?* before dutifully answering her question. 'Yeah, it's pretty big I guess.'

'It'll be fine.'

'For sure.'

'So, then what's wrong?'

'Nothing.'

'Just tell me.'

'Honestly, I just thought it really was Judy Davis.'

'So, she's still alive?'

'And it got me wondering if she's still married to Colin Friels—'

'Right...'

'And how he's only done TV and she's more famous and...' Adam paused wanting to see if she's interested. '...And whether it was true that she won the Oscar for Best Supporting Actor but that Jack Valance, when he was presenting the award, was too drunk and read out the last nominee's name as the winner which happened to be the new Spiderman's Aunt May... Moira what's-her-face? She was in *My Cousin Vinny*?'

'Marisa Tomei.'

'Yeah, exactly. So, because Jack was drunk, Judy got duped.'

'You were thinking all that?'

'Yeah... that and how she'd feel about it.'

'Okay...'

Sceptical, Nina swivelled around, checked out the woman who looked nothing like Judy Davis, and played along. 'Doesn't she have a letter from the academy saying they made a mistake and she'd actually won?'

'Isn't that what you told me?'

'I think Kate said that Paul was at their house once when he was living in Balmain and Judy showed him the letter.'

'So, I wonder what Colin thinks about all of that?'

'Thinks of what? The struggles of having a successful wife?'

'No, that—'

'You think you're Colin Friels?'

Is she joking? Or winding me up?

'Alright then, how is everything?' asked their waitress, who was not a fabulous gay man, but instead an English backpacker who behaved like an extra from *Wallace and Gromit*.

Adam fake-smile replied, 'It's great, thanks.'

'Can I get another glass of the rosé, please?'

Once she'd left, neither spoke. Adam didn't want to answer the 'Do you think you're Colin?' question but could feel Nina expecting a reply.

Have fun.

Adam sipped his beer.

Maybe she's flirting? I mean, I'm so out of practice, so maybe…

Adam took a different tack, hoping it is flirty. 'Anyways, I was reading an article about Julia Louis-Dreyfus telling a story about how she was doing a *Saturday Night Live* skit with Tina Fey and that blonde woman—'

'Amy Poehler.'

'Yeah, and they were riffing about whether they were too old to be fuckable and how all of a sudden Julia stopped finding it funny and—'

'What does this relate to?'

'Judy Davis.'

Nina leaned back. 'Go on.'

'And I saw *Husbands and Wives* when I was seventeen and it became like my roadmap to what marriage is about—'

'It's classic Woody.'

'Yeah, and after that film I saw my parents differently.'

'Why?'

'Well, do you remember how Sydney Pollack leaves Judy Davis for someone younger and—'

'You want an affair.'

'What—'

'Is that what this is all about?'

'No! At the end, Sydney and Judy get back together and—'

'You want permission to fuck around?'

'That's not what I'm saying.'

'That's exactly what you're saying.'

'No, I just, I've always used movies to make sense of life and—'

'You're wondering if you went off and fucked someone else would people see that it was my fault, like the bullshit way Woody made Judy's character into the villain.'

'Here we go!' With impeccable timing, the Wallace and Gromit waitress presented Nina with her rosé and picked up the side plates. Angry whispering now, Adam didn't wait for her to leave, 'You jump a million steps ahead, I just thought I saw Judy Davis and I started thinking about her and all of a sudden—'

'That's such bullshit.'

'It's not.'

'She's not Judy Davis and you're full of shit.'

As Nina made her point, her fork left the table. It hit the floor and clattered out of reach.

The less Nina cared about being overheard, the quieter Adam became. Back-peddling, he replied, 'That's not what I'm saying.'

'So, I'm just making it up?'

Five beers and three wines in respectively, Adam's point was lost in the sweep of what's implied and assumed. 'Kinki, you're not making it up.'

'Sure.'

'And there's no agenda.'

'Right.'

'I'm just saying, as a kid that film resonated and—'

'And you're identifying with it now as an adult—'

'Yes.'

'Because you're trapped.'

Adam stepped out one last idea. 'I don't think you understand what—'

'If you want to fuck around, just do it.'

'No, I—'

'I'm sick of this. That I'm not enough. Just fucking do it.'

'I'm not saying that—'

'Yes, you are. Just be honest.'

Adam leaned over, whispering, 'I'm just admin to you.'

'You're not a fucking housewife.'

'Everything I want I put second.'

'You think I don't?'

'No, I—'

'It's called parenting—'

'How could you get it, you're not a guy.'

Nina snorted.

Adam was incredulous. 'Are you telling me you identify with not just the mums, but also the dads at school?'

'Why not? We're just parents.'

'Riiiight… like Hamish. And fucking Pete? You can relate to them? They're guys who are basically just shitty blobs of domestic wetness and yet somehow you can relate—'

Nina, defiant: 'Yes.'

'Are you kidding me? They don't know what they want; I don't know either and yet you're telling me you, in that uniquely shit, male kind of way, you know how they feel?'

'Absolutely.'

'Imagine if I tried that crap on you.'

'It'd be great—'

'I mean, they're spineless fucks and they can't want that. I don't either. And I fucking hate sausages but I'm at fetes twenty-four seven, BBQing and packing the car and washing your undies and—' Adam's eyes darted around, looking anywhere but at her. 'If I'm not one of those sexless amoebas, then the only other option is to be a Shooter McGavin fuckwit with their checked shirts and low-carb beer, thinking they're all still players, laughing at everything like they've fucking got it all worked out, with their disposable income and ocean swims and they can bang whoever they want cause their wife's cool with it, if she knew, which she doesn't, so they're probably divorced which makes the whole thing so… Fucking. Ordinary.'

He spat out these final words, and glared at the table. Their glasses and the condiments spread out looked like the CBD. The word 'divorced' sat there too. She waited for him to look up and face her but he focused on his beer, tracing the edge of his glass with his finger as the restaurant chatter seeped in. He muttered, 'A new life awaits you in the outer colonies.'

'What—'

'The chance to begin again…'

'What's that from?'

Adam, not looking up, shook his head.

'Tell me.'

'Don't worry about it.'

'No really.'

'Blade Runner.'

'You and your fucking movies.' She snatched her wine, 'You only see what you don't have.'

They sat in silence. Got the bill. Walked home. He tried to touch her when they arrived back, but Nina avoided contact.

*

Within walking distance of his Airbnb, Adam finds a bar-restaurant with footpath seating. He orders his favourite travel meal – a Corona with a chicken burger and fries – and while waiting for his food, grabs his mobile and reads his emails. There's a bunch of questions from the office relating to things he can't fix until he returns to Sydney.

To avoid the stressful powerlessness of these office issues, and the looming expectation of the next day, he tries to distract himself by listening in on the two women sitting behind him. They are both in expensive active-wear and could be his age, or a decade older. The quality of their cosmetic surgery has Adam outsmarted, but his glance hasn't fooled anyone. One woman glares at him, happy to show her indifference to his eavesdropping.

Adam returns to his meal. As though to highlight that she isn't going to change anything for anyone, and certainly not for any man, the woman continues to recount her husband's noncommittal attempts at reconciliation. Loud and clear. Her conversation seems to be increasingly directed at Adam, so he gets busy with his burger.

Soon after, the women hug their goodbyes, unlock their silver SUVs, and drive off.

There's no way those women were going to look at me.

Why would they?

Hang on, I'm not a total flop. I got Nina to like me.

Yeah, twenty years ago.

And I hate mining, and conservative politics. I'm anti-homophobia. Anti-racism. Anti-sexism. Anti-corporate greed.

Gosh, want a biscuit?

No, I just...

Those women couldn't care less, so just get another Corona and act like it's The Fast and the Furious.

Yes, sold! And how good is Louie's impersonation of Vin, 'I don't have friends... I got family.'

So good.

See, Kinki, this whole 'I only see what I don't have' *is just not true.*

Wife, kids, house; I see it all the time.

ALTERITY

Adam's presentation is part of an HR and Technology symposium. Over the years he's tweaked his talk as the technology improves and the jargon changes, but essentially it stays the same, and the response is generally positive, so he keeps doing it. Or as they say in agency-land, rinse and repeat. But this gig is different because although he's travelled to other places to speak, he's never been to Silicon Valley, let alone presented at one of their tech conferences.

Driving to the convention centre he reassures himself that it will be just like all the others. It's not that he's complacent but rather, when faced with something hectic, Adam tries to control his nervousness by convincing himself that he is relaxed and on top of things.

Adam strolls into the convention centre foyer and reads the screen outside the Google Campus, Exhibition Hall 3A.

12:15 - Adam Robinson. First Leap Studios, Australia.

12:15? Hang on… isn't that now? But I thought I wasn't on till one?

He gently pushes open the doors.

Immediately, a freaked-out AV guy scurries over. He reminds Adam of Jack Black in *High Fidelity*, but is slightly better dressed, as he's wearing the staging company's uniform.

'We've been calling you all morning.'

'What?'

The AV guy scowls, takes the USB Adam's holding and returns to his tech desk.

There's over 300 people here.

On stage, the MC, a woman with rock-hard, wavy blonde hair and a tight grey corporate outfit is standing at the lectern, flanked by large TVs displaying the conference Twitter feed. Behind her is a cinema-sized screen with Adam's name on it.

The AV guy plugs in the USB. 'What's the name of the file?'

'Presso San Fran.'

'I don't have time to set up a lapel.' In response to Adam's confused, scared-cat face, he adds, 'Plug your laptop into the lectern and go off that. I'll use your USB to drive the projector.'

'Okay… so I won't be controlling the presentation. You will?'

'Yeah.'

'So, if I want to move to the next slide, I'll have to ask you?'

The AV guy looks up from the handheld mic he is prepping. 'That's correct.'

'Okay… cause there's nothing worse than having to say "next slide".'

'Well, that is the situation you're faced with.'

Adam nods. The subtext of, 'You should have been here on time, dickhead,' reads loud and clear.

Before Adam can get to the side of stage, the MC begins her upbeat intro, 'Prior to working at First Leap Studios, Adam Robinson headed up the digital content teams at a number of Australia's entertainment networks. He's collaborated with local and international artists including Lady Gaga, Taylor Swift, Katy Perry, Ed Sheeran and Coldplay. We're very excited to have him come all the way from Sydney, Australia to talk with us today about virtual and augmented reality, and the impact the metaverse will have on the future of learning.'

There's minor obligatory applause.

Was the bio too star-fucker? This is the Valley; Gaga was probably the keynote, and who gives a shit about Coldplay?

AV Guy hands him the mic.

'THANK YOU.'

His mouth is way too close to the mic. His opening words are deafening. People flinch. Trying to remain un-stressed, Adam heads towards the stage. 'I must admit, when I was asked to send through my bio, I thought it was just for the program's website. It didn't occur to me that it'd be read out as an intro... I mean, it makes sense, but hearing all that, I'm feeling a bit self-conscious.'

A few heads turn around, looking unimpressed at him starting his presentation from the floor. Adam thinks he overhears, 'Like we've never seen this before,' but decides to block it out.

'Plus, having to follow this morning's line-up has left me feeling a little bit daunted and...'

Do Americans get self-deprecating...? Like Hugh Grant or Timotea...
Timothée Chalamet?
Am I comparing myself to—
No!
And anyway, Hugh Grant's much older and better looking.

'So, thank you for giving me the opportunity to talk to you today.'

And stop trying to be likeable.

Adam takes to the podium steps two at a time.

'I'll just plug in my lappy. The AV team's got a copy of the deck, too, so I'll just give a little signal when I want to move to the next slide and we'll be sweet. I think a good game is a fast game, so I'm just going to rattle through. What I say and what's on the slides won't be the same because that's the whole point of the slide, to give you something new. And if you have any questions, please ask. Just interrupt and ask.'

He pauses to see if anyone nods, looking like they're a question asker. Adam loves a question asker because he can always say, 'Good question…' then talk about whatever he likes, but the crowd are on their phones.

'So, the first thing with VR and AR is that lately it's all being lumped into the metaverse, along with NFTs, blockchain, AI, crypto, you name it, and worst of all, people still want to call it XR, which to me isn't a great name, especially since the moment you say it people think porn.'

Tumbleweeds.

Quit with the boom-tish gags.

'So I'm not a fan of XR as a name, and just because VR, PR and HR all rhyme doesn't mean you should do it.'

Mate, seriously, how is that funny?

Adam nods to the AV guy to cue his first slide. It's a dramatic, bird's-eye view of a hiker perched on top of a mountain, overlaid with the title: The VR Landscape.

Ah good there's a couple of lookups. Excellent.

'Today I'd like to focus on virtual reality, and one of the things I'm always wanting to be clear about, is that before you allow your clients or boss to get drawn to the shiny new box, which is how lots of people still see the metaverse and VR, you should use these five principles to make sure it's suitable for your project.'

Adam gives a nod to the AV guy to move to the next slide. It's a gritty cityscape photo of a young woman skateboarding on the roof of an empty car park, overlaid with the heading: Presence.

'So, presence: the sense of being there.'

Why are they looking at me like this?

He cues the AV guy for the next slide.

'Empathy: the capacity to feel for others.'

Nod.

Now they're actually… what…?

'Interactivity: the ability to make choices.'

Why are they being like that?

'Agency: the freedom to change your environment.'

Usually, Adam walks around on stage, believing that this ad hoc energy engages the audience. Today, rattled by the start and the jaded crowd, he is cowering behind the lectern, awkwardly nodding as he jabbers through the slides.

'And Alterity, which is my favourite because it sounds a little made up but it's actually a real word, and it's the key to VR; it's the capacity to see the world from a perspective other than your own.'

He pauses, wanting this idea to land. It does not. It is definitely un-landed.

The entire audience is either whispering to their neighbour or looking puzzled. Adam looks over his shoulder, back at the screen.

His power point has no pictures.

Instead of his classy images, there's a default font saying, 'insert text' and empty boxes with a broken pic icon.

'Shit.'

Did I just say that?

'Sorry.'

Faaaaaaark!

'My apologies. But where are the pictures…? I plugged in my laptop and so that's what I've been looking at, and I gave the AV guy a USB with a copy of the presso, so I guess…'

Stop the stream of consciousness!

'Sorry for the technical difficulties.'

'I can see our AV guru is on his way.'

Mate, hurry the fuck up!

The AV guy lumbers up to the lectern.

Adam greets him with, 'If you can please copy it off my lappy and then plug it straight into the projector screen and I'll—'

'So, this isn't your presentation?'

'What's on the screen now?'

'Yeah.'

'No?!'

'Alright then.'

You fucking numbnut?!

He unplugs Adam's lappy. The big screen goes blank.

'Thanks. Thanks so much. Let's give a bit of a hand to the AV team today. They've done a great job.'

A few claps. Adam realises he sounds facetious.

'I mean this is entirely on me, I thought the USB had all the pics... but um...'

Stay chill. San Fran and chill.

To counter the crowd's collective, *'This VR dipshit can't even make a PowerPoint,'* and his rising freak-out, Adam offers, 'Think of this an ad break and... if it was, then on telly at home when I was a kid you'd probably hear, *"We're happy little Vegemites..."'*

What the fuck?

'"As bright as bright can be..." You guys ever heard of Vegemite? You put it on toast? Everyone hates it. But it's great. It's black.'

The audience in the Google Campus Exhibition Hall 3A don't care.

'It's, like, really big in Australia. Like Tim Tams? You heard of them... a chocolate biscuit that's kind of like an Oreo but not... Tim Tams don't have a catchy song, although, Cate Blanchett did do a Tim Tam ad – not to be confused with Nicole Kidman, who did *BMX Bandits*. I mean, she did lots of other stuff, too, but at the start she… how are we going back there?'

You fucker, what is taking so long?!

Internally, Adam is Amanda Plummer playing Honey Bunny in *Pulp Fiction*, standing on top of a café table, swinging a pistol around and screaming, 'I'm going to execute every mother-fucking last one of you!' Externally, he's a white guy with a burning red face, trying to act casual by referencing TV ads screened before the audience were born, in a country they've never lived.

'Have we got a thumbs up… yes we do!'

The MC strides down the aisle and hands him his laptop.

'Okay, so, now we're in business.' He plugs it in. 'Hopefully it's worth the wait. Does this make things clearer?' He looks around the room. 'Great! I can see a couple of nods.'

He can't.

'So, remember this one? Alterity. Seeing the world from a perspective other than your own? It's like standing in someone else's shoes, but a fancy word for it. So when you're back in the office and you need to slap down some buzzwords to prove you know VR, just pull out "alterity" and you'll be fine.'

Adam scans the audience. Everyone is facedown, on their phones, speed texting. There's movement to his right that catches his eye. On the large monitor by the side of the stage, the conference's Twitter feed is popping off. Adam's performance of the Vegemite song has been posted with the caption '*Australia's not Got Talent*' and a crying laughter emoji. It has seven likes.

Adam doesn't have Twitter. Just shame.

'And, fundamentally, that's the most critical element of VR. So are there any questions?' He doesn't wait to see. 'Okay, thanks so much.'

He closes his laptop. Its clean snap is picked up by his mic which prompts a couple of people to look up. The MC silent screams 'NO!!!' her grey jacket riding up her shoulders as she flaps her arms, shooing him to stay on the stage.

Are you kidding me?

Trapped, Adam takes a deep breath and starts again, 'In Australia, our public broadcaster is called the ABC, and a while back they asked me to do an interview.'

He nods to himself, remembering how validating it felt. 'This doco crew filmed me for thirty minutes talking about how great VR and AR and the metaverse is, and how it could be used for good or evil but how the good far outweighs the bad and...'

A handful of people are listening.

'After the interview, I told everyone to watch it – my friends, people at work; I even told my in-laws. And when the show was on telly, the only bit they used from my interview was, "VR is perfect for the military and porn."'

He shakes his head in disbelief. A couple of faces offer faint signals of amusement.

'So, yes... there's always going to be a hideous version of whatever we do, however...'

Adam can hear his voice, but it doesn't feel like it's coming from him. It's no longer the high-pitched sales babble, but instead is thoughtful and sincere.

'We also did a gig at this Sydney cancer treatment institute. It was based around patients who, once a week, get chemo and sit for eight or nine hours with tubes attached and nothing to do. They're all fighting different types of cancer, at different stages and different percentages of success and remission...'

He pauses, remembering the hospital conversations, the beeping equipment and the upbeat nurses.

'And the thing that surprised me was how so many of the people we interviewed said that it was the repetition that they hated. Coming back week after week and just having to sit there and wait.'

The room is with him now.

'They said it was boring. It was grim, too, losing their hair, getting sicker, hoping it'd work and not knowing, but the boredom and having all that time to think… So for diversion therapy we gave them VR goggles. We'd already shot a bunch of stuff for travel companies, so we had all this footage of beautiful places, like sailing in New Caledonia and diving off the Great Barrier Reef, and this one girl…'

Why now? Of all occasions, why would I bring this up?

'…she's not old. Maybe nineteen… She's wearing a little headscarf because of the chemo.'

He stops.

The audience waits.

Adam wants to keep talking but he can't block out the idea that maybe she's already dead. He finds himself talking quieter and slower. It's the only way he can keep it together.

'She's got tubes monitoring her and… she's got the VR headset on and… she starts swimming, doing breaststroke with the cables in her arms, moving around as if she's in the Pacific Ocean.'

Adam sees her vividly, her teeth so bright compared to her skin. Her pleasure as she swam.

'So yes there's a bunch of lousy ways that the technology's being used but there's some good ways too… And that's what I want to do, to… to help people escape their daily lives and make them happy, even if it's just for a moment. Thank you.'

He grabs his laptop and scampers off stage before the MC can stop him.

*

Crossing the foyer, Adam is walking quickly, struggling for breath.

Is this a panic attack?

Maybe it worked… maybe she's okay… Can I smell toast? It's just the exhibition carpet. It smells like burnt toast. It's the exhibition centre, it's not—

'Adam? Excuse me, Adam?'

A woman is trying to catch up, but her skirt and heels are slowing her down.

'I'm Jen, Gupta's EA.'

'Hi.'

'Hi.'

He waits for her to catch up.

'He wanted to make sure you knew where the shoot's happening.'

'Okay, great.'

'So…' She looks at him weirdly.

He adjusts his glasses, paranoid that he looks like he's been crying. 'I'm Adam.'

'Yeah, hi, I'm Jen. Jennifer.'

'Nice to meet you… Sorry… So is it a walk from here or should we drive?'

'In the Valley, everywhere's a drive.'

'Yeah, of course.'

'And congrats on your talk.'

'Thanks.'

'It was really interesting.'

'That's nice of you to say.'

'No, really.'

Adam grabs his mobile. 'Sorry, I've just got to…' He unlocks his screen and acts like he's just got a text. There's rows of missed calls from the event co-ordinator in the hours leading up to his talk.

Why did I leave it on silent?

'Shall I meet you out front?'

'Sure.'

'I'm in a white caddy.'

'Okay.'

'Just so you know it's me,' offers Adam.

'No doubt.' Jen resumes walking.

Her heels look so spiky.

In the exhibition centre windows, Adam sees his reflection. Slumped dad bod with no butt and stick legs, encased in his favourite outfit of black blazer, T-shirt, and jeans. Adam sucks in his gut, pulls his shoulders back and fixes his glasses. Once there's no risk of catching up to her, he follows.

GREEN SCREEN

How long was I talking with none of the pictures? And how'd I get the time so wrong?

Standing in a corner of the green screen studio with the crew hovering and the client waiting for his guidance, Adam deploys a psychology trick he learnt at a management workshop. It consists of remembering a specific moment when he felt great, and as he recalls that instant, pressing his pinkie finger hard against his thumb and stepping forward. The theory is that the unusual sensory cue of pinkie and thumb, combined with the powerful happy memory, will trigger a little rush of endorphins and create a high-performance state.

When we won startup of the year…

He presses and steps, but the positive energy does not arrive.

How about when I kicked that goal? In 6th grade? Sure…

He tries again.

Ah… What about something with the kids? Or Kinki and… There's too much clutter. I need a single precise moment of 'Fuck yes!' Okay… what if I combine telling the guys that I just won this San Fran gig with being Brad Pitt, and they're high fiving me 'cause I've 'pulled it out of the bag, bro!'

He presses and steps.

Well, this one job isn't enough… just channel Pitt's swag in… what?

Bullet Train. *Or* Inglourious Basterds. *I mean anything really, he's such a cocky fucker.*

He repeats the process.

Nope. Pitt's not the fix. Okay then, just keep it simple and think of the guys' faces and their relief.

Thought. Pinkie press. Step. Self-assess.

Fuck me. Get positive. Think positive.

Adam is practically breaking his fingers trying to get into the zone as Gupta, the CEO, introduces himself, not by saying his name, it's assumed Adam already knows it, but by saying, 'So, you're the director…'

Gupta Johri has an Indian American accent and the Stanford confidence of a man born to money.

'Yeah hi, that's right, I'm Adam.' He tries to read his face to work out if Jen has told Gupta about his presentation and, if so, how damning she'd been.

'Yes, I know.'

But Gupta's face gives nothing away, prompting Adam to ask, 'So, you looking forward to this?'

'Well, I don't know yet, no one's given me the script.'

'Ahhh righto…'

Adam glances over at Wayne, the chief marketing officer and guy in charge of giving Gupta the script. Wayne's face is a billboard of, 'Please don't throw me under the bus.'

Wayne, you numbnut.

It's Wayne's budget that is financing the gig, so Adam will always publicly support him. To Gupta's question, Adam replies, 'Oh, don't worry about that, we've got an autocue and—'

'I want to see it.'

'Of course, and you'll be able to make changes, so it'll be—'

'Good.'

'Plus, we've got hair and makeup too.'

Given he's bald, Gupta looks quizzical.

Adam glides over this reaction, adding, 'I think it's going to be a lot of fun.'

Adam learnt long ago that, among male execs, there are two types. The insecure. And the others. The insecure you had to defer to, pump up their tyres by asking lots of questions. For the others, such as Gupta, you had to own it. Be as casual as they were. Breezy expertise was reassuring.

Since the pinkie-to-thumb press wasn't working, Adam reverts to his own approach. His strategy to get to CEO level of breeziness was to repeat to himself a million times over, *It's all shit. And if everything is shit, then who gives a shit about this shit?* This logic, repeated endlessly, would gradually seep into his nervous system, and for a set period he could convince himself it was true. The trouble was that the presentation fiasco had ruined his bravado, and this job was a big deal.

First Leap Studios didn't have the cash for a fuck-up, so, having sent Gupta into hair and make-up, as Adam chatted to the camera department about the placement of the key light, internally he was trying to not let his sense of failure over the presentation stop him from successfully videoing Gupta and Wayne talking up their product.

The plan was to take this green-screen footage back to the Sydney office and integrate it with 360° graphics to create a dazzling VR marketing app that would impress potential clients and thereby increase sales. This was the idea Adam had pitched to win the gig, but the Australian branch of Wayne's global marketing team had told him that their boss' acronym-based bullshit was starting to lose traction, and that Wayne was a CMO searching for a way to keep his job.

It seemed to Adam that Wayne's response to combat this corporate quicksand was to work on his personal brand. His hair was freshly cut and strand perfect, and based on the suggested dress code, Wayne had arrived with five identical blue business shirts that screamed corporate integrity. None of this mattered to Adam since all he cared about was getting good content, but although he dressed the part, Wayne could not sell the sizzle. Throughout the filming, irrespective of Adam's attempts to elicit a half-decent performance, Wayne looked like a panicked pre-schooler on his first day of childcare. As they crawl to the end of the script, even with astute editing and a thorough milking of the several thousand takes, Adam accepts the best he could hope for is Wayne sounding vaguely CMO-ish and being Pinocchio-level wooden.

Meanwhile, as this train wreck plays out, Kelly the makeup artist is in the greenroom trying to pat down Gupta's head. His hair, or lack thereof, is the issue. To get the errant wisps down, which was essential for the green screen to look good, she uses lots of hair spray, but the effect of so much spray on a hairless head makes Gupta's skull too reflective. On set, the studio lights would bounce off his head like an old VW in the sun. To counteract the shine, Kelly pads it down with concealer, but the tone of the concealer is not the same as Gupta's skin, so when Adam walks into makeup to see how they're going, he discovers that Gupta's skin from the eyebrows upwards is a beige-to-brown colour chart.

'Hey mate, have a look at the script while, Kelly – can I please have a quick word?'

Adam gives Gupta a print-out of the script from his bag. One of Adam's golden rules is to always have a truckload of scripts on set, and he draws upon this little moment of competence to help lift himself out of his cycle of self-recrimination.

Kelly stops padding down Gupta's forehead and follows Adam. Standing out of earshot of the CEO, his EA, the CMO, cameraman, sound guy, auto-cue operator, studio manager, and the talk-too-much film school grad who was possibly the camera assistant and definitely the most annoying person on set, Adam quietly asks, 'Have you got any other tones of concealer?'

Kelly, who is circular, with overworked, streaky, blue-blonde hair, replies with conviction, 'No, I do not.'

'Cool, okay. Just stay here for a moment.'

Kelly nods.

'We're not saving lives,' Adam adds. He is trying to sound nice, like it's no big deal, but it plays the opposite, and she reacts with 'Excuse me?' just as Gupta pops out of the makeup room and says, 'There you are!'

Gupta hands back the script. There are markups all over it, words crossed out, arrows linking different paragraphs, and extra lines scribbled into margins. Adam gives it a quick scan, passes it over to the autocue operator to update the file, and asks, 'So, you love it?'

Gupta pauses, 'Is that a joke?'

'Umm, yeah…'

'Well, not as much as your presentation.'

Hilarious.

He nods to Gupta, 'Touché', who looks mildly electrocuted with his small assortment of erect hair tufts jutting out of his skull amid Kelly's concealer mosaic.

On days when the corporate can-do pinkie finger exercise works, Adam takes a situation like this and a CEO like Gupta, and explains the two tricks with green screens: one, you can't wear green or tight-checked patterns as they always flicker and strobe; and two, nothing too thin or fine can be visible, i.e., Gupta's ten-strand mohawk will bugger up the green screen and ruin the footage.

All it needs is for Adam to ask Gupta to let Kelly give him a quick haircut and wipe off the makeup, but he says nothing, he doesn't have the confidence to acknowledge Kelly's crappy work in way that won't make him feel incompetent, and so instead Adam buys into the fantasy that he'll be able to fix it in post, and says, 'Just come through this way and we'll get started.'

Adam brings Gupta on set and gives the cameraman a pre-emptive glare to stop him from commenting on Gupta's appearance. Once the CEO's in position, Adam can't help himself. He asks Kelly, 'Do you think he needs any touch-ups?'

Kelly tugs at her bangs as she looks at Gupta in the video monitor. He needs more than touch-ups; he needs a complete overhaul. 'No, he's good.'

Complicit, Adam calls, 'Action.'

Gupta reads out the autocue. His re-writes make no sense. The script has become a listicle of industry jargon, broken up by stock phrases; 'market-leading', 'globally recognised', 'customised enterprise solutions'.

It's a five-star shit show which Adam swats away with, 'Well done, you killed it, and that's a wrap!'

Gupta's beaming.

'Could you take a few pics for me on set?'

'Sure.'

He hands Adam his phone.

Fuck yes.

Adam sees Wayne lurking on the edge of the set, furious. All day he'd been stuck to Gupta like a fridge magnet and now Adam has his boss' phone. Prior to the shoot, Wayne had told Adam about his social strategy, to create a campaign using behind-the-scenes selfies of him and Gupta which he'd promote across the company's social channels and industry sites too. The subtext being it'd raise Wayne's profile and thereby protect his job. At the time, Adam hadn't seen the value in telling Wayne that no one'd give a shit, and now all Adam cares about is being Gupta's bestie.

He gets the CEO to stand unusually close to the lights; using their brightness to overexpose and blast out Kelly's make-up disaster. After taking several shots, as they swipe through reviewing the pics, Gupta asks Adam, 'Do you have kids?'

'Yeah, two. A boy and a girl. Twelve and ten. How about you?'

'A son.'

'Great.'

An only child often has a story, and it feels too personal for Adam to delve into that, but before he can ask a follow up question, Gupta says, 'How do you find the travel?'

Adam's thrown. He realises Gupta is that third and rare type of male exec, a CEO capable of not being the story. Every stumble-trip stress that preceded this moment culminates in this question catching Adam off guard. He wasn't ready to think of himself, and the fatigue of the prior events means he slips up and tells the truth. 'I like it.'

Gupta looks surprised. The correct answer is, 'It's hard not being with my family, but what can you do, blah blah,' as per the standard corporate father spiel. Gupta seems to expect that Adam would know the rules.

Not wanting to acknowledge his mistake, Adam selects a pic.

'I think this is the best one.'

Instead of checking out the photo of himself surrounded by

camera gear in the green screen studio, Gupta looks at Adam. Like a smoker who's quit and just succumbed, Adam acts like nothing's happened, but he can tell Gupta's not buying it. The rules are that you miss your family. Full stop. Feeling their connection breaking, future deals falling through, and his studio going broke, Adam scrambles for a sugar hit of good fathering, 'I mean, I like it 'cause of the whole going away and coming back ritual. I like giving my kids something hokey every time I come home, and when I leave my daughter gives me this.'

Adam pulls out from his little front jeans pocket Ella's panda finger puppet.

'She says it's to protect me.'

Gupta smiles.

It is quaint, reads father-daughter bond, and locks in the deal.

Thank fuck.

*

According to the cameraman, driving from the Valley to San Fran at this time of day would take an hour and fifteen. The sound guy thinks an hour ten. As they pack up their gear, and discuss this at length, Adam understands why one is single, and the other divorced.

From the large car park, Adam reverses his enormous white Lincoln. Work is now officially over, and he is free until tomorrow's flight to do whatever he wants.

Before arriving, Adam had imagined that Silicon Valley would be a place where you could actually see mountains and a valley, and that Google and Amazon would have futuristic-looking buildings framed by an impressive landscape, and despite his better judgement he'd think it was pretty great, but instead everything is hot and concrete and glass with only signs and car parks separating one block from the next, and as he drives away he realises the one element that is impressive about 'The Valley' is that the tech giants had sold the dream that it was cool, when on a whole bunch of levels it is not.

Adam needs to debrief, to unpack the conference and talk through the shoot, but he doesn't have the wherewithal to create a positive spin for the work guys about the presentation, and if he does call Nina, even though for a minute or two she would try to act interested, she isn't great at faking.

On the freeway, the traffic slows down and banks up, allowing Adam to feel confident enough to dial while driving. He can't help himself. He rings Nina.

'Hey, Kinki, how are ya?'

'Good.'

'Can you talk?'

There is a long pause, the silence punctuated by her typing.

'Is now not a good time?'

'No, it's fine.'

'It's bit after four here, so is it morning there?'

'That's right.'

Adam hears Nina's keyboard being massacred. She doesn't type, she bangs it out like she's Elton John at Madison Square Garden.

Nina asks, 'Is that why you rang?'

'Huh?'

'To find out the time in Sydney?'

'Exactly.'

'Well, yep, it's a bit after nine.'

Because her laptop keyboard 'e' and 'i' had been crushed, Nina had bought a soft, rollup keypad to lie over the top, but the 'i' key

Angus Stevens

had already come loose, so although it is still functional, it doesn't sound healthy.

'Thanks, Kinki, that's tops.'

'Is something wrong?'

'No, I just wanted to say hi and see how everything is.'

'It's fine.'

'Great.'

Either tell her what happened or get off.

The typing stops.

'There's nothing wrong?'

'Not at all.'

'Okay…'

'So what are you up to?'

'Not much, just work.'

There is a gap which Adam waits for her to fill, but then the typing gets faster and louder as she commits to the next paragraph, email, article. Adam, not wanting to sound like a martyr, but doing so nonetheless, says, 'Okay, well, let's catch up when you can talk freely.'

'I can now.'

On a train Nina would always answer her mobile. Adam would not. 'People don't want to hear what we're having for dinner.' 'They don't have to listen.'

Adam contrives a smiling, 'Sorry, I was just missing you and I just wanted to say hi.'

'Where are you?'

'I'm on the freeway heading back to San Fran.'

'So, the shoot went well?'

'Pretty much.'

'And the talk?'

'It was fine.'

'Amazing.'

'Yeah.'

Now for the exit. Adam wants her to say 'I love you', but knowing she won't say it with work people around, coupled with the fact she never says it first, he offers an uncommitted, 'Okay...'

'A-huh.'

'Look after yourself.'

'Don't have too much fun.'

'I'll try not to.'

He hears her 'work chuckle'... and that's that.

Hanging up, Adam feels lonelier than before.

Laid out before him, everything is faded and dry. The highway is blank and flat and then, like a mirage in the desert, Adam sees water. A huge piece of blue, on the edge of the freeway, shimmering and beautiful. It's unexpected and magnificent and flicks a switch in him, something that only travel can bring.

Adam lowers the windows, letting the freeway grit blast in as he turns up the air-con and tunes.

At least I'm alive.

Etta James belts out *At Last* as he drives back into San Fran.

THE APOTHECARY

Over dinner, Adam gets on his phone and researches the best pot outlet near Castro. Its branding is like a hipster gentlemen's club from the Jules Verne era of big beards and thin 1890s font.

Having shown his ID and registered at the concierge, Adam is given a leather-bound menu that presents different categories, along with their sub-categories and descriptions, like it's organic wine.

It's pot for fuck's sake.

But it is not. It is so much more.

There are chewy versions, vape friendly, wax, tropicals, hash, and buds, and every variation is accompanied with dizzying detail around what each hit would provide, from light buzzy, to chilled, to deep navy, to any number of other colours, coupled with its origin, such as Indicia Dominant versus Hybrid, as well as a TCH rating to illustrate 'potency per gram'.

It becomes a three-way toss-up between the Kaizen Kosher Kush Live Resin, the Beezle Punch 'N' Pie, or the Pineapple Chewy Hydro Gumballs.

Compared with Adam's experience getting weed from Kings Cross Chris, holed up in his ground-floor housing commission apartment with his Chihuahua and stinky bong juice carpet, or with Home Delivery Mark who'd always say he'd be there in twenty, arrive an hour late, stay for a quick smoke and, without fail, use

Adam's toilet and leave a dump so brutal that the whole house stank not of quality hydro but of Mark's apocalyptic turds, this leather-bound concierge experience is both deeply appealing and unsettling.

Back in the Lincoln, Adam opens his little tin of Pineapple Chewy Hydro Gumballs. The guy who'd been his apothecary assistant had said, 'Start with a half and see how you feel.'

How strong could they be? Plus, it'll take time to feel it, and it's already eleven.

Adam downs two.

The drive back to his Airbnb takes about twenty minutes. By the time he arrives he still thinks nothing is happening, and although reverse parking is problematic, Adam doesn't ascribe that to the pot, so he munches two more and walks up the street to get a second dinner.

The pizza shop is 1950s fabulous strips and stripes. Behind the counter the pizza guy has nailed the uniform: knee high white socks, a yellow-and-white-striped collared shirt; and he tops it off with a superb moustache that combines the precision of Salvador Dali's with the meatiness of the Village People cop.

As he stands under the bright lights and faces the pizza guy, a sea of super stoned-ness sweeps over Adam. A tidal wave of green bentness, numbing his entire body and paralysing all functions. The pineapples have arrived.

'What would you like?'

Adam can't say. Cause he doesn't know. Cause the pizza guy's moustache has taken over his brain.

What's the line after Whyyy em cee aaaa? *Is there one? Of course there is. I can't order now if I don't know the words to YMCA and...* Why em cee aaaa *is everyone looking at me?*

'Sir?'

Sir?

'What would you like?'

Oh, fuck I'm like some old stoner fucker for fuck's sake. 'Who gets this stoned when they're that old?' *is what this magnificent moustache man is thinking. And stop saying,* 'What would you like?' *over and over, I heard you the first time, I've heard you every time.*

'Sir…'

'I'll get the supreme.'

'The Salvador Dali?'

'Who? No, the supreme.'

'We don't have a supreme.'

'Really?'

'No, we have a Salvador Dali.'

'You've got no supreme?'

'That's right.'

'Oh okay… you have chicken?'

'We have the Foghorn Leghorn.'

'As in that big chicken?'

'What?'

'Okay, yes, that one.'

'Which one?'

'The chicken.'

'Okay…'

The moustache looks at him, eyebrows raised, with patient condescension.

What?! What now?!

Oh, money. Right. Of course. No problem.

Adam gets out his wallet. There is a queue behind him. He can feel it, but he doesn't want to look around. It sounds big, and he can hear people shuffling their feet, making sighing and huffing noises as he stares at his money.

It all looks the same. And why's it all green? And the same size. Mix it up, America.

Find a number, look for a number. Where is it? Somewhere near the face…? Einstein, use a card.

Cash is stuffed back into his pocket. Card is taken out, tapped.

Thank fuck. Step aside and don't look so stoned.

How… how can I un-stone myself? It's like un-throwing a rock and anyways…

Adam zones out staring at the menu displayed up behind the counter.

…none of the pizzas the moustache talked about are there… No supreme. No chicken.

'Eighty-six… Eighty-six…'

Louder and more irritated.

'Eighty-six.'

Everyone's looking at me. Not again.

'Eighty-six.'

The moustache man stares at him.

Oh…

Adam hands over his ticket, takes his pizza and acts un-stoned, badly.

*

Adam tries to enjoy the experience of walking through San Fran but is just too paranoid.

Two blocks to go. Just get it together. I'm being like I. Good old Withnail and I.

This flashback to one of his all-time favourite flicks comforts Adam. He arrives home with his pizza intact and his soul contained.

Sitting on the couch in his little Airbnb, looking at the spiral staircase that leads up into the roof, Adam wonders if he should have another little pineapple.

There's so many left and it's bad to waste things… But I'm so very, very bent. But I'm home and what could happen? That's true… but maybe I'll get all my stuff sorted now so tomorrow I don't miss my flight. But it's not till three, and the bedroom is miles away. It'd be good to watch TV. Yeah, but the zapper's way over there.

It is on the coffee table. Literally within reach.

Get a drink. But the kitchen's so… like, heaps… faaaaaaar…

The pot menu should have a distance rating. One pineapple and stuff is still feasible, i.e. you can get to the kitchen, but by five of these little pineappley gummy fuckers, a journey that far is like Marco Polo-level.

Adam sits watching nothing on the blank TV screen for an indeterminate period.

He looks at the zapper and the stairs. He zones in on each of the walls circling him and the pictures everywhere. The paintings are accompanied by wooden sculptures littered around the place. Big dicks. Big tits. Big butts all seemingly worshipping the gods of fucking.

This is so intense. Was this all here when I first came in?

What if each painting is a portal into like a different… um… world…? Then what are the statues? The little sculptures? Yeah, are they vessels for spirits to just hang out? And what if the stairs are still there cause it's more convenient for the resident ghosts? Why would ghosts need stairs? Oh man…

He closes his eyes. His belt feels heavy. He needs to unbuckle it, but it's too much of a hassle. His arms are fastened to the couch, weighed down by non-existent dumbbells. He opens his eyes. The zapper is still too far away, and the glass of water still empty. He looks at his gut which is rudely constrained by his overzealous belt. He digs deep, lifts his right hand and painstakingly, singlehandedly starts to unbuckle it. The task becomes too much for one hand to bear. He brings in backup and in the flurry of having both hands try to undo his belt he discovers he has more left in the tank. Adam decides to escalate things and actually get up.

Yes, motherfuckers!

He stands, shuffles past the Mexicans and Hawaiians and Africans on the walls, and begins his mission.

It is brief. And unsuccessful.

Upon arriving in the bedroom, he flops down on his bed and immediately regrets it. His plan had been to get some goddamn water. He'd barely gotten halfway down the hall. The empty glass is still in his hand, but that ship has sailed. Adam slides his arm over to the edge of the bed and then with calculated risk drops it. It hits the wooden floor with a thud but doesn't break. Pleased with this triumph in physics he rolls over onto his side, leaving his left arm dangling out over the edge of the bed. It's only then, upon feeling the incision into his belly that it dawns on him, there is still the issue of the belt buckle. In all his excitement it remains done up. One item of clothing leads to another.

I wonder if the Airbnb girl's come and got her bra and charger? Are they hers? Would she and her boyfriend come down when their guests are out?

He opens his eyes as though that will help him answer the question.

The room is so dark and quiet it feels like a cellar. The sound of the glass hitting the floor still hangs about… as Adam sinks into a stoned blackout.

*

Someone's here…

Fuck.

Adam's heart is beating crazy fast, but he doesn't open his eyes, instead he lies there listening.

What was that?

Like a slight squeak.

Listen. Listen.

He lies still. Shitting himself. Eyes closed. Too scared to breathe.

So, can I hear someone? If there was someone here what the fuck are they doing? Or is this a dream? It's too real. Just look. No!

Adam remains curled up on his side, his arm still hanging off the bed.

Is there pressure on the floor?

Ever so slightly, Adam opens an eye. He does it gradually so they wouldn't see him squinting. His body is a freaked out mess.

Separate the walls from the doorway.

Adam slowly adjusts his vision—

Fuck!

There's a guy standing beside his bed.

It can't be real.

Adam's so terrified he can't move.

It's a fucked-up dream.

It's the Airbnb guy.

There's no one there. It's a dream where in the dream I wake up, and then I think it's real life, but it's not, it's just another layer of the dream, so if I look I'll see there's no one there.

But he is there! He's right there!

Long and thin, the man's towering over the bed. Adam feels the world fall away. He's so scared he can't move. He tries to make a noise, but nothing comes out. He can't even whimper. It is the single most terrifying thing he's ever encountered. Physically, mentally, a total nightmare. He screams as loud as he can. But nothing happens. Curled up like a baby, he has goosebumps all over.

There's no one there, it's a dream, it's a dream, it's-a-dream, it's-a-dream, it's-a-dream, it's-a-dream.

'Dream.'

Hearing his voice stops the panic and breaks the spell. The light beyond the bedroom door becomes visible. The faint buzz of the fridge audible.

Is he gone?

Adam opens his eyes. Properly.

What was that?

He looks back at where the man had been, but there is nothing there. The shapes of the bedroom, the chest of drawers, the window frame, all return as though to mock him.

That felt like death.

To be totally certain he's awake, he slides over to the edge of the bed and scans the floor looking for the dropped glass.

Where is it!?

Everything screams back to eleven. He starts flipping out all over again. Heart going nuts. Fear jumping up through his throat.

There. There it is.

The faint light of his cheap mobile charger illuminates the glass.

Life is real. This is real. It's not a dream. It's okay. So turn some lights on and get your shit together.

Standing in the bathroom with a little mirror cabinet above the basin, Adam splashes water on his face. His eyes are sunken and flat. Three deep creases run across his high forehead. He stares into the mirror, trying to see the guy who moments earlier had been so shit-shakingly scared, but can't see beyond himself.

This pot business isn't as much fun these days…

He drinks water, checks the time of his flight, sets his phone alarm, then a backup, then a backup to the backup. Completing these simple tasks, Adam finds reassurance that all is normal.

He returns to bed, turns off the lamp and, peering into the shadows, tries to understand why he thought someone was there.

Wall. Bed. Door. It is all straight lines.

Ugh. Just sleep.

THE RETURN LEG

The three rounds of alarms do the trick.

The whole day is loose and foggy and although he knocks off a bunch of tourist activities and avoids looking at his emails, justifying his negligence with the excuse it is Saturday in Sydney, his hungover bentness means that everything feels like a task.

He drops off the car, and while on the light rail heading towards the departure terminal, Adam decides that travelling with his pineapple pot is too hectic, so before going through customs, he heads for the men's.

In the privacy of the bathroom cubicle, he jiggles the nine lollies in their tin, then drops one into his mouth. He licks off the sugar.

Do I really need to do this again?

He takes it out. It is wet and gooey and slips onto the floor.

The remaining eight sit innocently in their home, awaiting a purpose.

Do I flush you or leave you as a treasure?

He closes the lid, places the tin on the top of the multi-roll toilet paper dispenser and leaves.

Approaching security, it occurs to him:

What if some kid thinks they're lollies? No, they're for some Harold and Kumar *guys who believe in the Pot Fairy. Yeah, but what if some eight-year-old thinks they've hit the jackpot, eats them all and has a psychotic episode that never ends?*

Adam is in the line-up for departures.

I can't go back now.

Handing over his passport, he also presents his ticket on his mobile phone. The airport employee processes them and hands them back.

Anyways it'll be some college kid or a cleaner and they'll thank the Pot Fairy for sure.

He steps through the final stage of security, belt and shoes off, wallet and phone out with his laptop placed flat in the tray, past the metal detectors and the sniffer dogs and into the departure terminal.

Home sweet home…

2

2

PRE-FLIGHT ENTERTAINMENT

Stepping through airport security and funnelled down a corridor, Adam turns the corner and is presented with a sleek passenger experience. Whereas the rest of the airport had scuffed floors and mid-noughties technology, the departure terminal is entirely different. It has fresh paint and a new-car smell. The floor is polished concrete, gun-metal grey, with clinical white walls and bright LED billboards strategically placed throughout the terminal showcasing the latest in fashion, technology and luxury goods.

Among the display ads is an in-house promo for the terminal's all-new Pre-Flight Entertainment Centre. Even for Adam, who rarely noticed such things, this ad has cut through. It's more eye-catching than the mini-movie perfume ads that involve Portman/Lawrence/Robbie running through a European street/beach/hotel, and contains more stately poise than a Hemsworth/Clooney/McConaughey car/watch/whisky ad. Plus, it's hard to miss. The ad for the Pre-Flight Entertainment Centre app is everywhere.

It's a charming montage of attractive but relatable people of all ages and cultures, their faces illuminated by the light of their mobile devices, captivated by the content on their screens. It concludes with the unobtrusive statement: 'PFEC: take your departure to new heights'.

As Adam walks through the terminal, he can see its effect.

Having seen the ad, people fiddle with their phones as they download the app, and then shortly after sit down and start watching. It combines the intergenerational attention of Facebook, Insta and Tik Tok, as each new user's engagement is unabashed and committed.

Naturally, Adam has no interest in following suit. His rule of thumb is that anything that everybody loves is probably shit because generally people have no taste, or more specifically don't know better and will eat what they are given. Almond Lattes. Broccolini. Goji berries. Kale. He just has an instinctive suspicion of swimming with the tide.

This means he's missed out on a bunch of things. *Game of Thrones? The Avengers? Friends?* No, no and nope. And any Clint Eastwood film? A hard no. Adele? Never actively listened, but it is impossible to have ears and not have heard her.

With this personal history of contrariness, the behaviour of the passengers accessing the PFEC app has no impact on Adam. He isn't interested in his phone. He wants a drink.

Wandering down the terminal concourse, he sees before him the perfect table at the perfect airport lounge bar. Fake green-leather booths. Fake Irish pub-style decor with pretend wood panelling and a very real bar stocked with lots of everything. Above it several large TVs are playing NFL and NBL games. Plus, the table he's spotted is separate from the other travellers, but central enough that he will have a good view of the sports, and to top it all off, placed front and centre is an American-style two-foot-tall fold-out menu.

He settles in and checks out what's on tap. In addition to the list of wines, spirits, and cocktails, there are some pictures highlighting hero beverages. The image of a Blue Moon beer with a slice of orange in a glass big as his head looks good.

A beer with orange? It's like taking the Corona and lime recipe and shitting all over it.

And yet he is compelled to get one.

And those buffalo wings look alright. And maybe some fries, too. And a Coke.

Is this delayed munchies or straight-out gluttony?

There are no more tasks to complete, leaving him with a pleasant mulled over, beery slide back to Oz.

Yes, everything still feels a bit off and yes that guy last night was the most real and freaky nightmare I've ever had, hands down... but I'm still feeling so full-body dopey, what can I expect?

Adam blisses out and surveys the airport from his top-shelf vantage point. It's better than a frequent-flyer lounge: close enough to the airport concourse, so he can watch the world go by and sufficiently isolated not to have his bubble burst by randoms; plus, his table's placement means it is damn nigh impossible for large, unseemly groups to park themselves down beside him and cramp his style with piles of luggage.

It appears to Adam that the only glitch to this idyllic set-up is the guy sitting diagonally opposite him, who is probably five years younger, or perhaps he is the same age but painfully healthy. Either way, he is slick and tense and on his mobile talking to someone who is not his superior about some work bollocks. His excessively glowing skin looks fresh with a solarium hue. His hair is short back 'n' sides at CMO Wayne-level perfect. He is angular and sharp and is wearing a watch that deserves a full-page glossy magazine ad. While tapping his touch screen laptop and talking about so and so, he observes Adam giving his order and doesn't look at all impressed, as he's clearly been sitting there longer.

Adam watches Slick Guy swivel and click his fingers repeatedly and unsuccessfully try to attract the attention of the waiter. As Adam orders his meal, he can sense Slick Guy's rising irritation. If he wasn't so darn slick, Adam might have been inclined to let the waiter know but, given el Slicko likes clicking fingers to get someone's attention, Adam decides to leave him to his own devices and enjoy watching him fail.

Two women, both wearing leather sandals and carrying neck pillows, carefully navigate their way between the tables. They're both pushing carry-on bags, plus one woman has a small duty-free shopping bag, and the other a large, floppy hat. They look like retirees who are either widows or lovers; either way, they seem to be mid-way through their trip of a lifetime. The woman with the floppy hat drops it down on the table and accidentally knocks over her menu. Adam passes it back to her.

'Thank you so much.'

'No worries.'

What is it with 'Thank you so much,' why does everyone feel the need to add the 'soooo much', like, settle down people, 'thanks' is all that's required.

'Do you know how to download the app?'

'I'm sorry?'

'This airport app.'

'Not really…'

He feels the women drawing him in, the same way his mother asks for help with her internet. It is a powerful boomer ability, where their technological ineptitude drains the life out of all younger demos.

Adam looks for an escape. Walking along the border where their pub seats meet the terminal concourse is an airport employee.

'Perhaps she might?' Adam gestures to her.

The boomer with the floppy hat swoops.

'Excuse me? Sorry to bother you.'

'Yes?'

'Could you show us how to use the app?'

She replies flatly, 'The Pre-Flight Entertainment Centre app?'

'Please, yes.'

Floppy Hat looks to Adam to see if he wants a tutorial too.

'I'm good, thanks.' Adam returns to the TV sports combo.

The airport employee remains standing on the border of the pub and concourse, projecting her voice with the slightly heightened tone of a public-service announcement, ensuring she can be heard beyond this immediate group, 'The Pre-Flight Entertainment Centre or PFEC is the latest development in our departure terminal guest program. Upon downloading the app, the user is presented with a suite of content options, which can be calibrated to their specific needs and interests.'

She speaks as though she works in a call centre, scripted and faux friendly as her nasal voice cuts through terminal noise.

'The Home channel is our most popular. Although there are other channels for you to select from, including Work and Lifestyle, we recommend you begin with Home.'

The two women nod, responding to her monologue the same way they would to a waiter listing the day's specials.

'There is also a variety of viewing modes available, including a shared perspective for couples and small groups, and solo mode for those who wish to view alone. These options are presented in standard 2D viewing as well as a recently-launched immersion mode; however, immersion mode is not available for all users as it is currently in a limited beta release.'

Adam doesn't want them to know he is listening, but it does sound kind of cool, so he surreptitiously gets out his mobile and begins to download the app.

The woman's talking faster now. Her conversational tone is replaced with the monotone of terms and conditions being verbally skimmed over, 'In compliance with the current PFA Guidelines, it is my duty to inform you that viewer discretion is advised. Although every effort is made to ensure user safety, individuals participate at their own risk.'

Adam looks over at the two retirees. They are drawn right in. Like getting a briefing before a bungee jump, they acknowledge the warning with appropriate regard while thinking it's clearly not relevant. The woman momentarily pauses as the waiter, a young-dad-looking guy, edges past her and delivers Adam his forty-gallon Blue Moon beer and glass of Coke. Then as the waiter heads back to the bar, Mr Slick swings out his arm and physically blocks him. 'I'd like to order.'

'I'll be back.'

The waiter pushes through the outstretched hand and keeps walking.

Between el Slicko's battle with the staff, the TVs above the bar, and the PFEC app, Adam knows he's in for a good show.

The airport woman continues her PFEC introduction, shifting from her monotone legal voice back to her community announcement voice.

'Finally, some dos, don'ts, and FAQs... Do take your time to familiarise yourself with the interface. Don't rush the experience. Try to find a comfortable location within the terminal to access the content. Don't try to walk and view the content. Yes, the content is live and regularly updated. Yes, you can unlock fresh content based on your viewing habits. And yes, the app is free!'

With her final statement, she gives a little flourish with her hands and a gorgeous smile. But something strikes Adam as unsettling, as though she looks younger than when she first started talking. She notices Adam looking at her.

Please don't.

She comes over. 'Do you have any questions?'

'No, I'm good, thanks.'

'May I?' She gestures to Adam to hand over his phone. Reluctant, he obliges.

'Oh, that's interesting.'

Adam remains silent, not wanting to take the bait. Plus, he is trying to look at her face without her noticing. His disquiet with her looking younger is increasing. He was sure when she first arrived that she'd looked late twenties but, now it looks as though she isn't even sixteen. Or at least her face – her body is still an adult woman's, but her facial features look practically pre-adolescent. With near reverence she says, 'You've been granted Immersive Viewing.' She hands back the phone. 'You're the first person I've met who's got that.'

'Really?'

'May I ask what line of work you're in?'

'I run a VR and AR studio.'

'I see.'

Adam can't tell from her reaction whether she knows what that means so he adds, 'Virtual and augmented reality.'

She flashes her teeth with an expression that Adam reads as, 'Yes, I know what they are, boomer,' and points to his phone. 'If you select Immersive Viewing… see the pop-up?'

On his screen is text with an accept button.

'They're legal Ts and Cs that you have to agree to if you want to try it.'

'Okay...?'

She switches back into quick-speaking legal mode, 'This disclaimer acknowledges that the beta version of the PFEC Immersive Viewing can result in physical side-affects. While the pain during a session is not transferable back to the owner upon session completion, there have been cases whereby the physical symptoms persist. These have led to serious and, on rare occasions, fatal injuries.'

She reaches out and scrolls her thumb over his screen to the end of the text, and adds brightly, 'Will you accept?'

She's leaning over his shoulder, waiting for him to press the 'Accept' button.

'Um.'

'You might as well.' She presses it for him, like an enthusiastic kid corralling her babysitter into one more episode before bedtime.

'Excuse me? How do you know when it's downloaded?' The boomer with the floppy hat wants attention.

The airport woman says to Adam, 'Have fun!' and returns to the retirees.

Adam watches her assist them. Her age and unflappable zealousness feels like a combination of Hitler Youth and Apple Store shop assistants.

He puts his phone aside. There are more pressing matters to attend to, namely his mega beer.

It goes down an absolute treat, plus the Coke gives Adam the required sugar pick-me-up.

The timing of the wings and fries appearing at his table just as he takes the final sips of his first beer is exceptional. It allows Adam to order a double vodka and soda without having to wait, as he gears up for a sleepy boozy flight.

It's only once Adam has his food and his additional drinks that the waiter tends to el Slicko. Adam acts like he is looking at the TV, but really, he is listening to Slick placing his order. Once the waiter leaves, Slick throws Adam an investigative glance. It reads to Adam like Slick is deliberating over whether Adam's the reason he isn't getting service. Regardless, Adam isn't prepared to directly engage and instead focuses on his drinks and the sport TVs. His attitude when sitting at an airport bar is that anything that involves a ball is worth watching; NFL and NBL are both good enough. In the footy the white and blue team are winning, and in the basketball the red team. Adam decides to go for the other guys. Make it interesting.

How good was The Other Guys? *Like seriously.*

Will Ferrell is a genius.

And the director goes from that to Vice *and* The Big Short; *meanwhile, my career goes from shooting online interviews of bands I don't like, to VR training... Yeah, but he also did* Don't Look Up *and that was up its own arse, so...*

Adam hums a Ferrell-esque ditty channelling how Will Ferrell in *The Other Guys* typed his police reports, as he eats his buffalo wings.

Still, with my career success versus actual talent, I'm so punching above my weight.

Is it impostor syndrome if you know it's true?

I think so... I mean, isn't that the whole idea?

Or is impostor syndrome when you think you're not good enough and therefore an impostor, but you actually are good enough and thus you are suffering impostor syndrome?

Hmmm, good point and, fun fact, these wings are top notch.

Meanwhile, over at table twelve, Mr Slick's grenache blanc arrives. He inspects its greenish-yellow shade, sips, and winces. It is as though the wine has genuinely hurt him. Shortly after, Slick's salad arrives. He disassembles it with precision, scraping the creamy white dressing off the leaves, separating out the bacon bits from the anchovies and occasionally bringing some of it to his lips.

While Adam basks in the Ferrell-loving pinkish undercooked chicken scrawn of the buffalo wings, and the honest-to-goodness cheese-loaded fries, he imagines Slick is Mark Wahlberg's character in *The Other Guys*, highly strung and shitty, and with his orange-sliced beer and vodka chaser, Adam silently toasts to his good fortune.

As he tucks into wing number nine, it occurs to him, el Slicko isn't Marky Mark, he's more like DiCaprio. And it isn't *The Other Guys*, it's *The Wolf of Wall Street*.

What was the real guy's name?

Jordan Belfort.

That's right. What a dick.

Sure, el Slicko isn't wearing the era-appropriate business outfit, but everything about him is the present-day equivalent: cashed up and cheap. This idea propels Adam into the next one. He must get on the terminal Wi-Fi so he can experience the PFEC app extravaganza and see what movies they've got, but first he should get another round, and before that he needs to take a piss.

Adam considers the implications of leaving his bags unattended at his table.

If someone came and started to nick them, would Slick do anything? Hmmm.

If Slick's like Jordan, then not a chance.

There were so many things that gave Adam the shits about the whole *Wolf of Wall Street* story. He'd actually met the real-life Jordan Belfort, as he'd once done a motivational keynote to the senior management where Adam worked. It was a company-wide wank fest, and the higher-ups had thought Jordan was a good idea. Slime oozed off him. The conference had been held at Sydney's biggest casino. The film was yet to be released, and Adam had sat there looking at his colleagues.

They're lapping up this grease. Enjoying the fantasy of an ugly little man who gets Hollywoodised. Bragging about ripping off people and positioning it as the art of selling; what makes that motivating?

Then Scorsese goes and glorifies his fuckwittery by having DiCaprio play his life.

Why do people want this shit?

Or is it the lure of not giving a fuck about anyone or anything? Since they didn't have the balls to do it themselves, they're drawn to the orbit of someone who does?

Adam realises he has been staring at Slick as he trod through this work memory and since Slick is staring back, Adam fiddles with his vodka. He compares Slick to Jordan Belfort and considers how Leonardo looked nothing like the guy he was playing.

In the movie of your life… the crucial part is who plays you; because it's who is cast as you that defines the film's genre and therefore your life.

Okay…

The kids, Louie especially, loved to say that Adam looked like a combination of Ricky Gervais and Leonardo DiCaprio. Nina said he was more like Mark Ruffalo, but the kids were adamant Adam was a Gervais/DiCaprio combo.

Gervais is black comedy; DiCaprio action thriller; and Ruffalo moody drama.

Three different films equals three different lives, but which movie is me and who would I pick?

Actually, the real issue is I need to take a piss, and I'm not sure if old

Slicko will pinch my stuff, or watch as someone else does.

Adam places his laptop and overnight bag under the table, positions his jacket over the chair, takes out his mobile and makes eye contact with Slick to ask non-verbally, 'Will you keep an eye on my stuff?'

Just before gets up and heads to the gents, Adam glances down at his phone. On a whim he opens the PFEC app, selects Immersive Viewing – Trial Mode, and hits 'Play'.

THE WTF OF WALL ST

Adam's no longer holding his mobile phone, instead there's a glass of water. The accompanying tableware is shiny and expensive, and beside him is a floor-to-ceiling window overlooking Manhattan.

What the fuck?

Plus, sitting opposite is Matthew McConaughey with fluffy hair, thumping his chest and chanting, 'Mar-oomph… Mar-oomph… Mar-oomph-faa… Mar-oomph.'

Where the hell am I?

Adam looks around. He's surrounded by rich white men, all too interested in their own conversation to notice McConaughey's show.

Panicking, Adam grabs the glass of water and gulps it down, hoping that somehow that'll snap him out of it.

None of it's real.

He closes his eyes, shakes his head, wanting it to all disappear.

The thud of McConaughey's chest beating is gone.

Adam opens his eyes.

He is back at his table in the airport bar.

Fuck me.

He glances around. The retirees are watching their mobiles. El Slicko is picking at his meal.

This is crazy.

Adam is clutching his mobile. His hands are trembling. The PFEC app is open, and on its on-screen interface is a picture and the text box, '*The Wolf of Wall Street*'. At the top of the screen, Immersive Viewing – Trial Mode is highlighted.

Whoa…

He flips his phone around.

Is this really real? An app that immerses you? How the fuck does that even work? There's no goggles. Or headset.

His hand which had been gripping the phone is tingling. The tips of his thumb and fingers are red and puffy.

So, I never got to the bathroom? I just sat here, hit play, and then had lunch with McConaughey?

Adam chuckles. Excited. Nervous.

But did that actually happen?

Centre-stage on the PFEC interface is the button, 'Resume'.

Adam stares at it.

Honestly, this is the craziest fucking thing. I do not… I don't… ohhh man.

It feels like the first time he popped a pill, but there's no one egging him on, no cute girl, or a mate saying, 'Just have a half to start.'

This is on him.

There can't be that much risk… they wouldn't allow it.

Am I really going to do this?

He swivels around to check out all the people sitting around the bar. Everything is flat-pack normal. It's reassuring.

He finishes off his vodka soda chaser and presses the 'Resume' button.

Adam's back in the restaurant. It's like the scene paused and waited for him to return before it started up again.

The Manhattan skyline is still outside and McConaughey is still doing his weird chant, 'Mar-oomph… Mar-oomph… Mar-oomph-faa… Mar-oomph.'

Dressed in an overpriced late-80s suit and looking like a coked-up seedy rabbit, McConaughey gestures for Adam to join in.

Tentative, Adam does as he's told, hits his chest and starts grunt-humming. He feels stupid and skinny but can't work out if it's just because his cheap suit is so loose fitting.

Wanting to see his reflection, Adam scans the restaurant looking for a mirror, but is thrown by McConaughey saying, 'We're the common denominator.'

Who does he think I am?

McConaughey returns to his chant and adds at the end of each phase a bird squawk. He rolls his fingers to make Adam copy. 'Keep it up for me.'

Adam starts chanting, 'Mar-oomph… Mar-oomph… Mar-oomph-faa… Mar-oomph.'

McConaughey adds, 'Arh!'

*

Hang on!? What?

Adam's back at the bar. Everything's the same. Slick, the retiree women, the sports on the telly, the waiter: all business as usual. On his phone, the PFEC app interface reads, Immersive Viewing – Trial Mode Complete.

He lets go of his mobile. His fingers are tinging with the same pins and needles as before.

That was just a teaser... it's a pretty intense way to on-board people. I mean, I guess I could have started with normal 2D mode... but fuck.

He fiddles with his stuff, making sure his laptop, bag, and jacket are all where he left them and breaks out with a grin he can't contain.

This is unbelievable. Total immersion.

How many people have tried this? I'm selling the house and buying stocks. Who's the mastermind who made it?

Adam scopes his phone, wanting to find the About this App section and get all analytical and business-like.

The world... nothing's ever going to be the same.

He looks at the PFEC interface. The Trial Session has a green tick 'completed' icon, the Immersive Mode option is still highlighted, plus, alongside *The Wolf of Wall Street*, two new titles are visible. About this App can wait. He selects all three, takes one last glance around the terminal.

Was I just DiCaprio playing Jordan Belfort?

Adam takes a deep breath.

I gotta find out.

He hits 'Play'.

Inches from his nose is the fattest, longest line that Adam's ever seen.

To rack up or to not…

He snorts hard. It hits the back of his throat. Dry and clean. He's not coke fit, so he warbles through. Left. Right. Left. It takes him three passes. Marching along, military style. Ploughing up and down his coke paddock, missing bits and having to retrace his steps.

Fuck it's good.

Adam takes in the rest of the world. The joint is pumping, there's topless girls beside him and past the other strippers working the poles he sees in the mirror Leonardo DiCaprio grinning back at him, like the shit-eating cocky motherfucker that is *The Wolf of Wall Street*.

Adam bursts out laughing.

Are you kidding?

Adam is Leonardo, dressed as Jordan Belfort, looking thin and trashed, his unbuttoned Ralph Lauren shirt exposing his hairless chest, and feeling invincible as the massive coke-rush hits.

This is the greatest fucking app on the planet. Fucking yes!

Adam raises his martini glass and does a piss-take imitation of *The Great Gatsby* meme of Leonardo toasting.

It's still me… My mind… In Leonardo's body. Playing The Wolf of Wall Street.

The pumping bass vibrates through his

chest. Coke. Sex. A pulsating frenzy.

Okay... remember, this is just a game. Just a show.

The blonde on his right starts kissing his neck as the brunette rubs up against him.

And who are these women?

The brunette slides down past his chest. Adam in anticipation closes his eyes.

All the sensations stop.

Wait whaaaaaat? No! Come on?!

The music's gone. No touch. No beats. Nothing. He opens his eyes. He's no longer at the strip club. Instead he finds himself in front of a fireplace, fiddling with candlesticks.

What the fuck is going on?

In the reflection of the brownstone windows, Adam sees he's still dressed as the Wolf.

Oh, thank fuck.

And he still feels DiCaprio's invincibleness and Belfort's vanity.

Where's this scene in the film? Leonardo's waiting on something. The room's décor is shabby Vegas but it's not Jordan's house, it's...

That's right, Leonardo's is trying to make a fire, but why?

Behind him wooden glass-panelled doors slide open.

Oh yes...

Margot Robbie, who's playing Naomi the Duchess of Brooklyn, stands before him wearing thigh-high black stockings, stilettos, and nothing else.

It's not infidelity if none of it's real.

Adam tries to contain his flesh hunger, but in his excitement he stumbles on the fireplace rug and in doing so blinks.

Snap.

He opens his eyes.

Hang on hang on. What's with this app?

It's like a bad wet dream.

Adam looks around. He's in the back of a limo with vial of coke and Margot beside him.

I close my eyes and – bang – it cuts and...

She's in a low-cut mini, stretched out across the back seat.

I mean, it's not that bad...

As Adam starts to sprinkle the coke over her chest, he asks, 'Didn't you get an Oscar nom for this?'

'Huh?' Margot is dumbfounded.

The limo suddenly rumbles like there's an earthquake.

Don't fuck this up! Just copy the movie. Okay, okay!

Adam's DiCaprio finishes sprinkling out the Charlie, buries his head in Margot's cleavage, and goes to town. The rumbling immediately passes but the limo's suspension leaves them bouncing around, resulting in moderate levels of coke-snorting success.

Adam's happy to fail; smashed and loose, he licks up the leftovers and feels his tongue go numb. As he tries using his coked-up nose to push down her dress, the car lurches to a halt. Margot's laughing as the car door opens.

'Get out of the fucking car!'

A young Italian woman yanks Adam out by his collar and starts slapping him across the face.

Mother fucker! Who'd do that to Leo?

Adam peers through his coke haze and recognises Belfort's first wife.

'You son-of-a-fuckin bitch!'

Adam tries to slither back inside the limo but she keeps smacking his face.

I'm getting an earful and it's not even Kinki.

Bang, bang, bang. He shields himself and inadvertently closes his eyes.

And stop hitting my goddamn head!

YOUR FRIENDLY NEIGHBOURHOOD

In the darkness, the yelling of Belfort's first wife is replaced by the sounds of cars stuck in traffic and the thunder of an approaching storm.

Is she gone?

Opening his eyes, Adam sees in the evening drizzle Kirsten Dunst standing before him. She's got red hair and a tan overcoat, she smiles and says, 'I better run, tiger.'

Did she really just call me that?

As he watches her cross the street, Adam's brain switches into puzzle-solving movie-mode.

Kirsten's never been in a Scorsese flick... And every time I blink it takes me to a different scene, but just then my eyes were closed for ages and now it feels like a completely different movie... and there's only one person Kirsten's ever called tiger... and that'd mean she's playing Mary Jane which'd mean... I'm... Spider-Man?

He checks out what he's wearing, looking for confirmation. It's an inconspicuous shirt and jacket, but underneath it he feels a skin-tight garment. A sly Tobey Maguire grin slides across his face.

This is awesome!

The coke-drug smog of DiCaprio's Jordan is swapped out for Maguire's puppy dog Peter Parker. Pure energy. Lithe and adolescent.

This is just the best fucking app ever.

There's more thunder, and the rain gets heavy. Kirsten, aka Mary Jane, hurries around the corner.

Why's she going that way?

Adam sees two dubious-looking men start to follow her.

Oh shit, it's the mugging scene.

When Louie and Ella watched it for the first time, Adam had monologued over the racial stereotypes ingrained in Hollywood movies and how the *Spider-Man* (2002) version was no different.

'Low-level baddies in cartoon action movies generally are a person of colour. If not black, then Hispanic, and only in plot-related exceptional circumstances white.'

Louie and Ella nodded, more interested in the film than their dad's unoriginal theory.

'Then, as the baddies go up a level in badness, they're able to get whiter to the point where the arch-nemesis can be as white as the hero, and their second-in-command man can reference the Nazi Aryan tropes, like Hans in *Die Hard*, or Draco Malfoy and his dad.'

Realising he'd lost the kids, Adam directed the last part to Nina. 'This escalating scale culminates in the big baddie's whiteness being a reflection of the hero's anti-self which, to complete their journey, the hero needs to battle and defeat.'

She nodded, 'Gotcha.'

'But a low-level baddie, like a mugger whose role is a plot device, is pretty much always a person of colour.'

'Thanks.'

'I mean, I'm sure there's savvy academics who have nailed this point a lot better than me but, you—'

'Yeah, Adam, I get it.'

'It's like the same casual racism that makes all-white movies have black judges and high school principals.'

'Hmmm, I know.' Nina smiled, with a flirty undercurrent that triggered Adam's memory of the first time he saw *Spider-Man* (2002). They'd just started going out. He was a late twenties kidult who'd gone over to Kinki's little studio apartment in the Cross straight after the movie. It'd been great. He'd not left her bed until she dressed for her evening shift the next day.

Now, face to face with the thugs, none of that seems real. Adam is completely immersed in Peter Parker's world and his memory of this mugging scene doesn't reduce his fear.

In the alleyway, the goons chase down Kirsten's Mary Jane, rip off her coat and expose her sheer purple dress. The rain makes it cling to her body like a nightie.

As the muggers circle her, Adam's jumping across the rooftops in pursuit.

If I remember this wrong, will the outcome change?

As he rips off his shirt to reveal his Spidey costume, Kirsten's Mary Jane is thrown up against the wall.

The biggest of the tough guys hits MJ. Hard. Her face goes soft and pulpy. Up until this point, Adam had felt teenage excitement. Cartoon fun. But that punch wasn't. MJ's seriously hurt, face down in the gutter.

He jumps down. The asphalt jars up through his legs and all through his body.

Smack. He's king hit from behind; his body bends out of shape as he hits the ground. The alleyway mud jams into his mask. It smells like cat piss and bin juice, and seeps into his mouth. He spits it out. The gunk is obscuring his vision.

Ouff!

Where are my Spidey senses?

His ribs are smashed. The impact drops him back down into the gutter.

What the fuck is going on?

He struggles to breathe as they kick him deep into his guts and chest.

Then Adam feels a pinch. Clean and piercing. It pulses up through his body. Everything becomes elegant and slow. He hears himself, the blood in his veins, and the guy lunging towards him.

Adam effortlessly pushes himself up off the pavement, rotates like a ceiling fan and kicks the mugger under the chin, snapping his head back and landing him on his arse.

The rest is a blur. The other bodies rush at him. He dances. Ducking, weaving, punching them all. They charge at him and are sent away, flung into the alley bins and grey metal fences.

The hoodlums get up and come at him again. Adam finds angles and movements to deflect, hit and swerve, and has so much time it feels unfair. They're flattened like ragdolls. Again, they run at him and throw punches, but he snaps them in two, flipping and tossing them away.

Then, just as quickly as it began, it all stops.

Their groaning bodies are strewn around the alleyway. Unnerved by the fact that he's the cause of their pain, Adam web-slings away.

Aiming for anywhere that's the fastest exit route, he goes straight up. Zip. Three storeys high.

It's like muscle memory, but it's actually movie memory.

Looking down at the tableau of baddies splayed out, he watches Kirsten, aka MJ, get to her feet and regain her composure.

Hanging from his web, upside down, he lowers himself down to her eye level.

Kirsten Dunst gently unfolds his mask, carefully pulling it down past his chin to expose his lips, and kisses him. Her touch is so warm and soft. Their kiss is glorious, and over.

What!?

She smiles at him. He wants to keep kissing, but she's stepped back, so stunning and adoring that he knows it's his cue to leave.

That was done way too fast.

Adam retreats to peaks of the NYC skyline while beneath him Kirsten is euphoric, beaming with PG-friendly superhero kiss bliss.

Adam's not been with anyone but Nina in a long time.

Well, Kinki's spiky and she treats me like admin, and no one is getting hurt and...

Exactly!

Plus, Kirsten Dunst playing the most gorgeous Mary Jane, has just kissed me with a sexy loveliness that set up superhero cinema, so... why is it that I feel short-changed?

No! I don't. I'm good.

Maybe Kinki's right. I mean, I should really be able to fully appreciate this...

I am, I am.

Ugh!

From the top of the building, Adam, aka your friendly neighbourhood Spider-Man, blurts out to all of New York, 'A new world awaits you, dickheads!' Does a two-finger tap on the palm of his hand and - *sheuuw* - slings a web out across the street.

He free falls off the ledge until the pull of the web reaches its maximum length and, like a bungee rope, yanks him up.

He shoots out another, his heart in his

mouth like a kid on a swing being pushed higher and higher. The suit is tight but porous, so it feels like he's nude-swimming with the air rushing across his body like water. He can't help but shout, 'Whoooo!'

Adam's whoop even sounds like Spidey. 'Cause he is.

He's above the skyline, looking at the tops of the roofs like they're playground stepping stones.

The web ends. He starts to drop. Falling fast. The sound of the wind is deafening. He shoots out web which sticks to the buildings. He spreads his arms out like a star, then pulls them to his chest. The web stretches and tightens and flings him high into the Manhattan sky.

It's flying combined with a perfect game of slingshot. The speed starts to make his eyes water; he's going so quickly that the extremes of high and low are ever-accelerating.

How's the montage end?

Huh?

Remember in the trailer, how's Spidey stop?

Doesn't he just swing through the screen and the logo comes up?

Swoozzzz. Adam's web misses the building and fizzles off. Instead of curling around the corner, Adam is hurtling towards an apartment block.

I can't fuck this up!

He shoots webs all over the shop but crashes through. The red brick wall rushes towards him.

'Ahhhhhh!'

In a last-ditch effort to avoid the wall, Adam aims for a window. He ducks down, bracing for impact. He shatters the glass, as his legs smash through the frame.

NON-DISCLOSURE

Adam's back in the Irish Pub with his heart pounding. His table is a shambles. The vodka and beer glasses are split. The bowl of buffalo wings is scattered across the floor.

The retiree women are talking to each other in hushed tones. El Slicko turns away the moment Adam looks over.

The chair with Adam's jacket is teetering on two legs, banged up against a table, plus his carry-on bag is upturned and blocking the passageway.

Did I do all this when I crashed?

The hand that had been holding his mobile is burning. There's a searing pain coming from his right shoulder and his nose feels spread across his face.

Adam picks up his bag and rights the chair. This movement highlights new injuries. His right ankle and shin are throbbing. With his good arm he pulls up his jeans. His calf has a gash in it. Blood is sliding down into his sock. He feels his cheek. It's bleeding too.

I don't get it, I should be in agony...

'Watch out.'

'Huh?'

The waiter leans in close as he cleans up the mess. 'With immersive mode.' Although he speaks in hushed urgent tones, he keeps smiling, making sure his face and actions look like business as usual.

'I'm not allowed to talk about this stuff, but…' The waiter starts picking the chicken bones off the floor. 'I've only seen one other person get immersion access and it wasn't good.'

'What do you mean?'

'How's your hand? Is it kind of burning?'

'Yeah.'

'See, they've created the connection, but they can't control it. The boundaries, that is. It's… you're a test case. It's beta. It taps into you via your hand. It syncs in, but what you experience and how you get in and out, that's all still being worked out.'

The waiter trails off as he stands back up. The charade of cleaning the table can't be stretched any further without drawing attention.

'And don't die in there.'

'I'm sorry?'

'Whatever you do.' The waiter picks up the empty glasses. 'So, another Blue Moon?'

'Hang on—'

'Beer?'

'Yeah but—'

'And a vodka soda?'

'I guess.'

He mumbles, 'Have something that grounds you. To bring you back,' then heads back to the bar.

Fuck me, could that be more intense?

Adam feels Slicko observing him.

Don't look back. Don't draw attention.

Adam dabs the cut on his cheek with a napkin. The blood looks bright red on the white absorbent paper.

How are they allowed publish an app that can do this? And why am I a test case? Is it 'cause I know VR?

The two retirees grab their carry-on bags and neck pillows and rather than pass his table, take a longer exit route.

Adam feels isolated and unsettled.

And what's with the 'don't die in there'... like, righto, thanks for the tip.

He looks at his fingertips and rubs his thumb over them. The burning sensation has reduced back to a light tingle. He puts on his glasses and holds the phone up close.

What's he mean, 'it syncs with you'?

He inspects it with forensic attention, studying the edges where he usually holds it and discovers sitting at regular intervals beneath the side buttons within the matte metallic frame, tiny, almost microscopic, grey dots.

Were they there before?

Like anyone with a phone, he's familiar with the little hole that is pushed in with a paper clip to get the sim card out, but these dots are a zillion times smaller.

Is that the sync point?

He replicates how he held the phone while using the PFEC app to compare where the dots are in relation to his fingers and thumb. They match up.

I don't know... they could have been there all along.

But I'd have seen them.

They're microscopic. It's only because I'm looking for them that I can see them.

So, they've always been there?

I guess...

Adam looks at the PFEC interface. The rollover menu has

Immersive Viewing highlighted. The text and image thumbnails for *The Wolf of Wall Street* and *Spider-Man* (2002) have the green tick completion icon. The one un-viewed title, *Pretty Woman*, remains greyed over, presenting an unlocked icon and a play button. Juxtaposed against the viewed titles, it looks enticing.

I love Spider-Man, *and* The Wolf of Wall Street *has a certain who-gives-a-fuck charm, and, yes,* Pretty Woman*'s a guilty pleasure… but with all the films out there, why these three?*

Adam's reverie with the PFEC app and its viewing algorithm is broken by the waiter's arrival with another massive Blue Moon beer and accompanying vodka soda. Adam is pleased to see him. The drinks are a bonus.

'That was quick.'

'Thanks.'

'What do you mean, "don't die in there"?'

'Exactly that.'

'If the movies are tame, then presumably I'm safer.'

'I get the logic, but don't count on it.'

'Can I show you what I'm watching?'

The waiter replies, 'Yeah, but I'm not allowed to tell you anything beyond what you'd already know.'

Adam looks around. It feels like this is being said not just for his benefit. Nearby on the concourse, two airport staff slowly walk past.

'Gotcha…' Adam shows him the interface.

As the waiter looks at the screen, Adam studies his face, searching for any cues or reaction to the titles, but the waiter just shrugs.

'I haven't seen them.'

'*Spider-Man?*'

'I've seen the new ones but not that old one.'

'Not even *Pretty Woman?*'

'I dunno, maybe I saw a bit of it when I was a kid, but isn't it, like, really old?'

'No, it was made in ninety-one. Ninety maybe.'

'I was two.'

'A young Julia Roberts…?'

'It's your rodeo.' The waiter gives the table a perfunctory wipe over and turns to leave, but Adam's still fishing for more angles.

'It's a rom-com, so there's no fights or stunts, so I'll be safe, yeah?'

'Like I said—'

'And does closing my eyes take me from one movie to the next?'

'What?'

'Does closing my eyes affect the experience?'

'What you know is what you know, and…' he adds cheerily for all to hear, 'You want anything else? More wings?'

'No, thanks, I'm good.'

'Okay then… just stay *grounded*.'

He nods at Adam wanting to make sure he gets the message.

'Got it.'

'Good.'

The waiter leaves, and Adam sips his beer. The cold glass soothes his tingling fingers. The pain in his shoulder's reduced to a faint ache. He leans down and inspects his leg. It feels pretty good.

As long as I stick to the script, I should be fine.

Adam eats his orange slice. Takes the slice of lemon out of his vodka soda and sucks out the juice.

Why did I get chosen?

Just have some balls and do it. Be a goddamn pioneer.

No, I'm more like a straight-to-video version of Inception.

Adam slips his hand into his jeans and pulls out Ella's little panda.

But instead of a spinning top… I've got you.

Adam takes a mental snapshot.

Bag and jacket secure. Drinks sorted. Slicko's still here but the old ducks have gone.

He puts the panda back in his pocket.

Here goes nothing.

He takes a swig of vodka soda and then, with the swashbuckling rush of Errol Flynn diving off his ship, hits 'Play'.

PRETTY HOPELESS WITH WOMEN

Adam immediately hears canned TV laughter. It sounds suspicious. He slowly opens his eyes and discovers he's sitting on a beige, patterned couch.

On the TV is a black and white show with a barefoot woman running around in a wooden barrel, squishing grapes.

What am I watching?

Nearby there's giggling. It's Julia Roberts in a blonde wig eating strawberries and drinking champagne.

Adam sits up. This causes the papers on his lap to rustle. She clocks that he's stopped working and crawls over. When she arrives at his crotch, she is momentarily distracted by the *I Love Lucy* comedy playing out on the TV.

The whole room looks lavish and dated. Julia's the classiest thing here by a mile, but she's being weird. Adam feels disconnected and sober. Then the penny drops.

I'm Richard Gere?! Oh, man. This is a double-edged sword. It's the head job scene.

Richard Gere's character, Edward, has thrown a ton of cash at Julia's hooker-with-a-heart-of-gold character called Vivian.

This is not...

Adam's slacks are light and loose, and as her hands slide up his thighs, it feels frictionless, like he's covered in Teflon.

Ahhh, it's so cringe.

She starts unbuttoning his shirt.

I wonder how many takes Julia had to endure doing this?

Hang on... I know this way too well... It's the sequence where Jules loosens his tie and unbuttons his top button, then it cuts away to the TV but when it cuts back to her, and she's sliding up his legs, his top button is once again done up.

Aged sixteen, Adam watched this film a million times. At the time he was smitten with a girl called Sasha Leightly, who, as far as he was concerned, was Julia Roberts' twin.

Sasha had been the head girl at Adam's high school when he was in Year 7. He had admired her from afar. Lusted and adored. Big brown eyes, big brown hair, and a big smile offered to everyone, from little Year 7s to the cool kids. She always stood with her feet at a right angle like a ballerina, which Adam thought was sophisticated and European; and out of the blue, four years later, she returned to choreograph the end of year musical.

Adam did not have a big part, but that didn't matter, 'cause the big deal, the show-stopping miraculous deal, was that Sasha Leightly aged twenty-one, studying drama, and recently broken up with her boyfriend of three years, found herself kind of interested in this god-knows-what-she-saw-in-him kid called Adam.

Seven weeks later, she pulled the pin. Plunk. She told him that he was too young, and she had to face up to the fact that her high school years were well and truly over, so she gave him a note and broke up with him in the car that had been their relationship home. A Ford Laser hatchback with a radio that didn't work but a cassette player that did.

The Laser that she'd parked outside his house and they'd spent hours talking and kissing in. She'd drop him off after rehearsal, he'd go inside, tell his folks he was going to bed, climb out the window and be back in her car within minutes. The Laser with a shoebox of mixtapes. The Laser where she'd introduced him to Billy Bragg and a soundtrack that would accompany Adam through to his early twenties. The Laser that, one night, because she'd left the engine on for so long so they could keep the stereo playing, the battery had run flat.

It was before mobile phones so, to rectify the situation, Adam had snuck back into the house, called road-side assistance and returned to her. The Laser that, after picking him up from school and en route to the river, Sasha had run over a blue-tongue lizard sunning itself on the road. They'd both looked back and seen its body flattened on the tar as its detached tail flailed about.

Before getting dumped, *Pretty Woman* came out.

The breakup note was given to him ten days before Christmas. It talked about islands and motorbikes. Adam spent the summer reading it over and over again, heart-broken as only a sixteen-year-old knows how. Bottomless.

So, what do I do?

I mean I'm here in this extraordinary app and I'm the totally gross Richard goddamn Gere?!

Yeah, but Julia Roberts isn't gross, and Sasha Leightly wasn't, and…

Julia undoes his zipper.

It's not cool. Times have changed. Would Julia do this role now?

Pretty Woman *wouldn't get made now, so it's irrelevant.*

Or would it? Things haven't changed so much.

Mate! The point is to enjoy whatever my head and this app comes up with. If it's a dream, embrace it.

And if it's real?

Then, really, how real can it be?

Adam recognises his Richard Gere reflection in the TV screen. Seeing himself with a grey-haired quiff, behaving with the entitlement of a rich man who's paid for sex, feels truly ordinary.

You're an idiot. The point is not to think about the gender politics or the current Hollywood landscape and its relationship to women both narratively and professionally.

Isn't it?

No! And yes, this scene doesn't have The Wolf of Wall Street *greed absurdity and it's without irony or sarcasm or whatever that miraculous ingredient Scorsese has that both shits on and celebrates the chauvinistic money power-plays, but it's Julia Roberts for fuck's sake, and she's just like Sasha, and no one's getting hurt, so...?!*

And with that, Adam leans back, sighs a greasy Richard Gere sigh and, settling in for the ride, closes his eyes.

The hands. The touch. Gone. Nothing. He opens his eyes. The TV is on, but the room is empty.

You muppet! Stop closing your eyes!!

Adam springs up from the sofa and heads straight out the door.

Julia is at the breakfast table nibbling a croissant, looking soft and tousled, her blonde wig swapped out for her natural locks, and wearing nothing more than the hotel's bathrobe.

'Hi.'

No, no, no! She's playing morning after! I'm still after last night.

What did I expect? It cuts away in the movie so of course it's going to…

Adam spins away and heads back to the TV room.

Can I get back to the champagne and make it last longer?

He opens the TV room door, but it's empty. I Love Lucy is still playing on the telly, but no Julia.

He returns to the brekkie table, but she's gone.

What the fuck?

Looking around, he sees steps leading to the bedroom.

It's like each room is a different scene.

Adam bounds up and enters. It's bathed in sunlight, with thousands of pillows on an acre of bed. But no Julia.

Then he hears a squeak coming from the bathroom and bursts in. She's in the bath, covered in bubbles, singing Prince's classic, Kiss.

Startled, Julia's Vivian quickly shifts from finding his arrival invasive, to acting cute. After all, it's her job.

'Don't you just love Prince?'
Adam re-writes the smarmy scripted line,
'More than life itself,' and instead yells
out, 'Yes, I do!' and leaps in.

BECAUSE YOU WATCHED

Nuts. This bastard app.

Adam's back at the fake Irish Pub, with a barely drunk beer and a tired vodka soda.

His neck is sore. His mind and body are out of whack. Slick's still at his table, but there's different matches on the TV. It's hard to know how long he's been in the terminal. The airport lighting is like a shopping centre or a casino. It's mid-morning and late afternoon, all day.

The worry that he might have missed his flight has him scampering over to the departure board. The flight to Sydney is yet to be assigned a gate.

That's cool... I've still got time. Which means in the app, time passes at a different rate. It's like five minutes in the app is maybe a minute in real life.

Adam returns to his table. He's not hungry but regardless scans the menu. He feels groggy, like he's had a nap that's slipped into a heavy sleep, only to wake up at dusk. He makes sure his jacket and carry-on bag haven't been touched then checks out his mobile.

The PFEC app shows Recently Viewed: *The Wolf of Wall Street*, *Spider-Man* (2002), *Pretty Woman*.

Righto... an arsehole with fucked up marriages, a teenager with his high school crush and a hooker fairy-tale. I feel guilty and I'm not even having sex in my dreams?

I'm so whipped and such a dick. If this dream immersion movie thing is going to play, then at least have some fun with it.

Adam rolls his finger along the screen and finds the adult content. Compared to the internet, it's dated and tame, but the titles are top-shelf: *Ass Ventura Crack Detective; Edward Penishands; Good Will Humping; School of Cock.*

Across the titles is a parental blocker. Adam types in his pin. The numbers are wrong.

What?

1111 is his password for everything. He tries 1234. Block. The text interface announces one remaining attempt before he's locked out for twenty-four hours.

Did I do 1111 the first time? Maybe I mishit a key.

It's high risk.

But it's always 1111.

He slowly types it in. 1111. Blocked. And locked out.

For fuck's sake. I mean, seriously.

Adam scrolls down the list. *American Booty; Game of Bones: Winter is Cumming; Drill Bill; Saturday Night Beaver.*

Hang on… The Case of the Smiling Stiffs is unlocked? You have got to be kidding me.

Adam's finger hovers over the play button.

Am I really going to watch this…?

Given how his earlier sessions have gone, Adam glances around. Aside from Slick who is busy on his laptop, there's no one else nearby.

No one's going to care.

Yeah, but still…

Adam's reluctance is more due to the film. It was a seminal work of his pre-adolescence. Scott Perry, for his Year 5 birthday had a sleepover party. His older brother, Gavin, being edgy, rented a porno, and after *Night of the Living Dead* and *The Lost Boys* as they lay about in their beanbags, Gavin chucked into the VHS player *The Case of the Smiling Stiffs.*

That year was a big learning curve on the sex front. At a school holiday tennis camp, Adam argued with absolute conviction to a bunch of kids, including Pepper, who he had a crush on, and her best friend nick-named Salt, that yes, obviously Prince Charles and Diana had sex, but there was no way. No way! His parents had. Ever.

For the rest of the camp, he was called Jesus.

In any case, the rumpus room at Scott Perry's sleepover party got pretty quiet when *The Case of the Smiling Stiffs* was put on. Not much rustling of the bean bags. But no hands were visible either. The plotline was burnt into Adam's consciousness. Two dick-tectives track down a vampiress who kills men through severe dehydration. Each victim is discovered with a massive hard-on. And a smile on their face.

Do I really need to take this trip?

No. He did not. Instead Adam scrolls down and finds *Melancholia* which he'd always wanted to see and which Nina wryly noted would be his cup of tea, 'Kirsten Dunst gets her kit off, and it's arty and moody, you'll love it.'

But he'd never found the right moment, and it was locked, too.

Nymphomaniac. Locked.

The adult content restrictions combined with the preceding events culminate in Adam rejecting playing the grown-up. Feeling petulant, he button-mashes the PFEC app. Alternative and recommended options are presented, and in an irritated flurry he selects them all. The films land on top of each other like lots of files being opened at once. This interface crescendo builds and builds, happening so fast that he barely sees the title before the next one appears.

He takes a sip of his vodka soda. The ice has melted, it's watery and flat but still has the faint taste of vodka. He licks his lips, leans back, stretches out his legs and hits 'Play All'.

ACTION WO-MAN

Adam's peripheral vision reduces and darkens like an Instagram filter, but directly in front his view is 8K, crystal clear.

A waitress sashays towards him carrying a tray of drinks. She looks familiar. Realising he's gawking, he turns away only to feel a splash of drinks spilling over his crotch.

'I'm so sorry, that was really clumsy of me.'

She's knocked her tray onto him and it feels fake, like a spy movie sequence with the sexy co-star working the mark to get the security code.

He looks up at her, wanting to understand why, but instead finds himself standing on a porch, in front of a glass door with a retractable blind.

Suddenly it zips up to reveal Cameron Diaz's Charlie's Angel, butt dancing. She's wiggling about with green slippers, and Spider-Man panties. Wiggle wiggle. She beams her platinum Diaz smile, takes the parcel

Adam's holding, and with a swoosh of her ponytail becomes—

Angelina Jolie *Tomb Raider*ing in a black singlet running down ancient stone stairs. Her breasts bouncing in front of Adam's face. Hypnotic. Shooting her guns directly past him, Adam follows the gunfire and turns around to see her target—

Winona Ryder stands in the *Heathers* high school gym shower. Her T-shirt is soaked through as the water flows over her face. She is mournful and murderous, slicking her hair back as the bathroom tiles collapse to reveal a high-rise rooftop at night and—

Scarlett Johannsson's *Ghost in the Shell* Japanese heroine jumping off a skyscraper. Her body is wrapped up in a black second skin that falls into the twirl of—

Jennifer Lawrence's *Red Sparrow* trench coat opening to reveal her naked Russian spy body, that shifts into—

Patricia Arquette on her knees in *True Romance* self-defence, laughing, bloodied, and battered in her red bra, holding a bottle opener above her head which she plunges down into—

Is this what I grew up with?

JLo's arse inside the boot of the *Out of Sight* car being jauntily tapped by George Clooney's suave and presumptuous fingers that slides into—

Halle Berry's black leather *Catwoman* suit as she crouches and meows over to—

This depiction of women?

Jamie-Lee Curtis dance-stripping in a little black mini for her creepy Schwarzenegger *True Lies* husband.

Is this what shaped my view?

She pirouettes into—

Kirsten Dunst in her *Bring it On* cheerleading uniform, faux-innocent singing, 'I'm sexy, I'm cute, I'm popular to boot! I'm bitchin', great hair, the boys all love to stare,' to—

But it's not what I think.

Molly Ringwald's *Breakfast Club* white panties being leered at under the high school table—

Sheesh.

Before landing on Maggie Gyllenhaal's *Secretary* bent over a desk. In the dark sheen of the leather chair, Adam sees himself as a tightly wound-up, early forties James Spader.

Submissive and compliant, Maggie rests her arms on the desk, her fingers spread, the line of her stockinged legs leading past her tight pencil skirt.

He gets up close, standing directly behind her, feeling the quietness of her anticipation.

Don't blink. Don't look away.

In the film, James Spader's Mr Grey tells her to lift up her skirt and pull down her stockings and panties, but Adam breaks away from the script and instead gently turns her around. Maggie looks fragile. He frames her face with his hands and starts to kiss her. She pulls away whispering, 'You can't do that.'

As she steps back, she loses her balance and grabs onto the desk. The office is listing and rocking like it's the inside of a boat.

Everything stops feeling solid and starts to fracture and rumble.

Maggie's indignant. 'You did this.'

'No hang on—'

The telephone and intercom slide across the desk. The story has unhinged. The room is spilling out.

Adam feels seasick and doughy. Rubbing his chin, his jawline feels like plasticine. He kneads his forehead, pushing his fingers way back into his skull, trying to shove away the strangeness.

RUN, ADAM, RUN

Adam opens his eyes.

He's back in the Irish Pub, sitting at his table, sweating and clinging onto his phone. His fingers burn. It's the longest session he's experienced, and he feels disorientated.

He casts his eyes over the PFEC app. The screen is covered with the pop-up text, In Session.

In session? But this is the terminal. I'm not... This should be real life.

He rummages around in his jeans' pockets.

Where's Ella's panda?!

And comes up empty-handed.

The waiter said to keep grounded.

Adam recognises the TV screens and the big table menus.

Look, it's okay... but if it's in session then...? I've got to find the panda.

He again scrounges through his pockets.

I can't have lost it if I never pulled it out. Then where is it?

He crawls around under his table, getting increasingly worked up.

What if my app session and real life have smooshed into one and that's why I can't find the panda?

Crouching on his knees, Adam pops up over his table and asks Slicko, 'Have you seen…'

But instead of Slicko there's a man in a pale grey suit, watching Adam like he's a lab rat.

'Are you right, there?' It comes out louder than Adam intended. Grey-suit Man acts like he didn't hear him and reads the menu.

He's like the shithead dad whose kid suicides in Dead Poets Society. *Or the father in* The Talented Mr Ripley.

Adam goes through his jacket, then double checks under his seat. The scratch of a chair scraping over the terminal floor grabs his attention. It's Grey-suit Man leaving.

Screw you.

He's like all of them, like every CIA sneaky fucker.

Grey-suit Man weaves his way through the crowd.

What does he know?

Adam starts to follow but the messiness of punters' luggage gets in his way. By the time Adam's out of the Irish Pub, the Grey-suit Man is barely visible.

I'm not a test case.

Adam starts to jog. The further away the Grey-suit Man gets, the more Adam believes he holds the answer. The Grey-suit Man starts running, and Adam chases like he's in *Mission Impossible*, with his hands and feet pumping up and down like pistons.

He jumps over an airport trolley, side-steps a Gen-Z couple, then almost takes out a kid with a Buzz Lightyear wheelie-bag. Adam catches his reflection in the shopfront windows.

Shit, I really am Tom Cruise! Outstanding. Run, Tommy, Run.

Grey-suit Man ups the ante, cutting through the narrow queues of passengers, and slips through a Staff Only door.

Adam, aka Tom, bolts over, pushes it open and finds himself in a concrete stairwell. Hearing the footsteps of the Grey-suit Man several flights below, Adam jumps over the banister and drops down the stairwell. He's graceful and fearless and with perfect timing he grabs the railing and pulls himself back to safety.

Too swept up in the moment to consider his *Mission Impossible* skills, Adam hears a door below slam shut.

He bounds down the stairs, yanks it open and enters a commercial kitchen full of cooks yelling and gas-stove flames.

Several waiters are carrying platters. The Grey-suit Man bumps into one, sending a tray of desserts into a spin. They teeter and wobble, but as the waiter regains control Adam crashes into him. It sends the tray flying and Adam to the ground.

In the mayhem, Grey-suit Man gets away.

Adam jumps to his feet and keeps chasing.

He pushes through the kitchen's doors into a café courtyard with a jacaranda tree and a girl with a cute pixie haircut serving coffees. Adam is about to run into her, but she deftly steps aside.

Was that Nina?

Adam tries to catch a second glimpse, but she's gone. Returning to the chase, Adam sees the Grey-suit Man enter the café's bathroom.

Gotcha!

Adam runs to the men's, opens the door, and discovers he's inside a shopping mall.

Okay... so we're portal jumping... like The Adjustment Bureau.

The Grey-suit Man dashes across the plaza, into a department store, runs past the bedding and menswear and into the changing rooms.

Adam follows. The walls and doors are lined with mirrors.

Kinki?

He spins around and sees Nina trying on her wedding dress. This image bounces from mirror to mirror. Adam swirls around, and pushes open a changing room door.

Instead of finding Nina, Adam is inside a childcare centre. The Grey-suit Man scuttles past the toddlers and their sandpit toys to the far side of the playground.

A little boy with bright blonde hair is talking to his cicadas. Adam almost runs over him, jumping out of the way at the last moment. The boy yelps. Adam recognises that sound.

Louie?

The toddler runs inside the sandpit cubbyhouse. Adam changes course, crouches down, and sticks his head through the cubbyhouse door.

Immediately Adam's struck by a huge wave and is swept off his feet. Choking on saltwater, Adam thrashes around struggling to get to the surface. Another wave crashes over him and down he goes. Overhead, little feet paddle past as a girl floats by on her boogie board.

Ella?

Adam swims to the surface. As he breaks through, the girl catches a wave, squealing as she sails away.

Why these memories?

More waves roll over him. He fights to stay afloat as his clothes drag him down. He loses his bearings, drowning in the surf.

The waves crashing overhead sound like trucks at night on a freeway.

I've got to shut my eyes and keep them shut.

He feels his lungs contract as the saltwater burns.

The waiter said that people get lost.
Just hold on.

The pressure becomes overwhelming. His body starts convulsing...

YIPPEE KI-YAY

What is that? No waves? Nothing?

Immediately he sucks in massive gulps of air. Hyperventilating and gasping, he opens his eyes and realises he's leaning against a large office window.

It's okay, just breathe. Breathe it in... no rush.

Outside are the night lights of a city.

I've gotta get out of this immersion mode.

But who was that guy?

He steps back from the office window and sees his reflection. He's barefoot, bloody, wearing a torn white singlet and black pants, and is holding a gun. Adam looks at it, stunned.

How is this possible?

He stares at himself. He's John McClane. Or more precisely he's Bruce Willis playing McClane. Muscular. Intense. He leans back against the window.

It's... fucking confusing, sure, but... am I really now in Die Hard?

Yeah, motherfucker. Yes.

Adam chuckles to himself. It gurgles out unintentionally.

Did I just McClane laugh? Fuck me.

He steps back to the window. Thirty storeys below, a police car circles the driveway and leaves the premises. Adam bangs against the glass, 'No, no, no!'

His actions feel out-of-body, it's not his style to whack windows, but it is Bruce's John McClane style.

The patrol car's leaving and McClane's on an empty office floor... so next is?

His movie memory recap is interrupted by the barrage of gunfire ripping the place apart. Sheets of glass shatter around him. Adam dives behind an office partition and sees the blonde baddie with big mullet hair reload his machine gun.

Gruber's brother?!

Adam looks at his pistol and checks the bullet count.

What am I doing?

Adam's never held a gun in his life, but now it's an extension of himself. He reloads and acts out two classic Willis manoeuvres.

One: Nervous puff-puff breathing, trying to catch his breath.

Two: Sneaking an in-out look around the corner to spot the baddie.

But he doesn't get much payoff, as Gruber's brother unleashes another round of gunfire before Adam can properly see anything. Glass shatters above him. Adam covers his face and feels it cut into his arm and shoulder.

Fuck this hurts!

If I die here, what happens in real life? I can't break the script. I did that with Maggie.

He scrambles across and cowers under a desk.

I've gotta do everything just like the movie, get back in sync, and hopefully that'll get me back.

The gunfire is everywhere as the office is demolished.

Think. Think it through. What scene's this?

Rounds of machine-gun fire rip through the building, followed by more glass showering down.

Of course! It's the barefoot sequence!

The fire exit is twenty metres away, down a highway of broken glass.

That's just self-inflicted agony.

If I die here, then there's no way back.

Adam starts running.

The pain is obscene. Deep angular shards tear up into his feet, stabbing and brutal. He drops his shoulder and breaks through the door. Loud. Violent.

He crashes into the stairwell and slams the door behind him.

His feet are shredded, with glass sticking out at all angles.

He limp-drags himself up the stairs.

This is so fucked up.

Adam pulls the glass out of his feet, rips his singlet into strips and, as he wraps it around trying to stop the bleeding, unleashes a thunderous bellow.

His cry reverberates around the stairwell. Trying to regain his composure, he takes stock of the rest of his body and, feeling blood trickle down his face, he uses his arm to wipe it off. As he does so, he inadvertently blinks...

Okay, the scene's cut! Fuck yes! Genius and accidental, but I'll take it.

He's shooting wildly into the air, sending the hostages running back into the building, as the FBI chopper fires at him.

It's the rooftop scene! Oh, hell...

Adam starts laughing McClane style, sardonic and crazy. The pain in his feet has rapidly dulled.

Hang on, this is brilliant... The moment the scene cuts and the location changes, the pain level resets.

Plus, if all I need to do is shut my eyes to cut, then getting out of here's a piece of cake.

Adam scampers across the rooftop, jumps off the ledge and lands beside the industrial air vent. Ignoring the gunfire around him, he closes his eyes.

Come on what's going on? I've been like this for ages.

The brilliance of a helicopter searchlight sweeps across his face and the light cuts through his self-imposed darkness.

Why isn't it working?

Maybe I've got to complete the scene first?

The continuous stream of bullets ripping through the air vents compels him to open his eyes. Above him is the FBI chopper, firing at him.

Adam knows the drill. McClane is penned in and there's only one way out.

Adam grabs the firehose and wraps it around his waist.

Well... I guess I've gotta trust my theory... just stick to the script and—

He runs and jumps off the building.

'Yippee ki-yay motherfucker!!!!'

Swinging out high and wide with the hose gripped around his waist, he leaps out. As the hose pulls him back towards the building's façade, he fires at the window, shattering the glass moments before he crashes through.

The helicopter and rooftop explode. He feels the searing heat as they erupt behind him, and, shutting his eyes, he braces for impact.

The scene's complete, now take me back.

The inertia from the explosion keeps going long after the blast. He opens his eyes and discovers he's behind the wheel of a fast and furious car.

You've got to be shitting me.

The speedo is on 170 and he's crashing

through office partitions like they're paper. His fat-ass fingers are wrapped around the steering wheel and his arms are bigger than his neck, puffed up like protein meringues. He looks in the rear-view wanting to see the destruction he's carved out and instead sees his big bald head.

I'm Vin goddamn Diesel?!

Framed alongside him are the windows of a high-rise tower, and with the end of the floor fast approaching, he fangs it.

The adrenaline and fatalism he felt during *Die Hard* remains, but now Adam's gumption is on steroids.

This is the best stunt of the whole franchise.

He hits 190. The office partitions snap and scatter as Adam drives headlong straight through the window. His red sports car soars out of the building and high off into the Abu Dhabi sky.

Adam feels weightless. He's in a car. Flying. It begins its elegant drop as gravity gets involved, while the building that Adam/Vin is trying to land in remains a long way away.

He feels like Wile E Coyote running off a cliff.

The car's bonnet dips downwards. His hands are glued to the steering wheel. The car is falling, not flying. His stomach goes up into his throat. Dread starts to rise. Pointless though it is, Adam floors it. Thousands of feet in the air with his wheels spinning.

Hey, Kinki...?

He tries yanking the wheel upwards like it's a plane's joystick but it doesn't move.

What the fuck!

The building looms large. He might land it, but the angle's too steep. It's clear that the moment he smashes through the glass wall the car will just crunch into the floor and he'll get mashed. The building comes up fast as he keeps flooring it. According to the speedo, he's at 210. He's never seen a dial go that far to the right.

As the window wall of the building zooms towards him, Adam hunches down.

This is it...

The bonnet shatters the glass, the car crashes into the floor, Adam whiplashes into the wheel and his eyes slam shut.

In the darkness, Adam feels the momentum.

I'm still going.

The car bursts out of the dirt, its wheels hit the ground and continues hurtling forward.

He opens his eyes, but rather than office debris, he's surrounded by desert sand flying everywhere.

The car is belting along a dirt track. Each

turn of the wheel makes it drift wildly.

The sleek European dashboard is no more; instead Adam's faced with 1960s dials and a skinny steering wheel. His wrists are no longer Christmas hams; they're thin with bangles, and his hair's so long it wisps across his sunglasses. He checks out the rear-view mirror.

Behind him is a cavalry of cop cars with sirens blaring, chasing him across the plains. In front is the Grand Canyon.

The cops fan out. He's completely fenced in.

'Do it.'

Surprised to discover he has a travelling companion, Adam turns to his passenger. She's wearing a headscarf and sunnies and has flaming red hair.

'Go!'

She's emphatic. Adam looks at her, 'Thelma?! Geena?'

It's impossible for him to see her behind all the stuff masking her face.

'You sure?'

This scene only has one ending and if I replicate what happens in the film, what'll happen in real life?

'Do it!'

Her conviction is unwavering and the scene is so iconic that Adam commits. He accelerates. Dust billows as the roar of the convertible drowns out the cops' sirens.

Adam pushes it to new motoring heights, hitting the cliff-face sooner than he expected. It feels way more dangerous and real than any of the previous stunts. Instinctively, he grabs his passenger's hand.

As the car bonnet dips, he looks over at her. The wind has whipped off the scarf and her sunnies have come loose.

It's Nina.

Whaaaaat!?

She's ablaze.

She squeezes his hand and whoops an almighty whoop.

He joins in whooping and hollering.

The ground comes up fast.

Hang on. What if this isn't right? What if...? Kinki!

Bang.

Black.

3

FILM SCHOOL

Like the silence of being underwater, this darkness is quiet. It's difficult to get any sense of time. There's no panic or anxiousness. It's as though his soul has hit pause. He doesn't feel anything, not his arms or legs or even the weight of his eyelids. All he feels is absence, and the absence of absence, as if nothing had a feeling and then that nothing feeling was emptied out.

It's unclear if he's standing up or lying down. He feels both vertical and horizontal as each sensation cancels out the other. He tries to get a sense of where he is. A context. But there's nothing to see or hear.

In his mind, he hears himself saying, *Try to listen*, but he can't tell if it's him thinking this or if it's him listening to himself think he's saying it. This absence fills the space, then loops back in on itself, back into nothingness.

He stops listening or looking or speculating over whether he's standing up or lying flat. He stops trying to make sense of it.

So, this is nothing.

It's euphoric and sad. Any effort to try to pin it down feels restrictive and counter-intuitive so instead he lets it all spool out of him. He lets go of everything, every thread of a thought or a care, and as he allows himself to completely dissolve into the absence, he hears a single note.

It comes from a piano. A second note follows. The strand of these two notes wrap around him like time and space. They offer rhythm, fill out and form a tune, one that he's heard before and liked, and as he tries to remember how he knows it, other elements start to congeal.

I'm Hamish.

I've two kids.

I'm Adam.

I'm married.

I'm Simon?

Not Pete?

Or divorced?

He multi-choice questions through his life. Splitting his memories, separating what is his history from the other people's. Real or fictional.

Simon isn't me. Or George.

I'm Adam.

He's always found his name onerous.

Maybe now I'll change it. Be less biblical.

No, no, not at all, I want it all back. Back the way it was. I want to get home. I've got to get home.

He hears a woman's laugh. It bubbles over the melody and brings with it the bright sound of cocktail glasses clinking, spotlighting the space.

I know that laugh.

CRAZY STUPID

The spotlight expands to reveal a bar.
Elegant. Lit like a speakeasy. And the woman
with the laugh is smiling at him. Generous
and beautiful.

'You're ridiculous.'

Nina specialises in expressing love through
these types of words: 'ridiculous', 'absurd'.

Only once has she said 'monstrous'. Each
syllable slid into the next. It was whispered
to him outside the Iguana Lounge. It was so
cold, he could see her breath as she rolled
out the word and he felt so good and so
astonished that she would like him, let alone
call him that. It was twelve-stars, splendid.

Now, sitting at the bar with a drink in
hand, he's 'ridiculous'. Happy. And confused.

There are elements of the Irish Pub woven
into this nightclub setting, but his desire
to understand where he is, is superseded by
Nina's arrival.

'You're looking good,' she says dryly.

Adam, trying to catch a glimpse of himself,

looks behind the bar, past the spirit bottles that line the wall, to the mirror. She's right. He does. He's Ryan Gosling good.

She looks different too. She's morphed into Emma Stone. The only way Adam knows it's Nina inside Emma's body is by the glint in her eye.

'You're no slouch either.'

Nina's Emma Stone leans over and slowly slides her hand across Adam's Ryan Gosling-ed chiselled chest.

'So, Mr Gosling... what was your character's name in *Crazy, Stupid, Love*?'

'Umm.'

'Actually, who cares because this is already our best date night. Ever.'

'You're such a perv.'

'You don't say.'

She sits back on her stool, knowing her short dress has slid up, and crosses her legs. She's looking playful and gorgeous. Her soul is beaming through her Emma Stone casing as she lights a cigarette.

'So...' She takes a drag. 'What the fuck is going on?'

'I have no idea.'

'Well, you must have some.'

Adam grabs a cigarette and lights up.

Nina's Emma offers her signature arched eyebrow, 'And I see you're smoking these days.'

'Like you said, no one ever quits, they're just waiting for something fucked up enough to give them an excuse.'

'And this is that time?'

'A-huh.'

'I see.'

'Plus, Kinki, it's all nuts.'

'I know—'

'Like "I might be insane" nuts.'

'Okay.'

'And I've got a shit-ton of questions and I don't know much at all.'

'Right…'

'And meanwhile you're acting pretty damn calm.'

'I'm looking like Emma Stone, you're Ryan Gosling, and we're in the bar from *Crazy, Stupid, Love*… I'm just working with what's in front of me.'

Adam smiles at her summation.

'So, what's going on?'

He takes a moment to answer, wondering where to begin.

'Well… in the San Fran terminal, when I was waiting to fly home, they offered me this new… what they call a pre-flight entertainment app which has all these content channels as well as an immersion mode.' He pauses, wanting to give this info emphasis.

'Okay…'

'But it's a beta version so not everyone gets the immersion mode, but I'm one of the lucky ones.'

Adam can see she's trying to keep an open mind, like she's interviewing a dubious witness.

'And so, in the app I select Immersive Viewing, chose from a list of my favourite movies, hit play, and then - bang - I'm inserted into the actual film.'

'What?'

'Yeah, like, it's nuts… the app puts me in the movies. Literally.' Adam takes another drag. 'At the start, to get back, I just had to close my eyes, and the app would shut down, and I'd return to the airport. But now I close my eyes, and nothing.

'And this waiter at the airport warned me. He said I was a test case and not to get hurt or die in the immersion mode 'cause if I did, it'd change me in the real world and I thought maybe if I died in a movie I'd die in real life, but then I lost Ella's panda—'

'Her little finger puppet?'

'Yeah, it's become like my version of the spinning top in Inception.'

'Wow…'

'And it's helped me know when I was out of the app and what was what, but then I lost it and I was in all these action films and

it didn't matter whether I blinked or not,
or how extreme things got, I'd still be in
these movies and then we crashed at the end
of *Thelma and Louise*—'

'You were in *Thelma and*—'

'Yeah, you were with me—'

'I was?'

'We drove off the edge together and—'

'What happened?'

'That's what I'm saying, 'cause of that
ending and us dying in the film, I think
what's happened is that…'

He stops.

Reluctant to say what he's thinking, Adam
takes one last drag of his cigarette before
gently stubbing it out.

'Adam?'

Looking down at his drink he mumbles, 'I
think I'm trapped in this halfway place where
the immersion mode of *Crazy, Stupid, Love*
and my memory of the airport bar and of you
are all bleeding into one.'

'Okay…'

'It's the set of the film and we're
characters in it, but we can say and do
whatever we like, and the extras are just my
memories of people I know and—'

'The extras are people you've met?'

'Mmm.' He leans in closer to Nina, speaking
softly. 'See that barman? He looks like the

waiter who warned me.'

'Really?'

'But how could he be here unless he's my memory of the waiter?'

'Adam…'

He pulls away, 'I told you its nuts, like, I'm not joking, it's actually insane. Seriously…'

He's usually good at reading her face, or at least thinking he is, and maybe it's because she looks like Emma Stone, but her expression leaves Adam at a loss.

'Kinki?'

'What?'

'What do you think?'

'Adam, it'll… I'm not…' She abruptly finishes her cigarette and jams down the butt hard into the ashtray.

Adam waits for her to finish her sentence. A silence grows between them. It becomes fat and awkward.

Adam, wanting to fill in the gap, blurts out, 'Well, thanks for coming.'

Nina's laugh is unbridled and unexpected. It breaks the confused tension of his explanation, and for the first time in a long time, he feels okay.

She holds out her glass. 'My pleasure.'

Clink. They cheers.

He finishes off his drink. 'Want another?'

'Sure.'

To the barman, Adam says with his dazzling Ryan G face, 'We'll have two more, thanks.'

'Whisky sour?'

'Yep.'

Nina pulls out another cigarette. Adam offers her the lighter. They're channelling Bogart and Bacall, dressed as Gosling and Stone.

'You know, Kinki, the thing is, in a crisis, when nothing makes sense, you're completely there.'

'I know, right?!'

Adam grins. The answer is so Nina. Cocky and self-mocking.

As the barman works on their drinks, she whispers into Adam's ear, like she's an undercover agent on the prowl for the mole, 'Is he the guy?'

'Who?'

'The waiter who warned you?'

'Kind of.'

Adam's enjoying the buzz of their banter, it feels like the early days of their romance. He nuzzles into Kinki's neck and murmurs, 'He's my memory of the waiter who warned me, and then I've brought that memory of him into this *Crazy, Stupid, Love* bar.'

'Cool...'

The way she says cool has a playfulness, like she's up for the challenge.

She sits back, taking it all in. 'In that case, I'm not leaving until we've done the *Dirty Dancing* scene.'

'I'm just glad you're here.'

'You just like the dress.'

She smiles at him in a funny kind of way, almost rueful. Adam's not sure what to make of it but before he gets to ask, she jumps in with, 'So, what've you been watching?'

'Here.'

Adam shows her his mobile. She flicks through the PFEC interface.

'*Fast and Furious*? *Catwoman*? *Tomb Raider*?'

'Yep.'

'Why not *Wonder Woman*?'

'It might be a rights issue.'

'In your memory?'

'Or maybe I wasn't as into it as the rest of the planet.'

'You think?'

'All I know is it has to be a film that on some level I've connected with, and if I try to change it too much then it just glitches out. And at the start, like I said, I'd close my eyes, and the app session would end, and I'd be back at the airport like I was just watching stuff on my mobile, but now I can't get back. I can't get to the terminal, I can't get home, I-'

'It's okay.'

Adam nods, trying to remain composed.

'So, let's see…'

She flicks her finger up and down the Viewed list, like a doctor looking at the patient's records. It's intimate and he feels scrutinised. It's a familiar dynamic and one that he usually hates, but now Nina's an ally.

'*The Case of the Smiling Stiffs*?'

'A seminal film.'

'No doubt.'

'And please note that it's unlocked but not viewed.'

'And what happened with *Secretary*?'

'I tried to kiss her and—'

'You missed out with Maggie!' Nina's face lights up as she flat out laughs at him, 'I love it!'

'Anyway, Spader's a dick.'

'I hear he's a gentleman.'

Nina hands back his mobile. She's finished examining the patient's records.

'Well… you're watching all the wrong movies.'

'*Die Hard. Spider-Man*. I don't think so.'

'*Pretty Woman*?'

'I was sixteen when it came out.'

'Let's just go through it, beat for beat.'

Adam can see she's in journalist, working the story, fix-it mode.

'You select a movie?'

'Yeah.'

'You get taken into it?'

'Yep.'

'But now when it ends, instead of returning to the airport and leaving the immersion, you're stuck here?'

'Exactly, I'm left in this weird hybrid of movies and memories.'

She leans back. Adam sees her brain rattling through the various options, 'You've seen *It's a Wonderful Life*?'

'No.'

'You haven't seen it?'

'I love how you repeat a question when you don't like the answer.'

'It's just, I can't believe you've not—'

'Well, I haven't.'

'So, I can't choose that for you.'

'I guess not.'

'Are there any good films in here?'

'They're all good.'

'Are there any where the hero's trapped in a dream or a loop, like you are now, and they've got to work out what they really want. Like that rom-com with the guy from *Brooklyn 99*.'

'Andy Samberg?'

'Yeah.'

'Haven't seen it.'

'Well, that's why I'm thinking *It's a*

Wonderful Life, but—'

'Well, yeah I haven't seen that either.'

'Well, what have you seen?'

She grabs back the phone. She's incredulous.

'*The Wolf of Wall Street*?'

'That's what started it.'

'Of course it did.'

'I'm sorry?'

'So typical.'

'I don't actually like it, I—'

'Cashed-up drug fantasy about not giving a fuck, with Margot Robbie as the eye candy.'

'So what?'

'Don't you see the pattern?'

'I don't know if they're the same ones you're—'

Exasperated, Nina cuts him off. 'Two of your first three choices have older blokes fucking younger women!'

'But I never do!'

'So you keep saying!'

Adam sighs.

Nina inspects her Emma Stone dress and flicks off a piece of non-existent dirt.

'Alright… what are the rules. Can we jump to different parts of the movie, or do we have to do it sequentially?'

Adam doesn't reply.

Nina's flustered. 'Do you want me to help or not?'

The barman intrudes, wiping the bar and placing down a new tray of nuts.

Knowing she's waiting for his answer, Adam uses the barman as an excuse to delay replying as he thinks through what he's going to say. Once the barman moves down the bar, Adam offers, 'Yeah, I do.'

'Really?'

'Yeah, I really do.'

Nina doesn't acknowledge this and instead takes a drag on her cigarette. Adam studies her face, curious to see if she's silent 'cause she's got the shits or because she's waiting for his attention. Upon making eye contact, she locks him in. Quiet and self-contained, she asks, 'What do you want? Like, actually, genuinely, really want.'

'I want to get home.'

'Why?'

'Because I love you, and I love our kids.'

'You don't have to sell it.'

He tries to mask his flush of indignation by focusing on his whisky.

'Adam… you sound like you're trying to convince me. Or yourself.'

'Not at all.'

'But it doesn't work that way. It has to come from you.'

He looks at her as he speaks softly, 'I want to come home. Big time.'

'Okay then.' She smiles. Warm. She usually only ever offers this kind of look to the dog or the kids. Adam's touched that she's giving it to him, her gentleness and compassion, and yet he also hears a shitty little voice wondering,

Why are you so stingy with being nice to me? Why's it only offered when things are really shit?

Looking pleased with herself she hands him back his mobile. 'This was unlocked.'

Adam looks down at the PFEC interface.

'No way!'

'Yep.'

'You're a genius.'

Adam raises his glass.

'Thank you, Kinki.'

Clink.

'No worries.'

He hits 'Play'.

GROUNDED

Sonny and Cher's version of *I Got You Babe* warbles out from the tinny bedside clock radio.

So now I'm in a film about a man who's trapped playing the same day over and over again, while I am trapped in a reality that is my memory of my favourite films. Sheesh...

Even though Adam's convinced of his theory about why the PFEC app and its immersion mode works the way it does, as he lies under a patchwork quilt in the *Groundhog Day* hotel, listening to the radio announcers say, 'It's coooooold outside,' it still feels weird.

The numbers on the bedside alarm clock flip over to 6:00.

Adam, aka Bill Murray, opens his eyes, yanks off the sheets, and gets out of bed. He's feeling different. Good different. Energised and congenial. Plus, unlike the previous characters, in *Groundhog Day*, Adam is playing a character who's the same age as he is.

I just need to get home.

Adam is speaking to a news camera with the townsfolk of Punxsutawney around him. He is tearing through the original script and it rolls off the tongue.

'When Dostoevsky stared down the barrel of another long bleak winter, he saw a season bereft of hope, but'—

Where are these words coming from? I can't believe I remember this. It's got to be Nina.

—'standing here among the good folks of Punxsutawney, basking in the warmth of their hearts, I couldn't imagine a better fate than a long, snowy winter. From Punxsutawney, it's Phil Connors. Adieu.'

The crowd around Adam/Bill/Phil claps. The muffled sound of snow-gloves' applause has a friendly small-town feel. Larry, the cameraman, finishes recording and addresses Adam with earnest appreciation.

'Phil, you touched me.'

Adam raises a Bill Murray eyebrow. Larry's line sounds sexual, but Larry doesn't register the double entendre. Adam likes the innocence and is genuinely pleased to have impressed him. Adam feels the townsfolks' warmth as they cluster around, and he offers it right back by the bucketful. Shaking hands. Kissing babies.

But the thing that delights him most is that Nina is with him, as Andie MacDowell, playing Rita the field producer.

Groundhog Day has Nina and Adam history.

They watched it with their kids as one of their 'Friday-night movie nights'. And they watched it during their mid-twenties pre-relationship friendship phase, stoned and debating the art of the rom-com. Nina had all her stars out, listing with theatrics and precision the multi-faceted gorgeousness of Bill Murray and why *Groundhog Day* was a scriptwriting masterpiece.

Adam, in return, posited his Andie MacDowell hair theory. Namely that her characters' emotional states are defined by her hair.

'If she's cross, it's in a tight bun. Sexy and playful; it's out. Confused: high ponytail. Falling in love: pulled back with a few strays that she can coquettishly tuck behind her ear.'

'I need specifics.'

'*Green Card;* big, continental and curly 'cause she's falling for a Frenchie. *Sex Lies and Videotape;* repressed and pulled back till it isn't. *Four Weddings and Funeral;* the first scene she's the mystery woman, so she's wearing a hat, by the end of the flick when she's love struck, and standing in the rain, its sexy and slicked back like she's just stepped out of the shower. And the Oscar for Best Supporting Actress goes to… Andie MacDowell's hair.'

Nina grimaced. 'You think Andie MacDowell's sexy?'

Back at the rotunda, Adam, aka Bill Murray, moves through the crowd. He is stopped by Nina's Andie. 'That was surprising.'

'I surprise myself sometimes.'

'Well, would you like to get a coffee?'

Nina tucks a loose curl of her MacDowell locks behind her ear and leans in, offering Adam a chance to boldly sneak in an unscripted kiss, but Adam, fearful of breaking the rules, replies, 'Gosh, I'd love to. Can I rain check?'

He gives her a boyish Murray grin.

I've got a montage of selfless acts to do.

Wearing an oversized dark duffle coat and matching gloves, Adam walks along a tree-lined street. He checks his watch. He's going to be late, so runs ahead, arriving just in time to catch a boy falling from a tree. As the kid runs away, Adam nails his lines.

'What do you say? Huh, punk? Not once have you thanked me. I'll see you tomorrow. Maybe.'

On Main St, three elderly women fuss about. Their car has a flat. They're sitting inside, debating what to do, when it starts to bounce and hop about. Outside, Adam is jacking it up, changing the tyre as they cry, 'It's an earthquake?!'

This is fun homework.

Adam buys the complete suite of insurance products from the perky bald salesman.

'Bing!'

Ticking boxes.

By the time of the charity auction, Bill Murray's character is the man of the moment. He's made so many folks happy that the whole town wants a date with him. Standing on stage, Adam feels all eyes upon him.

Is it the character Phil Connors that's getting sweaty palms, or me?

With the action films it was just remembering what to do, and when to jump, but once this auction ends and we're on a date... I know this film's about learning to do good without expecting it in return, but...

The town hall erupts. The results are in. Nina's Andie MacDowell, having dropped some serious cash, has gazumped all rival bidders.

... right now, standing on this stage, Phil Connors doesn't know that he'll wake up tomorrow with the spell broken and he's learnt his lesson. But I do.

But if I know what happens next, how do I know that I'm not kidding myself?

But I'm not.

No...?

So, what's the problem?

The penny drops.

There is no problem. I love her, pure and simple.

Adam smiles at his realisation, and in response to the money she's splashed out, he gives the crowd a classic Bill Murray 'can you believe it' grin.

As scripted, the scene cuts to Punxsutawney's town square. It's idyllic, with wooden park benches, neatly pruned bushes, and a light dusting of snow. Adam/Bill and Nina/Andie are tucked up in their coats in the cold night air. Andie's hair is super boofy and loose.

Adam puts the finishing touches on the ice sculpture of Andie MacDowell's face and rotates it around for the big reveal.

Nina is gobsmacked by its beauty. 'How'd you do that?'

She's radiant. Adam sees her anew, and as he delivers his lines, their meaning and weight sneak up on him, resonating with unexpected depth.

'I know your face so well I could have done it with my eyes closed.'

He looks at her, searching past Andie MacDowell to see Nina. He'll see it in her eyes, whether his feelings are reciprocated.

She replies, 'I think I'm happy, too...'

It starts to snow. Accompanied by a swell of strings playing a rom-com soundtrack, they kiss. It's intimate and lovely.

Adam closes his eyes.

Please let this be it.

The kiss that sends me home.

WOODY, YOU DIDN'T DO IT, DID YOU?

Adam keeps his eyes closed for as long as he possibly can and only opens them when he no longer feels her touch.

He's not in the park. It's not snowing. And Nina's not there.

What am I doing wrong?!

Adam finds himself standing in the doorway of a sumptuous art deco Manhattan apartment. Everything is black and white. Beyond the architrave is a stunning room ideally suited for Fred Astaire and Ginger Rogers to dance up a storm. There are enormous windows, matching velvet chaise lounges and a bar so well stocked it'll outlast prohibition.

Where am I?

His companions deposit cumbersome suitcases near the entrance. They are looking fabulous. A woman with blonde bombshell hair and a sparkling cocktail dress glides by Adam.

'I hope you like your martinis very dry.'

A debonair gentleman with a pristine necktie saunters to the drinks cabinet and announces in a foppish English accent, 'The Copacabana floorshow starts in ten minutes, so hurry up, children.'

In an ornate golden mirror, Adam sees his reflection. His complexion is matinee movie-idol white; he is wearing a safari suit and holding a pith helmet.

I can't believe I still remember this... The Purple Rose of Cairo.

To the group, Adam proclaims, 'Only twenty-four hours ago, I was in an Egyptian tomb, and now I'm on the verge of a madcap Manhattan adventure.'

There is only one film that Adam has seen with a character unironically dressed in a safari suit. There's only one television commercial too. The 1988 commercial depicts a heart-throb adventurer seeing a girl in the cinema audience eating Twisties. He stops what he's doing in the movie, looks through the screen, thereby breaking the fourth wall, and asks the girl if he can have some. Given they're both hot, and hot to trot, the ad ends with him stepping out of the movie screen to hang out with the girl and eat Twisties. As far as ads go, Adam thought it was pretty damn good. Two weeks later, in his Year 10 English lesson, Mr Buchan showed the film that the ad had ripped off. It was made when Hollywood's heroes were played by Harrison, Arnold or Sylvester. Thirty or more years later it could have been one of the Chrises – Hemsworth, Evans, Pratt, or Pine – but instead the leading man was played by an actor's actor with a friendly but forgettable face.

What's the name of that guy again? He did that Aaron Sorkin drama about TV news and was in Dumb and Dumber...

Of course – Jeff Daniels!

If I'm Jeff, playing an adventurer, then I guess I'm on a quest...?

To do what? Well...

Adam walks up to the screen and stares through the fourth wall, past the light of the film's projector, to the matinee audience.

To find Nina? But why would she be here? Well, why am I here?

To find Nina...? Then that must be my quest.

He peers into the actual cinema. There are not many people watching the flick, but near the back is a woman sitting alone.

Is that Kinki?

From inside the film, Adam, looking like a young Jeff Daniels, holds his pith helmet in one hand and a martini in the other. He talks through the movie screen and addresses the woman sitting by herself. 'My god, you must really love this picture.'

He can't quite make out her features, but the moment she answers with that distinctive waif-like voice Adam recognises her.

'Me? You mean me?'

Oh my god, it's actually Mia Farrow.

'I've got to talk to you.'

M-I-Adorable Mia!

And just like the ad and the movie, too, Adam steps out of the screen and into the cinema.

The usher screams and faints.

The black and white Manhattan set is immediately replaced with warm sepia tones and Adam's complexion gains a healthy glow. As he clambers over the cinema seats and heads towards Mia, she sinks down in her seat.

From the cinema apartment, the English gentleman calls out, 'Listen, old sport, you're on the wrong side.'

Adam ignores him and keeps going.

Slumping lower into the chair, Mia looks like she's trying to disappear. Her delicate, light-brown dress accentuates her frailty. Adam, aka Jeff Daniels, arrives, and with his matinee charm asks, 'Who are you?'

'Cecilia.'

He looks into her eyes, and he realises that Nina's not there.

'Oh.'

Adam is baffled.

What's going on?

From the silver screen, the bottle-blonde cries out, 'Tom, darling, come back.'

Maybe Nina's the blonde? I think I've made a terrible mistake!

Adam/Jeff/Tom crabs across to the aisle, hurries back to the screen, and takes a running jump back into the movie.

Thwack!

He bangs against the screen and hits the floor like a sack of potatoes. It's inelegant and unbefitting of an adventurer.

'I say, old chap.' The Englishman is appalled.

Adam sits up, dusts himself off and tidies up his suit.

'Tom!' squeaks the blonde. She tries to

pull him in, but her knuckles crunch against the screen. He is locked out. Adam closes his eyes and rubs his brow.

Just take me back.

The cinema goers start to crowd around him. Adam keeps his eyes shut and tries to block them out.

Please send me back to Kinki at the Crazy, Stupid, Love *bar.*

The noise of the cinema audience cuts through.

'I didn't pay for this tomfoolery.'

'What's the ruckus?'

'Where's the manager?'

Adam gives up and looks over at the screen. The cast is pressed up against it, staring out into the movie theatre.

The bottle-blonde pleads, 'Tom, darling, come back.'

'Really, old sport, this is most uncalled for,' moans the fop.

In Groundhog Day, *Kinki spelt out to me what I had to learn, but what's the lesson here?*

Beyond the commotion of the cinema patrons clustered around him, Adam sees Mia white-knuckled, clutching her purse.

I just adored her... and Woody, too.

But she's not Nina.

Sure, but maybe she can help. Or I help her, or we help each other? Either way, so many quests are about the hero saving the girl and, in doing so, saving themselves and then realising that the girl never needed saving, so... I just have to stick to my plan and try and find Kinki. I mean, she's the point, she's the quest.

Adam gets to his feet, brushes past the folks buzzing about him, and offers Mia his hand. 'Would you like to join me?'

The moment Mia accepts, the whimsical clarinet arc of Gershwin's *Rhapsody in Blue* starts to play.

'We're here to find Nina.'

'Who's Nina?'

'Never you mind, doll face. Never you mind.'

Adam gives Mia a gold-class smile. As the vibrant wail of Gershwin's big band kicks in, they run up the aisle and through the swing-door exit.

Manhattan at night. In the thirties. Cinema beautiful.

On the depression-era streets the cars have sideboards and honk like a clown's horn. As they dash through Downtown, the nightclubs' neon lights crossfade and montage around them. Flashing martini glasses. Dancing girls. The Banana Lounge and The Ritz. On the sidewalk, a cop working the beat idly swings his truncheon as a newspaper boy yells, 'Read all about it.'

Mia, breathless, asks, 'Where are you taking me?'

'The only place I know.'

'Will Nina be there?'

'You never know your luck in a big city.'

'Gosh, I'm not so sure—'

'Cecilia, this is our quest!'

An excited little smile sneaks across her face.

Arriving at the flashing lights of the Copacabana, the doorman steps aside as Adam escorts Mia down the red carpet. They're greeted by the wafer-thin, top-hat and tails manager, 'So good to see you, sir.'

With a grand sweep, the manager opens the nightclub doors and leads them through the dancehall, past the chorus line of high kicks and ostrich feathers to a circular booth that's pink and cushioned. The manager snaps his fingers, and immediately a swarm of waiters appears.

I don't remember this happening in the movie...

Why is it that we're able to be here, unscripted and everything's okay?

Maybe it's not the immersion mode at all?

Maybe it's my mind trying to work shit out...? So, when the Groundhog Day *kiss failed to get me back to the airport, I've gone into some other part of my brain to try and work out what's going on?*

Pop! A magnum of champagne bubbles over. Adam and Mia are surrounded by sparkles and laughter.

Just roll with it and find Nina.

How can I if it's all unscripted?

Maybe that's the point.

A cigarette girl in a flouncy dress with a

red ribbon slung over her neck to support her tray full of smokes arrives at their table.

Adam takes a packet and hands over the cash. The girl looks at him strangely.

'Hey, mister, what are you playing at?' Her Brooklyn drawl undercutting her classy attire.

Adam replies in his Jeff Daniels explorer voice, 'I don't know what you mean.'

'I mean this.' She shows him the notes. They're blank.

'Prop money. Yikes!'

'What'd you say?' asks the cigarette girl.

Mia is mortified. 'Here.'

From her purse, she scrounges together enough coins to pay for the smokes.

The cigarette girl takes her money. As she walks away, Adam knows the clock is ticking. They're skint, with no way to pay for the champagne, and it's just a matter of time before they get ratted out.

There's only one option. Adam grabs their glasses, fills them to the brim. 'Bottoms up!'

The dancehall's band becomes the soundtrack to Adam and Mia's escapade. The horn section gets brassy as the cigarette girl cuts across the dancefloor, past the black-tie gentlemen and their ring-a-ding-ding companions.

It plays out like a Buster Keaton-style silent movie with the physicality of characters' actions telegraphing their emotional response. The cigarette girl starts flapping her arms about, giving the barman the inside skinny regarding the behaviour of Adam and Mia. He responds with, 'Shock and dismay!'

He looks across the dancefloor and sees them neck their champagne. 'Indignation!'

He runs to the manager and points an accusatory finger their way. 'Outrage!'

Mia and Adam grab their coats and hats and run outside. The manager and doorman are in hot pursuit. Adam holds Mia's hand as they dash down the street and brush past the truncheon-twirling cop, who spins around like a turnstile.

Just as he regains his footing, he is spun back around by the Copacabana staff pursuing the bill absconders. Blowing his whistle, he joins in the chase.

Mia's shoes clatter on the sidewalk, as she struggles to stay on her feet and keep up with Adam.

If we get caught, then what? Can I get locked up? In my own mind?

In a moment of cinematic coincidence, a swanky car pulls up at the sidewalk and a portly chap who looks like W.C. Fields and is dressed like the Monopoly man, complete with monocle and walking cane, gets out. He barks orders at the little white dog yapping in the back seat, 'Stay there.'

As W.C. heads towards a five-and-dime, Adam slips past, opens the car's front door, and ushers Mia inside.

The wheel and dashboard are threadbare basic. Adam shifts the heavy gear stick, crunches the gears, and floors it. The car putters off down the street.

With the noir-style contrast of the streetlight framing her face, Mia watches the sidewalk high jinks.

Shocked to discover his car is being stolen, W.C. lumbers after them. His pursuit down the footpath is indirect and erratic. He collides into the manager and doorman, and shortly after the cop crashes into them too.

Mia mutters, 'Oh my.'

The dog, in response to this hullabaloo, puts his front paws over his eyes. Physically impossible, but none-the-less cinema cute.

Mia turns to Adam. 'Where are we going?'

Duke Ellington horns punctuate each question—

'I don't know.'

—with brassy soundtrack flair.

'What are you doing?'

'I'm not sure.'

'Are we fugitives?'

Adam nods.

'On the run?'

'I believe so.'

'Well it's a fine mess you've got me in.'

Driving in front of them, various old Model T Fords zip about.

It's as though they're filmed from a different angle.

Adam shifts around in his seat, sliding from left to right.

When I move, everything inside shifts but outside the cars stay the same...

'Look, Cecilia, those cars on the road have been filmed separately and then projected into the scene.'

'What are you talking about?'

'It's like an old school green screen, it's rear projector cinematography.'

'Mister, I ain't buying what you're selling.'

'Well, I'm just sayin—

'Some quest this is.'

Mia folds her arms looking more like a sulky lost girl than a devil-may-care dame.

As they drive through Manhattan, the streetlights flicker past in a white blur, the neon signs are long gone, and within moments it looks as though they've driven miles. The shopfronts lose their detail and become small squares of light, as if the art department, being smart with their budget have cut holes into black sheets and shined torches through to create the evening streetscape passing by.

In the front seat it's snug; the radio plays a swooning oboe melody and as the film-set street rolls out before them, Adam's thoughts road-trip drift.

When Woody Allen made *The Purple Rose of Cairo*, he was living with Mia. They each had an apartment on Central Park, and Woody would float between their two houses.

Adam idolised them, and as he was falling for Sasha Leightly he was cutting out Woody and Mia press clippings and sticking them on his bedroom wall. *Annie Hall. Husbands and Wives. Hannah and Her Sisters. Manhattan. Crimes and Misdemeanours.* It was his roadmap to adulthood. While Adam as a teenager was discovering Woody's films, Mia was dating and co-starring with the director, who in turn was co-parenting his future wife, Soon Yi, a girl the same age as Sasha.

Uncomfortable with this knowledge, Adam readies himself to tell her everything.

But she's in character right now, she's playing Cecilia, not being Mia, and even if she was Mia, what right do I have to tell her about her family's future? Would I want to know my own?

Adam keeps his eyes on the road, but the road is changing. The city lights of Downtown are gone, there's not another car to be seen, and beyond the headlights is darkness.

'Tom,' whispers Mia, 'I feel faint.'

Adam looks over. She's fading out of the scene. Semi-dissolved. Adam can see her, and through her to the seat she's sitting on. He looks over to the backseat.

The dog's vanished.

The car's interior, the seats, window, and
chassis are no longer solid. Instead, they're
a pencil-lined sketch. A single frame in a
storyboard. Adam turns back to the front.
Mia's gone. No purse or hat. Not a trace.
Plus, the car's gear stick, dashboard, and
seats are now lead-pencil drawings, and the
steering wheel he's gripping is a thinly
drawn circle.

Fuck.

FIX IT IN POST

In the darkness, Adam carefully turns the paper-thin steering wheel and guides the car over to the side of the road. He gently pulls down the hand-drawn doorknob, opens the door, and steps out.

By the sliver of moonlight breaking through the clouds, he can make out the two-dimensional outline of his stolen car. Every line looks flimsy.

He softly closes the door, worried that too much force will tip it over like a cardboard cut-out, but instead, the moment the door clicks shut, the clouds block out the moonlight completely and the car disappears into the darkness.

From a distance, moving towards him and getting louder and louder like a jumbo jet taking off, Adam hears a loud generator-sounding whir. It's accompanied by a series of thunderous booming bangs as rows of lights turn on.

Bang, bang, bang. Lights, lights, lights.

The 1930s film artifice is stripped away and, standing under the bright floodlights, Adam discovers he's in an empty shell of a sound studio. It's like a giant snow dome. It's so huge that he can't discern between the white space and the white walls that house it. He drops his pith helmet which rattles about when it hits the floor. His heart is racing.

He inspects the space from different angles, searching for a break in the endless white, trying to find something real to focus on.

When I tried to kiss Maggie and broke the Secretary *scene, I knew why. There was the film logic and I broke it, but ever since then I just seem to be getting further lost… and… I just want to get back. To find Nina and snap out of this and—*

'HELLOOOO! Is anyone HERE?'

His loudest most mighty yawp goes out into the world, with no echo or bounce back; it disperses without impact. His great explorer outfit feels stupid, so he kicks off his shoes, removes his jacket and shirt, and strips down to his boxers. Circled around him, Adam's safari suit looks so feeble.

If I'm dying, just kill me. If I'm dreaming, wake me. Whatever's placed me here, subconscious or not, fucked up id or whatever, just stop this!

All these thoughts rush through in a simultaneous barrage, like when little kids slam their hands down on a piano, banging a million notes at once.

Adam sits down on the ground and lies on his back.

'Nina… Kinki… are you there?'

His words float as cartoon text bubbles over his head. The floor is cold against his shoulders. He spreads his arms out like a T. 'Can you help?' More text bubbles appear.

'Ahhhh!'

The letters crowd out over his head. He shuts his eyes, trying to hide from what he can see, and listens to the silence of the space. Then he starts to hear his breath. It sounds kind of distorted, almost metallic, as though it's coming through a tube. Speculating over whether he could hear the buzz coming from his tube-breath, his mind drifts and he loses perspective on how long he's lain in silence with his eyes shut... unsure if it's been hours or minutes, but without any great care or thoughtfulness, he lies like a patient insomniac and tries to differentiate the buzz from his actual breath. It seems odd. Almost mechanical. Then he hears underneath it other sounds and tries to pick them out too.

Is that a hum? A very low, deep hum. Like a wind turbine? Is there a beeping? Like a truck reversing? No. It's more like a monitor maybe... Hang on. What's that? Is that shoes?

Adam sits up fast and looks around, thinking he'll spot the shoe wearer, but nothing's changed. The text bubbles still float above him. It's too much. His mind and body shut down. Overwhelmed with fatigue he lies back down. Sleep. Thick, sumptuous sleep arrives.

*

'Adam... Adam...?'

Nina?

'Come on, up you get.'

Where's her voice coming from?

Bleary-eyed, Adam tries to get his bearings. He feels the cool floor on his cheek. His belt is right beside him, almost touching his nose. His other clothes are scattered nearby. Beyond them there is nothing but white. He feels ambivalent and resigned. It's oddly freeing.

'Nina...?' He speaks quietly. 'Where are you?'

'Up here.'

Adam rolls onto his back. The text bubbles are gone.

Thank fuck.

He looks up at the white, domed roof. With no reference points it could be as high as a tree or the clouds, and regardless, he can't comprehend how she'd be there.

Busy Minion-style clatter begins, with screws being loosened and then a sharp crack rings out as, above, a panel swings open like an attic door. In the endless sweep of the studio roof, appears a little black square and peering over the edge is Nina.

'Hi.' She gives a cute little wave. He can barely make her out. She's up at least eight storeys high. 'Nice undies.'

'Thanks.'

'I've got an idea.'

'Great.'

She sounds excited but he sounds facetious. Her head moves out of view, and the panel flips back into position.

'Nina?'

The complete dome is back. Adam gets to his feet. Panicky, he yells, 'Nina!'

He hadn't meant to sound like a dick. It just came out that way.

The panel swings open again. She sticks her head over the edge. 'Hang on.'

Just try to not be an arsehole.

SCREEN-TIME

The dome morphs into present-day New York City.

Nina is standing on the rooftop of an old apartment block, smoking. She looks down. On the street corner, a shopkeeper is hosing down the sidewalk as a boy cycles past.

Adam is on ground level. The shopkeeper can't see Adam and almost splashes him with water as he avoids hosing the boy riding past.

Even though she's hundreds of feet above him, when she says, 'You showed me this movie,' her voice cuts through the street noise, like she's inside Adam's head.

'I did?'

'*Stranger than Fiction*. Emma Thompson plays an author and Will Ferrell is being serious.'

'I don't remember.'

'Your Maggie Gyllenhaal plays a baker.'

'Ah, yes! She makes cookies.'

'Total rubbish that she'd fall for Will, but—'

'She's so great.'

'No doubt—'

'In both that Batman flick and *The Kindergarten Teacher*—'

'Have you actually seen that?'

'*Batman*? Of course.'

'No, the—'

'*The Kindergarten Teacher*? Not yet, but—'

'You'll watch it after *Moonlight*.'

'I will.'

'Adam, seriously, it's a brilliant film.'

'Kinki, seriously, straight after *Moonlight*.'

'Alright, whatever.'

'I'm not joking.'

'Anyways, you know how Ferrell hears Emma's narrator voice in his head and—'

'Yeah, it's just like you with me, she's in his head, puppet mastering him.'

Adam knows his quip is uncalled for, it's a knee jerk reaction.

'You know what, forget it.'

'But in a nice way!'

The city disappears and the surroundings return to the all-white studio dome.

Nina is sitting on the edge of the open panel way up high in the roof. Adam, with his head pointed straight upwards, yells, 'It was a joke.'

'How was that funny?'

'Man!'

'You ask for my help but twist it so—'

'Gees, Nina, it's not a big deal—'

'Somehow it always comes round to this thing that I'm controlling you.'

'After our *Groundhog Day* kiss, Kinki, I thought we'd be better—'

'Then why say that?'

And even though there are eight storeys between them, they're still able to talk over each other. 'Honestly… Nina…?' Adam can see her feet are still hanging over the edge, so not all is lost. 'Kinki…? I'm sorry. It was uncalled for.'

'You're a dick.'

'Yeah, maybe sometimes…'

She pops her head out. 'Sometimes?!'

'I'm not a dick 24/7… am I?'

'Probably not.'

'But it is possible?'

'Well, the evidence is inconclusive.'

'Please let the records show,' Adam's head is tilted straight up to the ceiling, shouting out into the empty studio, 'I'm so into you and that was a bad joke that wasn't funny and I've no idea what urged me to say it and it was lame, and evidence is irrefutable that you rock, and I am, on occasion a bit of a dick.'

'Yes, you are.'

Adams smiles, relieved her punk-kid-ness shines through. 'Thank you—'

'Stop trying to be funny.'

'Okay… and Kinki… this isn't a joke—'

'Good.'

'But can I ask, *The Purple Rose of Cairo*, did you choose it for me?'

'Yeah, I did.'

'Why?'

'Because how often have we argued over Woody?'

'To boycott him or not?'

'And whether you can separate the artist from the art, and that got me thinking you can't. Nor can you wash away his influence on you growing up.' Her arms are waving around to emphasise her thoughts, 'And that got me to *Stranger than Fiction*.'

'Which is an absolute cracker.'

'Exactly. So my idea is that we have to plug in all the films about films that you love.'

''Cause movies fix everything?'

''Cause that's how you see things. You've said it yourself, it's how you make sense of the world.'

Adam nods. He stares up at her framed in her black box, surrounded by the vast expanse of studio dome, her insights dropping down on him like truth bombs that splatter.

'Okay…'

'And it has to be movies where they break the fourth wall 'cause we've got to see how they do it and then maybe we can reverse engineer it to, you know… get you back.'

'I love it!'

'Good.' She leans back, tucks her skinny punk legs inside, and pulls up the latch.

The moment it closes, the curved, white walls of the studio become a massive all-encompassing 360° movie planner. Thousands of films and their promo images surround him, and in the transformation of the space, he too is transformed back into his favourite black jeans and T-shirt uniform. But Adam doesn't notice this, he's too entranced in the vision before him as images from every film he's ever loved swoop around him. It's glorious. *The*

Favourite, Bad Santa, Miller's Crossing, Be Kind Rewind, Attack of the Killer Tomatoes, Un Coeur en Hiver, everything.

The dome is now a touch screen interface the size of an IMAX, combined with an enormous collection of the best graphics from every slick sci-fi flick he's ever seen. He swipes, rotates, flips and switches with a wiggle of a finger and immediately the system scrolls through lists of his favourite directors, eras, actors. The touch screen's sound effects buzz and zip throughout the studio.

'Nina? Can you hear me?'

Her voice is directly linked to the interface. Like Scarlett's voice talking to Joaquin Phoenix in *Her*, it plays around him.

'Yep.'

'Is there a limit?'

'Time's the issue, not the number.'

Adam starts selecting his favourites: *Blade Runner, Once Upon a Time in America*, both the director's cut versions; *Withnail and I; Carol.*

'And if I've got room for one more... *True Romance* or *Three Colours: Blue.* Decisions, decisions.'

'What are you doing?'

'Kinki, you rock.'

'These aren't on brief.'

'I know, but they're so—'

'We don't have time!'

'But—'

'I want your top three movies about movies. Not your all-time top 5.'

'But—'

'Adam, don't fuck around. It must be movies about movies, and how they break the fourth wall. That's it.'

Adam hears Nina's edginess.

'Kinki—'

'Maybe we'll find a clue in there, I don't know… it's just the best thing I could think of to get you home.'

'Okay…'

He flicks, swipes, and selects, then announces, 'Here they are… drum roll please… my top three movies about movies. *The Player. The Last Tycoon. The Truman Show.*'

He gestures, drop mic.

Nina, after a suitable pause, asks, 'Is there anything you like in the past decade?'

'I guess not.'

'*Once upon a Time in Hollywood…?*'

'You said only three.'

'You're so nostalgic.'

'Does that matter? I'm answering your brief. These are the films that, if I'm feeling crap, I'd watch.'

'*The Truman Show* is a film about a TV show, not a film about movies.'

'It breaks the fourth wall, and, Kinki, these are the three. I mean, personally, I'm impressed that I've been so quick and decisive.'

'You're amazing.'

Adam grins, 'No, Kinki, you are.'

The spark between them, and the pleasure of joining forces, has rejuvenated Adam.

'Press "Play", motherfucker!'

The dome immediately transforms, and as the white panels swap out to become the biggest screen the planet's ever seen, Nina appears by his side and whispers, 'Let's do this.'

CELLULOID DREAMS

And so begins *The Player*.

As the opening sequence plays out, with director Robert Altman's artistry unfolding in all its glory and cynicism, Adam and Nina, rather than being characters in the movie, are instead commentators, and while the opening shot rolls, they tailgate the action, shadowing the camera like ghosts, and watch the drama unfold.

The Player's first frame is the clapper board snapping down. The camera then tracks out to reveal the exterior of Hollywood studio offices, an EA is rushing off to find the mail, and a gruff Fred Ward is complaining to a freshman assistant that, 'Movies these days are all MTV, cut, cut, cut', and that nobody makes them like Orson Welles and the start of *A Touch of Evil*.

Driving into frame in his black four-wheel drive, is a late thirties Tim Robbins. He is greeted by a writer pitching him a flick as he walks to his office. The camera eavesdrops on their conversation before panning to a minor car accident, and tracking Bonnie bustling

across the lot in her early 90s power suit
carrying a pile of scripts.

While the action unfolds, Nina asks, 'Why
this movie?'

'What's not to love? The whole world is
introduced in a single shot. It's like a dance.
And how many people have we seen already, each
entering at a specific moment, like, what,
twenty, thirty extras and main cast.'

'Yeah but—'

'And it's the start of the movie, so we
don't know who's who, and there's cars parking
and buggies crashing and the camera never
stops moving, plus Fred Ward's character is
talking about this exact style of film-making
occurring in another film and how much better
the old flicks are compared to the new stuff,
but whenever someone suggests a related film,
Fred's not seen it so he's just full of
crap like the execs whose meetings we see
from outside their window, and all of this
happens in the opening shot which is like
eight minutes long and, for my money, Altman
after this shot could have easily packed up
his bags and gone home.'

Adam feels like he's back at uni, getting a
kick out of discovering something and loving
it. He keeps commentating, 'But Altman doesn't
stop; instead, he just keeps tightening the
screws, getting the film inside the film to

ridicule the very beast it's celebrating. Check this out.'

Adam swipes his hand, and the studio lot is immediately replaced with—

Head office. Nina and Adam are inside observing the Hollywood powerbrokers meeting, as Peter Gallagher is introduced to Tim Robbins.

Peter pulls out a newspaper and reads out a few headlines to prove his theory that stories are everywhere, which causes Tim Robbins to mock his suggestion that writers are superfluous.

Adam walks around the frame, 'I just love how Peter Gallagher's a smarmy hustling bolter, and Tim Robbins gets rattled seeing his own strengths reflected in his enemy.'

'Sure, but none of this explains why you chose this film.'

''Cause it's the business of show. It celebrates spin over substance.'

'But that's not you.'

Adam swipes again, and the studio office slides away to be replaced by a high, wide shot of Tim Robbins cruising his red convertible down his enormous driveway.

'Look, Kinki, Tim Robbins' character ends up remorseless and rich and shacked up with Greta Scacchi, the woman whose boyfriend he murdered.'

'But it's all fantasy.'

'But he makes it real.'

'But even Tim Robbins' reality is a fantasy.'

'Kinki, the whole film is. And this ending is perfect.'

'If we're going to crack this open, you've got to be honest.'

On the steps of his mansion, Tim kisses the beautiful and pregnant Greta, as Adam replies, 'It's a film about film-making that celebrates the art of artifice.'

Nina grimaces. 'I don't buy it.'

'You don't think that's clever?'

'You're not telling the truth.'

'I'd love to be Altman. To be able to do that. Create something authentic and scathing while enjoying the trappings I mock.'

'How would that work?'

'I don't know, but—'

'Greta's character's laughable.'

'No, she's—'

'No woman's like that. I mean, would you actually like me to be some Icelandic shower-curtain artist?'

'Some days.'

'Who's totally cool with you murdering my ex?'

'Definitely.'

'It's not Altman you love, it's Tim Robbins with his fantasy life and his fantasy wife.'

'Ah, Kinki, it's the movies.'

'Sure…' Nina looks unconvinced.

Adam, shaking his head, chuckles, 'You and your "I don't buy it" face,' then swipes. The entire set swaps out to reveal—

A 1930s studio backlot at night. A damaged water tower is flooding a wild west frontier town.

Adam and Nina watch as the crew rushes around trying to minimise the damage. Water pours through the saloon and streams down the street. It's hopeless.

Adam leans over like they're at the movies, and whispers, 'I love this scene. *The Last Tycoon*. Robert De Niro is the studio wunderkind who runs the place. There's just been an earthquake, and faced with this disaster he sees her, his dream girl, dressed as a 1920s flapper, sitting on the head of a sphinx floating down a gold rush street. I mean, how cool is this? All the different movie eras being washed away, and among the chaos is De Niro not giving a shit about the money going down the drain 'cause he's so transfixed by her.'

'Does it work out?'

'Kind of. She says no for ages and then finally he wins her over, only to realise he's more into the concept of her than—'

'Real-life?'

'Yeah.'

'Bummer.'

Nina wears an ironic grin.

'Don't start with me, Kinki.'

'I'm not.'

'This feels like a setup.'

'You're the one choosing these fantasy women.'

'It's a stitch-up.'

'By your own hand.'

Adam loves her mischievous face. They're standing close, almost close enough to kiss. Enjoying the charge building between them, Adam swipes.

The dome now transforms into blue skies and the open seas. Heading towards them is a skiff.

Initially the sails mask who the skipper is, but then they whip across, to reveal Jim Carrey holding the till.

'Oh, I love him. *Liar Liar* is genius.'

Adam, revelling in her ability to offer an opinion that he's heard a thousand times as though it's something fresh and new, replies, 'Is that so, Kinki?'

'It is, actually.'

Sweeping orchestral strings accompany Jim. He sails into the blue unknown until the boat's bow abruptly punctures the horizon. He's hit a plasterboard wall. He looks astonished as he clambers past the mast and rigging, to the front, and while it seems to be an endless ocean, he reaches out and feels the finite reality of the studio wall.

'This is when it starts.'

'What?'

Nina waits for him to continue, and Adam, enjoying her attention, adds, 'It's the end but really the beginning too, and I just love how, the moment the boat pierces through that wall, Truman knows for certain that all the pressure to play by the book and do what he was told was all crap. That his instincts were right, his whole life was bullshit, and he knew it, knew it all along.'

Adam feels lighter. The freedom to express himself feels good.

Within the dome's painted set of sky and clouds, a door opens. Jim walks up the steps that protrude from the wall, like he's stepping through the sky, bids farewell to his audience, and exits *The Truman Show*.

The soundtrack stops.

With no hero in the boat, and no score to accompany the action, it feels empty. Bittersweet and moving. The water laps against the studio wall as Nina reaches out to take Adam's hand.

Throughout their relationship it's always been an issue. In the early days, walking home from the pub she'd take his hand and he'd freak. He didn't mean to, it just happened, like an electric shock.

'What?!' she'd say, and Adam, unwilling to admit how suffocating he found it, would contrive some excuse to let go.

Now, standing on the set of The Truman Show moments after the climax, as Nina takes his hand, Adam doesn't pull away. Not because he wants to be nice but because it feels nice.

She nuzzles into his shoulder. 'So, why these films. Above all others?'

'Well, before I answer that, I'd like to add a bonus flick if I may?'

'Is it relevant?'

'I believe it is.'

'Well then,' Nina demurs, 'you may.'

*

Adam swipes and Truman's set is replaced by a streetlamp, and the flickering cityscape of La La Land.

They are sitting on a park bench. Adam is wearing a modern take on a 1950s look, with a fitted white shirt and a thin black tie. Beside him in a yellow dress, Nina changes her heels for flats. It's the second time that they've channelled Ryan and Emma, but unlike the earlier encounter, this time it's Adam and Nina as themselves.

Continuing their flirtation, Adam kicks dirt at Nina in time with the horns honking out the *La La Land* soundtrack.

Nina, affronted, hits his leg on the beat. The swing of the horn section compels Adam to jump up and start tap dancing. Nina follows suit.

They are feeling fine and dancing beautifully. It's intimate and frisky and, given that throughout their romance Adam's always been a show-stoppingly bad dancer, the fact he can keep up with Nina means they're both enjoying the shoe-shuffling sexual charge.

Nina offers a come-hither flick with her dress, which entices Adam to slide over. They step closer and closer as the brass reaches its full horn crescendo.

Nina's mobile starts ringing, but she ignores the call and keeps slowly, in time with the music, stepping towards him until there's barely a whisker between them. Their lustful tension is oblivious to the ringing phone, or the potential risk of glitching out.

They kiss. Roughly. Passionately. She grinds up against him. They grab and paw at each other, not giving a fuck about anything. Hands, necks, lips, fingers faster. Tie off, shirt off, pants off. Nina claws at his torso. His hands are cupped under her. There's no time to waste, the bench is too far away, the road will do just fine. He lies back and she rides him, her dress drapes down as she arcs forward wanting him. He grips her tight as she slams down on him.

Fuck yes.

LA LA PLEASE

They've glitched out.

Fuck what?! Oh, my fucking what the fuck, you have got to be shitting me. What now?

But not back to the *Crazy, Stupid, Love* bar - just to a different scene.

Still Adam and Nina. Still dancing. Still in *La La Land*. But now they're in the observatory.

Okay... so, not great, but not a total disaster.

Adam's practically steaming he's so overcome with sexual frustration. His balls are blue. His face is blue. His hands, fingers and toes are blue too. He's bluey the blue-est of Royal Windsor blue, blue balls.

They are circling each other, prowling around the observatory. Nina shoots a sideways glance at Adam in his tailored suit, looking sharp. She slides her hand along the rail. Her dress is tight across her bust, constraining her like a corset, but loose and flowing from her hips. Her chest is heaving.

For so long, there'd been no chase. When

she ever offered the slightest suggestion, he was all over her, but seeing the way she's looking at him, Adam knows this obstruction is driving her crazy. It feels amazing.

They're walking slowly, in time with the music, towards each other, loving the tease. When their paths meet, he's unsure what she'll do. She breaks their gaze by looking up at the stars above, as though she's alone and lost in her thoughts. All the while he keeps staring at her.

Please, yes.

Their paths meet. He can do whatever he wants. She makes this clear with her eyes and body.

He takes his hands out of his pockets. She leans forward in anticipation, and with the self-control of a saint, Adam, rather than grabbing her and shoving her up against the wall, ever so gently takes her hand. Their fingers lightly touching is exquisite. Her ankles and wrists are so precise and dainty, her movements are so graceful. Their bodies are so close, yet achingly separate. He steps behind her. She spins and faces him. As they waltz, he looks at her with such longing and pleasure. She moves forward to kiss, but the music momentarily pauses and holds its breath, and they too pause, cheek to cheek, lips parted...

He savours her.

With a lightness he's never experienced, Adam finds himself being smooth and unselfconscious as his body moves, for the first time in his life, in sync with how he's feeling, and the overriding emotion is one of gratitude and love. He can't believe his luck. To be with her, the most brilliant and superb woman he's ever known, and here they are dancing, and it's sublime. He slides his hands down to her waist and gently pushes her upwards. Nina's dress billows out. She drifts up off the ground. Adam pushes off and floats up to join her.

The observatory roof no longer shields the night sky; instead it presents the Milky Way laid out before them, queening the heavens.

Floating on starlight Nina wraps her arm around his neck. He smiles at her and she at him. It's loving and lovely. Their history and nuance all expressed in this dance. She purrs, 'I didn't know you could do this.'

'You showed me how.'

High in the *La La Land* night sky, they kiss.

Unlike the *Groundhog Day* kiss, this kiss is uncluttered. There's no great objective, it's just a kiss by lovers wanting to kiss.

Wrapped up in the moment, he closes his eyes, then panics.

What if she's gone?

He opens them. She's still there. Relief.
Gratitude. It feels real. Gentle and sweet.
He closes his eyes and again they kiss.

4

THE HOMEFRONT

Nina's slunk down in an armchair, with her laptop and a blanket, trying to stay asleep.

She hears herself breathing. It shifts from being in sync with the beeps of the heart monitor to increasingly out of step. The sounds of the hospital ward overwhelm the *La La Land* soundtrack. She gives up and opens her eyes.

To her left lies Adam.

He has tubes up his nose and in his arm. There's a mask over his mouth, and several wires attached to his body.

She gazes at his face, and wonders if during the movie his heart beat faster.

Behind her, crouching down and gently shaking her arm, is a nurse.

Nina ignores her.

Past Adam, on the other side of the bed, are Louie and Ella. They look tangled and uncomfortable as they lie in their armchairs.

Nina knows what the nurse will say, she's said it to her so many times before, but Nina doesn't want to leave, she wants to sleep. To stay sleeping with him. To just sleep and sleep.

Her heart is slow. Her movements sluggish. Reluctant, she turns to face the nurse and looks at her with weary concession. The nurse waits until Nina complies and closes her laptop. The muted clip of it shutting is a unique sound among the symphony of the medical devices.

Without saying a word, the nurse gets up and leaves.

Nina knows what she must do, but instead opens the laptop and resumes the film.

DEUS EX MACHINA

Inside Seb's bar. The place is full. Adam's feeling Ryan Gosling sharp in his black collared shirt, with his sleeves rolled up and his jacket hanging off the end of the piano.

He's leaning over the keys, spot lit and isolated, as he plays the film's love theme.

Across the room he sees Nina, forlorn, standing at the exit.

But the kiss was real.

He returns to a variation on the same melody, and as he riffs and expands the tune, he delves further and further inward, lost in his own thoughts.

Why didn't it work?

The spotlight framing him becomes brighter, more intense, cutting out the surrounding tables and patrons.

What am I missing?

Adam keeps playing. It harnesses his thoughts. The same way his dance with Nina gave him self-expression, the piano now offers an outlet. He finds himself watching his own hands as they glide and pounce.

Dark, mournful, swirling, his music builds on itself, restless and relentless.

We were doing this together. So, why's she's standing at the door, looking to leave?

Adam attacks the keys, each note a separate thought struck.

Adam shakes his head, imploring her to stay.

What did I do wrong?

The music ends, and he's left with the residue of the last few notes that hang about and then fade.

Across the club, with the slightest of movements, Nina offers Adam a little flicker of a love note.

Adam watches her leave, then tracks her shadow as it follows her outside and away.

He stares at the exit. It feels even more bare without her.

*

Nina wakes feeling empty.

The end credits for *La La Land* are scrolling. The film's closing track is nestled among the noise of the monitors beeping in the hospital room.

Beside her, Adam remains an absent presence.

He doesn't know that she drugs herself and sleeps beside him, watching his favourite movies. That in her dreams she joins him in his coma, lost in an unworldly place, hoping she can unlock something in his unconsciousness and bring him back home.

She props herself up and sets her laptop aside. Ella immediately stirs. Louie follows suit.

She knows they're eager to go. She knows they hate the place. They hate it when they're away, but they hate it when they're here. She knows how much they hate seeing their dad lying there and the hospital smell and the looks offered by the staff, but, like getting ready for school, they've built themselves a routine and, irrespective of the time when she's ready, they do what they're told. No fuss.

Ella then Louie give their dad a hug. It's loose. Their bodies barely touching. And strategic. It has to be, due to the cabling in and around his body. Now it's Nina's turn. She holds his hand, and on the small patch of skin that's not obstructed by devices, kisses him on the forehead. She whispers, 'See you soon.'

The kids hover by the door. The room is pale.

Nina turns away but can't bring herself to leave. 'How 'bout we stay just a little bit longer...?'

Louie sighs.

'It won't be for ages.'

Ella huffs.

'Do we have to?'

Nina gives a parental nod.

Ella flops down back down on the grey vinyl armchair. Nina returns to her nest beside his bed and opens up her laptop. Shielding it from her kids, she uncaps the Ambien and taps out two tablets. 'We'll leave soon. I promise.' And swallows the pills.

*

Adam looks up.

The light has changed. It's no longer focused precisely on him; instead it's broadened out to a vague, generalised glow. The tables have swapped out too.

I'm back at the bar!

He looks around. Excited.

It's worked! Kinki, we did it!

Adam swivels around.

Hang on, shouldn't the TVs be there?

He pivots back, searching for the departure gates that line the airport concourse, but instead sees scrappy looking tables in a dingy room lined with old photos. It's not the airport's fake Irish Pub, but rather a genuine drinking hole.

This app is so shit.

Adam glares at his phone. The PFEC interface reads, Now Playing: *Adaptation*.

Kinki... fuck... I haven't got anywhere.

Holding out for a miracle, Adam reaches into his jeans hoping for Ella's panda puppet but comes up empty.

His frustration is further exacerbated by once again having the sensation of being watched. He scopes the joint and immediately spots a guy slouched at the bar eyeballing him. Totally caught.

And what is with the constant goddamn observation. I'm so over it. Test case or not, they can all get fucked.

But slouching guy doesn't avert his gaze, instead he gestures for Adam to join him.

Adam strides over, gunning for a fight, but up close the guy doesn't look dubious. In fact, he looks ordinary. He's got tightly curled hair, is starting to go bald and is sweating profusely. Given the climate-controlled environment, this strikes Adam as particularly unfortunate.

The woman behind the counter lays out a tissue-square on the bar, and gestures for Adam to take a seat. 'What can I get you?'

'G and T.'

Adam pulls up the stool and asks, 'Mind if I sit here?'

The balding guy frowns. 'Why would I mind?'

He sounds so familiar...

The woman delivers Adam his drink as the guy says, 'So, you came.'

I know that voice...

'I didn't think you'd come, but how amazing is he?'

Adam gives his neighbour a closer inspection.

Ohhh, okay, wow... it's Nicolas Cage. But he looks like shit ...?

Past the spirit and liqueur bottles that line the shelves, Adam catches his own reflection in the bar-mirror.

Fuck me. I look just like him... Identical...

His sweaty drinking buddy persists with his questions.

'Charlie?'

'Huh?'

'He's amazing isn't he.'

'Who?'

'McKee, Charlie, the god of scriptwriting, who else?'

Oh my god, of course, I'm Charlie Kaufman. I mean, I'm Nicolas Cage playing Charlie Kaufman. And he's Donald, my twin brother who's also played by Nick Cage.

Donald offers a toast, 'To Robert McKee!'

Adam/Nick/Charlie raises his glass, 'To McKee.'

They cheers.

Adam takes a sip and then starts laughing. He can't stop himself. It's a compulsive nervous twitch. He finds the notion of him being Nick Cage playing Charlie Kaufman straight up funny.

Nick, aka Donald Kaufman, starts laughing too. 'This is too funny.'

'Like, really funny.'

They laugh some more. And then some more again as though it's hilarious, like when the hero and the baddie laugh at each other in the climactic standoff. But it's not. It's fraught and complicated and neurotic. It peters out and ends with Adam feeling slammed by uncertainty and doubt.

Why am I Charlie Kaufman, now?

He feels his gut pushing against his caramel

trousers and the weight of his mind as it starts to eat itself.

Charlie Kaufman, the scriptwriter who writes a film about writing a film and then writes himself into the film as a character called Charlie Kaufman. And now I'm that guy. It's like I'm reflecting on myself so much that I'm a reflection of the reflection, and nothing gets me out of this hybrid immersion mode...

Plus now it's so much worse 'cause Kinki's gone.

In this claustrophobic state, as sweat trickles down his back and between his arse cheeks, Adam starts babbling to his brother. 'I don't know, Donald, I mean, it's good to see you and all, but what am I doing here? I mean, I don't know what to do but maybe you can tell me? Maybe you can point out Robert McKee at the bar and maybe this is that scene – the "Kaufman brothers toast McKee then bump into him at the bar" scene. But that doesn't happen in the movie so how can he... how can you give me the answers, Donald? And my journey, the hero's journey, how does it end? How do I end the movie and get out of this hybrid state? I can't even have a car chase. I mean, doesn't McKee say, have a car chase? But I already did lots of that before and—'

'Does he?'

'I'm sure he does, and anyways, I remember Meryl Streep impersonating the sound of a dial tone and it's amazing. The best acting ever. So funny. So good. And I'd like to see

Nina as Meryl doing that. Can we do that? Get
Nina here? Please? I mean, do you know how?
Or… or am I straight out just losing it…?'

Donald appears confounded and unsure what to
say. They sit at the scungy air-conditioned
bar, sweating. Adam/Nick/Charlie reaches out,
takes a cocktail napkin. He offers one to his
twin. They dab their faces.

'Do you want another?'

'I guess.'

The woman behind the bar pours, mixes and
hands them their drinks.

On the wishful hope he'll see Nina, Adam
scans the bar, muttering, 'Maybe Kinki,
instead of being Meryl, will turn up as
Catherine Keener?'

'You know Catherine, Charlie?'

'That'd be so perfect. In the movie of
her life, Kinki would totally be played by
Catherine Keener. Not now, but if the movie
was made fifteen years ago, definitely. I
mean, if Keener was in her early 40s now,
that is. Maybe that's why I'm here. Maybe
I was supposed to ask McKee to help me but
instead I got you and my half-baked memory
of the film…?'

Donald Kaufman continues to look utterly
out of his depth, but nevertheless offers a
supportive nod. Adam/Nick/Charlie sips his
drink. His twin does this too. Adam then

twirls his ice around with his straw. Donald does too. To attempt to stop himself from being irritated at his twin mirroring his every move, Adam focuses on trying to recall the movie's plot and, thinking out loud, asks, 'What happens at the end?'

'Of what?'

Adam doesn't answer.

'Charlie... of what?'

Adam ignores Donald's questions and keeps talking it through. 'Meryl gets high and does the dial tone scene, then hooks up with the toothless orchid guy and then somehow we end up in the swamp getting shot at and... Ah, that's right! Of course! Donald, do you remember in the swamp talking about that girl in high school that you loved?'

'What swamp?'

'It hasn't happened yet.'

'Charlie, is this a flashback? McKee says that flashbacks are—'

'Donald, in the swamp you said that even though she was mean to you—'

'Who?'

'That girl in high school that you loved.'

'Sarah Marshall?'

'Yes! That's it, her! You said that Sarah Marshall would tease you behind your back to all her friends and—'

'Yeah, I knew she was teasing me, but I

didn't care because it was my love.'

'But so what?'

'So what!? So what!? Charlie, it was my love to give, however I wanted. Mine and mine alone and no one could take that away from me. Not her. Not anybody.'

'Ha! You're so right.'

'I am?'

Adam's fired up. 'I've been going about this all the wrong way.'

'What do you mean?'

'I can't expect her to adapt for me.'

'Who, Charlie?'

'Nina.'

'Keener? She's my friend. You can't hit on my friend Charlie.'

'No, not Keener, Nina, my Nina.'

Adam pulls out his mobile, 'I have to go to her. I have to choose the movies she likes.'

In the PFEC app, Adam does a title search for: *The Outsiders*, *The Way We Were*, *Say Anything*, *The Philadelphia Story*. All of them are locked, except *Say Anything*.

Adam raises his glass, 'Wish me luck.'

Donald looks baffled. 'Good luck…?'

Adam reaches out, clinks his glass, gulps down his drink, and hits 'Play'.

DON'T SELL ANYTHING

Adam is no longer old and sweaty; instead he's transformed into a young John Cusack playing Lloyd Dobler, trainee kickboxer and recent high school graduate. Athletic and lanky, with a dark floppy fringe, he is wearing a light-brown trench coat and basketball shoes as he bounds up and knocks on the flyscreen back door.

Diane Court, class valedictorian and the girl Lloyd's been crushing on, self-consciously steps out to meet him. She has a hibiscus in her long, curly hair, and is wearing a white dress with a matching shawl. It's an outfit that's better suited for a charity ball than high school graduation house-party.

The moment Adam sees Diane, he feels Nina's presence. The spark in her eyes is pure Kinki. It's an outfit that's a million miles from what she would normally wear, and her pleasure in playing dress-ups shines through.

'Hi.'

'Hi.'

Kinki, I'm so glad you're back!

All night from different spots around the party, Adam/Lloyd sneaks glances at Nina/Diane. Every time he sees her, he uses it as an opportunity to flirt, telling her with his eyes time and time again, 'You are so cool.'

After the party, Lloyd agrees to drive a drunk kid home. Diane, as his dutiful date, joins him. As they drive Lloyd's beat-up semi-sports car, Adam and Nina, encased in the teenage lovers Lloyd and Diane, sit quietly, enjoying the buzz.

The drunk guy takes them on a random tour, saying, 'It's the next left… oh, no, that's not it, try right down this road…' then nods off.

With the drunk guy passed out, Adam bites the bullet and, risking a glitch out, breaks away from the scripted dialogue. '*The Outsiders*, *The Way We Were*, *The Philadelphia Story*, and *Say Anything*.'

'What about them?'

'I knew you loved these movies and—'

'I don't think *The Outsiders* really counts.'

'I should have watched it with you.'

'I doubt it holds up.'

'I should have watched them all.'

'Why?'

'To know what makes you tick.'

'You don't know by now?'

'I wanted you back, and I thought if I chose a film you loved you might come back, but the only one I'd seen was *Say Anything*.'

Nina/Diane turns away.

With a Cusack baffled whisper, Adam asks, 'Hey, was that wrong? Do you not want to be here?'

'I course I do, but it's just… been a long time…' Nina steadfastly looks out the window as she murmurs, 'Since you've really wanted me around.'

Adam doesn't know what to say.

In their silence, a deep rumble starts to build as the car starts to rock and sway like it's on water. The steering wheel goes loose and floppy, the roof starts to bend in the middle, and the dashboard becomes rubbery. Everything starts to lurch and unravel, falling apart just like it did when Adam broke away from script of *The Wolf of Wall Street* and *Secretary*.

Nina squeals. He lunges for her, not wanting them to be separated, and in that moment the scene glitches out.

Adam looks around. He's still in the car and Nina/Diane's still beside him, but now they're alone and parked on a headland where they can see planes take off across the bay.

She looks at him with an incredulous expression. Adam raises his eyebrows in a silly reply. She giggles and Adam immediately knows that Nina's still with him. He loves that sound. It's so rare and such a delight. It bubbles up and she doesn't realise how adorable she's being.

It's raining.

Outside is the distant noise of the airport. Inside it becomes quiet.

In moments like this, Adam would always speak and then see her disappointment as his dumb-arse words broke the spell, but this time, in the Seattle drizzle, he doesn't say anything. Instead he looks for music. As he reaches into the glovebox his arm brushes her knee and the hem of her skirt. She watches it slide between her legs as he riffles through the cassettes. He takes his time, using the excuse of selecting a tape to have his arm linger. Flirtatious and charged. She edges towards him. It's so sexy and restrained and unfamiliar. He finds what he's after, then slowly snakes his hand back and slips it in the car stereo. The synth and drums of Peter Gabriel's *So* kicks in. Not making a sound, listening to the music, their teenage lust builds.

Suddenly Nina hops out of the front seat, swings open the back door, slides inside, shutting it fast before the rain gets in.

Adam doesn't bother getting out of the

car. He stretches out towards her with his
body draped over the seat. They kiss. They
just want it. Each other. Badly.

Adam drags himself over the seat and into
the back.

His grey sweater gets in the way. Nina pulls
it over his head. Clumsy and cramped in the
car, arms and legs all over the place, they
keep kissing each other. Their bodies are
new, and their touch and actions are like it's
their first time, like it's their whole time,
as they kiss and strip away their clothes
and caress each other, touching and kissing
everywhere, moreish and charged, not wanting
to miss a moment, to savour every sensation
and more and more again, much more. In the
back of the car, it's a mess. A stunning
mess. Monstrous.

For a long time after, nestled in each
other's arms, they lie in silence. *In Your
Eyes* plays on the stereo. Through the
fogged-up windows, the rest of the world is
irrelevant.

Cradling him, Nina speaks but doesn't break
the spell. 'You're shaking.'

Adam shakes his head.

'Yes, you are, you're cold.' She wraps him
in her arms.

'No… I'm happy.'

THE WARD

'Mum?'

'Mummy?'

Nina feels her arm being shaken.

'Mum.'

It's hard to tell their voices apart.

'Mummy.'

Whispering, they sound the same, especially when she's half-asleep.

'Mum, come on.'

She doesn't want to wake up.

'Please…'

She feels herself being dragged from one realm into another, but she wants to stay buried.

'Mum, come on.'

'Nina.'

She hears the nurse join in, and feels the weight on her legs lighten. It serves as a trigger. She opens her eyes and in the haze, sees her laptop being taken away. She grabs at it. 'Don't!'

Her speech is slurred, 'Leave that alone.'

Louie gives it back. 'But can we go?'

The laptop screen is frozen on a wide shot of Lloyd's car at night parked by the water. Nina stares blankly at it.

'Mum?'

'What?'

Louie's standing by her chair, pale and tired. He needs a wash. He immediately looks down at the floor, but she sees his anxiousness.

Ella plonks herself on Nina's lap, forcing her to move her computer. 'I want to go home.'

Nina squirms out of Ella's cuddle. She wants to see if there's moisture on Adam's breathing tube but Ella's blocking her view. She needs to know if anything's changed, if he felt her in the movies. She wants to believe it, but how can she know?

Ella takes the hint and gets up. There are dark bags under her swollen eyes. She wipes her nose.

'Nina.'

'Yes?!' She hears her own voice snapping at the fucking nurse. It sounds louder and further away than usual. Louie flinches. Knowing he hates a scene of any kind, Nina tries to ask calmly, 'What is it?'

The nurse crouches down beside her, 'Can I have a word?'

It takes her a moment to understand that she wants to talk in private. Once this idea lands, Nina asks Ella, 'Darling, can you just grab a drink or something?'

'I'm not thirsty.'

Louie reads the signs, 'Okay…'

As the elder statesman, he leads his sister outside.

The nurse waits until the kids are out of earshot, then flicks a switch. Her gentle tone replaced by sharp precision. 'Hey? Are you there?'

The nurse clicks her fingers in front of Nina's face.

Nina is thrown by the Jekyll and Hyde turn. The nurse holds the container of Ambien. 'This'—she rattles it inches from Nina's face—'must stop.'

Nina wonders how she knew about her stash, but her speculation is cut short by the nurse scolding, 'I've watched you come in here and disappear. Put on your computer and watch movies and sleep. Eating these 24/7.'

She rattles the pills at Nina like she's just about to shove them up her nose and through her brain.

'They see it too. They see their dad lying there, and now they're watching their mom join him and—'

Louie and Ella walk in. The nurse immediately stands up and returns to the role of cheery caregiver, 'If you need anything, just press the button.'

Nina wrestles with how intense the nurse was, and her desire to return to Adam in Lloyd's car.

'You didn't give us any money.'

She hands Louie a few notes.

'Get chocolate if you like.'

'Do we have to?'

'Find something nice.'

She offers by way of explanation as much to herself as to them, 'I can't drive like this, I'm still half asleep, so I just need to rest a bit and…'

She opens up her laptop, and avoids their faces.

Say Anything is standing by. As Nina gets settled with her laptop, Ella grumbles, 'Don't touch me.' She's shaking, trying not to cry as she brushes off her brother's hug.

Nina wants to say something, but they're gone before any words come to mind.

She hits 'Play'.

MARITAL PEN FRIENDS

Adam/Lloyd is driving. Nina/Diane is beside him. He accelerates to the lights. They're red and he leans across to quickly give her a kiss.

Success! Puppy-dog pleased with himself as he drives to the next intersection, searching for a moment to quickly kiss her again, he starts to ramble, telling her about how he feels and how he thinks he knows how she feels, and in the middle of this gushing rant he glances over at her, half-expecting a chuckle of affection but instead Nina is head down, fiddling with a little box in her lap.

'Stop.'

'Huh?'

She turns to him. Resolute. Her green eyes sharp and stunning. Pure Nina.

'I think we should stop.'

'I'm sorry?'

She holds out the little box, 'Here… Write me.'

Oh no… fuck no…

Adam feels his guts sink out through his seat, past the sewers and into shitsville.

Motherfucker fuck! It's the break-up scene. The 'I gave her my heart and she gave me a pen' moment... why didn't I see this coming?

On autopilot he takes the box.

'Adam, I can't do this to the kids. I can't. It has to stop, I have to stop, I have to...'

It doesn't make sense and he's not listening. Nina gets out of the car. It all washes over him. He doesn't register that she's called him Adam. It's too fast. Too brutal.

In a trance, Adam progresses through the film's breakup sequence. He drives aimlessly, walks aimlessly, hangs out with the guys at the 7 Eleven as they rap-sympathise, 'Lloyd, Lloyd, all null and void', before ending up, in the evening gloom outside Diane's bedroom window holding his boom box above his head, playing *In Your Eyes*.

But we've got to be together, and it has to be now – it has to be.

He imagines her hearing the chorus and running downstairs into his arms.

Come on, Kinki.

The song ends. He stands frozen, listening to the whirr of the cassette tape turning over.

Maybe she can't come. Maybe if she met me, the film would glitch out completely and we'd never see each other.

He lowers the boom box to the ground and stares at Diane's bedroom window, knowing Nina's inside.

So, she broke up with me because she knows she's got to follow the script...?

Because she's trying to get to 'happy ever after' ending...?

Adam is nodding. Lloyd Dobler-style self-affirming.

Right!

And that's why she mentioned the kids, because she's trying to give me bits of our real-life without losing me. But, Kinki, we've cracked it, it's okay, I get it. The whole hero journey thing is about me realising how lucky I am, and I get it!

The momentum of his revelation kicking him into gear, he dumps the stereo and runs towards the house.

It's not like Groundhog Day, *or* La La Land *where I'm into you but not actually seeing you for who you are. I'm 100 per cent into you, Kinki.*

He jumps up onto the porch and charges through the front door.

'Kinki! I love you! I love everything about you.'

He takes the stairs four at a time, yelling out, 'Kinki!' as he yanks open her bedroom door.

HOME-LESS

Suddenly he's in a corridor with blue linoleum floor and fluorescent lighting.

Louie and Ella!

God yes! It's fucking amazing it's worked, it's actually worked!

Adam runs up to them.

'Louie! Ellllaaaaa!'

The whole world can see his joy, 'Come here!'

He launches into a big daddy-bear hug. Grabbing them from behind, he pulls them in tight. But they simply walk through his arms, and down the corridor.

It stops Adam dead in his tracks.

The sinking gut feeling of the *Say Anything* break-up scene is nothing compared to what he feels now. Everything becomes warped. Like a car crash.

Adam watches his kids push open a door and step into the room. Refusing to let them out of his sight, he slips inside. Nina is asleep, crumpled up in an armchair. Her laptop is open, sitting on her lap. Adam sees a body, his body, in the bed beside her.

What the fuck is going on?

Adam bites his tongue. Hard.

If I can feel that, then how can I be there?

Adam feels the trauma. The absolute fear.

This is so… What's happened, Kinki?

She's sleeping heavily, issuing little snores. He holds her hand and, resting his head on her shoulder, he stares at the man in the bed.

That can't be me. How could I…?

Cradling his wife, he breathes her in.

I can't be in a coma? That's not me.

He wraps his arms around her and fixates on the heart monitor. Each beat brings him closer to acceptance.

Adam gently shakes her, whispering into her ear, 'Can you hear me? Please. Did you come to San Fran? Is that where I am? Kinki?'

Louie and Ella's card playing chatter cuts through the medical wheeze and beeps.

'Four jacks…'

'Cheat.'

Adam's focus shifts. He becomes transfixed by his children sitting across the room, munching chocolate and playing cards. They are vibrant and dazzling and illuminate the room.

Ella counts out from the pack, 'One, two, three, four.'

'Yeah, and what about this one?' Louie pulls out the fifth card that Ella had tried to slip in.

'Oh, yeah…'

Ella collects the pile.

'You always try that.'

'That's the first time in ages.'

'No, it's not.'

'Yeah, I did it all last game, but you never saw.'

They are so incredible.

From Nina's laptop Adam hears Lloyd say, `You just described every great love story.`

`Diane and Lloyd are holding hands, on a`

plane, about to live their happily ever after.
Ding. The movie ends.

Kinki what's going on? Am I lying there listening to the movie? All the movies?

He leans into her. 'Nina, can you hear me? Was it you? Did you…?'

She must have played the movies and somehow joined me.

'Kinki?'

Nina stirs.

'God you're amazing.'

*

Nina knew something was wrong immediately after the 'Lloyd holding the boom box' scene; from that point on she didn't feel Adam's presence at all.

Especially at the end, when the plane took off and she kissed him, it felt wrong. She looked into Lloyd's eyes, and knew Adam wasn't there.

But now this feels different. Her eyes are closed as she listens to the room. She hears Ella denying that she always puts down five cards and Louie's exasperated counter-arguments. She hears the machines beside her in the bed. But there's something else. She hears another breath.

It's in time with her own. It's hard to pick out, but it's definitely there.

She slowly opens her eyes and immediately recognises the arm flopped over her.

And that face! Adam is inches away from her. Staring intently. She squeezes him tight and actually feels him against her body.

'Adam!'

'I'm just so sorry for everything.'

She looks at the bed. He's there too.

Her face drops, 'Adam…'

'I missed the point, and seeing you and Louie and Ella, and I had all this stuff, and I was bitching and moaning about crap and—'

'How can you—'

'Now I can't get back—'

'Be here?'

'No matter what I do.'

Nina hears crying. Ella's terrified. Louie has his arm around his little sister, trying to keep it together, but he's freaking out too, 'Who are you talking to?'

Adam whispers, 'I love you.'

'I can't do this anymore…'

'Mum?!'

'Adam, I have to stop… I wish… I thought I'd cracked it but… I can't do this anymore.'

Her face is tight. Crushed.

Louie's hugging his sister. They're shit-scared.

Adam follows Nina's gaze and in doing so, sees everything from her perspective. The kids camped out in the hospital. Her bedside vigil. The lengths she's gone to connect.

His family is unravelling, and his presence is causing more distress.

'I'm their mother and I have to…'

Adam starts to feel lighter. She's crying now. 'Adam…?'

He is holding her hand, as the rest of his body is floating upwards. He's being turned upside down. His feet are lifting up to the roof as he clings to her.

'Adam, please…'

Adam's body is being pulled up and away, like reverse gravity.

She looks up at him. 'I love you.'

He's stretched out trying to stop himself from floating away. She is all that holds him to the room. Adam feels her loosen her grip.

'I'm sorry...'

She lets go of his hand.

'No! Nina!'

Adam feels the last connection slip away. Unable to hold her, he drifts above them. He yells out, but they can't hear him.

Louie and Ella hug their mum. Their trio is a blanket, wrapped up in each other, as Adam goes higher. Higher than the roof. Higher and higher he keeps drifting, up and away until all he can see is his bed and their bodies beside it. Then higher still as they become smaller and smaller until the room is a tiny box, surrounded by darkness which is so expansive and black that it crowds out the last speck... and then they're gone... and Adam is alone in the pitch black.

Adrift.

BETWEEN THE GAPS

As he floats in the darkness, out of the back of his head Adam feels a corridor ever extending and himself sliding further and further backwards down this tiny route. He grips on tight to the memory of the hospital.

It's the only thing that he can pin his life on, but he feels himself being pulled further and further away as everything leaches and saps out of him and flows down this long narrow corridor.

His memories are like a fire sale. He can feel them angling out of his reach, being snapped up and dissolved.

He can't comprehend how fast all this is happening. It's faster than a thought. So quick and so much fuller. It's a bulging elephantiasis slop of life that's fat and messy. Unwilling to let his whole life play out before him, his initial reaction is to shut it all down, but to switch it off is to sever the thread that links him to his hospital room, so instead he goes against this impulse and lets go.

The sweep of life cascades over him. Enormous and tidal. It washes and bathes him. Every deception. Every light-bulb insight. The greatest moments are smashed up with his most shameful, and he can react however the hell he wants because it's all his. It's a clean living, smoking and drinking, piss-taking and self-praising, participation award, and fundamental to this mashed-up bundle of highs, pain, anger and love is Nina. He loved others, but with her there was a magnitude that kept expanding, a snowballing, steamrolling, mountainous sweep of Nina. Louie. Ella.

That's it.

He feels his body unclench.

Simple.

As he continues to drift down the ever-extending vortex spiralling out of the back of his head, he retains the wispy thread that links him to the hospital and his family.

Adam lies in between these two dimensions, seeing his life and death. The powerlessness is empowering. But if he had to choose... he'd not be going now. He wants to play Cheat. He wants to slap down six cards, look Louie in the eye and say straight-faced, 'Four queens.'

Then with his next hand say, 'One queen.'

And watch Ella yell 'cheat' and revel in her flipping the card and seeing a queen and with her realisation that she'd been conned, smile and be incensed with the deception of her dad.

Let me live.

All of this plays out in the time it takes to press a single letter in a text. And, *bang*, he's done. The start end.

5

THE DEPARTURE LOUNGE

At first it's tricky to know what's what. But then he stops trying so hard and allows things to unspool and loosen… and in this vague state he feels his hand pressing against a thing.

Seeping out of the darkness, his focus gradually sharpens and reveals a heavy dark wood, which he's leaning over, so close it's almost grazing his nose.

This… is wood… and I'm touching it.

There is another object too.

The cloth in my hand. They're real. And if they are, then so am I.

He starts wiping the same section over and over again. He needs to feel it. To be grounded by it.

It feels mythical… like the tree at the end of Shawshank Redemption.

With each wipe, he feels other parts of his body slowly return. Hand, elbow, shoulders. Sound soon follows and with it the hum of other people.

He's back. At. The. Bar. But in a different position, as he's now standing behind it. On autopilot, Adm pours wines, beers, spirits, doing as requested. He doesn't feel connected to himself or his surroundings. His body feels separate, as though the hand pouring the beverage belongs to someone he used to know.

At some point in this ritual, an idea drifts into his head to acknowledge the folks that he's serving. The guy at the end of the bar, with initials on his cufflinks, looks kind of familiar. Adm stares at him, trawling through his muddled brain.

I know I've seen that face before… is he Jordan Belfort …?

But hang on that's not Leonardo… it's…

The guy stares back at him. 'Yes?'

It's too intense for Adm. He turns away and in the mirror behind the spirit shelf catches his own reflection.

Looking back at him is Jordan Belfort.

How is that me?

Adm spins around to check out the guy at the bar. He's dressed like Jordan but with Adm's face.

How can he look like me? Why would I be here dressed as Belfort?

'Can I get a beer, please?' a young guy asks him.

He sounds familiar. Retreating from his own questions, Adm the pours an ale and drops in the requisite slice of orange. As he hands it over, the kid says, 'Thanks.'

Adm looks up. The kid grabbing the beer is Adm dressed as Peter Parker.

Am I really… is that actually me…?

This half-formed idea is interrupted by an entitled, 'Two fingers' worth, and don't make me wait.'

Adm free pours a robust, grow-hairs-on-your-chest, double, and hands it over to the impatient boozer.

It's Richard *Pretty Woman* Gere. But it's not. It's Adm dressed as Gere. Adm checks out the rest of the folks sitting at the bar. His repressed Spader; his chest beating Bruce and Vin; his fearless Geena. Groundhog Bill, Purple Rose Jeff. They're all hanging out, even Cusack's kickboxing Dobler.

Is my psyche fracturing into little pieces?

All in character but with Adm's face. A self-referential costume party, where he's serving drinks to himself.

But if I'm lying on a hospital bed right now, then who are these people? Should I ignore them? But aren't they me? How can I ignore myself? Or some version of me?

Away from the bar, Adm notices a group of people that look truly unfamiliar. They are sitting around like it's after-work drinks and they don't know what to talk about. Someone says, 'The weather's so bi-polar.' The others nod in agreement.

I can't make up people I've never seen.

As Adm beelines towards them, a woman at a nearby table leaves cash for her bill and heads off.

Kinki?

Adm can't see her properly, but he calls out regardless. 'Nina!' His voice sounds high-pitched and antsy. The woman keeps walking.

How could she… she can't be here.

'Nina!'

It's her for sure.

He weaves through the tables. 'Wait up!'

In response to his yelling, the woman turns around, looking annoyed.

She's nothing like Kinki.

Adm recoils. 'Sorry. I thought you were someone else…?' It feels like a failed pick-up line. The woman ends their exchange with, 'Okay then,' and walks away.

He feels like he's made a scene and looks around to see if this is the case, but his doppelgangers are nowhere to be found and the after-work people aren't watching.

Adm's breath is shallow. Everything is compressing. His mind is skipping. Reactive and disjointed. He's feeling amped, and spots, out on the concourse, the departures board.

Would my flight be on there? If I'm in hospital, how can it work?

He hurries over and scans the flights. QF11 San Francisco to Sydney: go to gate.

Fuck yes.

He searches his pockets for his ticket. Nothing.

Why would I have a ticket if this whole place isn't real?

He puts his hand into his emergency money pocket.

Please be there…

The panda puppet pops out.

Oh, thank fuck. So, if I have the panda, then this is actually real. But if I'm in a coma then…?

His thinking's muddy clear.

Is the app real? Is any of this? But when I got here, I did have my stuff and now I have my panda, so…

Adm hurries back into the Irish Pub.

I've got to get my stuff and get on that plane.

Adm returns to the table that had once been home to buffalo wings and perfectly timed beverages. It's bare.

He scavenges around on the ground, searching for his things.

Maybe it's the wrong spot?

He sticks his head up, double checking he's in the right place.

No… this is it.

There's nothing to show for his time with his carry-on bag and the PFEC app. He sits down at the empty table. Everything that previously felt normal and familiar is laced with the knowledge that he's lying in a hospital. This idea belittles the reality laid out before him. It's disorientating and rudderless.

Adm opens his palm, 'Don't you leave me. Not again.' The panda's black and white fluff-eyes gaze back at him. 'And where's all my stuff?'

Ferreting around in his empty pockets, Adm cycles through the actions of searching for his passport and his tickets.

Was I worried they'd fall out, so I put them in the front pocket of my carry-on bag? But where's my bag?

His thoughts keep looping.

If they're not in my pockets then they must be in my carry-on bag. Which is where? And all those people at the bar, how could they be me? And if I'm in the hospital, what is this place?

His mind churns and flings about.

But if I can get my bag, and find my ticket and passport, then maybe I can fly home… Maybe they'll let me board without it. But if I'm in a coma, did I even ever make it to the airport?

Adm surveys the concourse, searching for a distraction. Anything to stop his noise.

He spots an airport employee stacking bags onto a trolley cart. With their little wheels and retractable handles they look similar to Adm's. A steward pushes several more over to the trolley cart.

Is that mine? Did that fucker take my bag?

The airport employee adds them to the pile, hops into the driver's seat and starts to motor down the concourse.

Adm takes off after the cart.

EXCESS BAGGAGE

By the time Adm's side-stepped through the tables of pub patrons, the baggage cart is over a hundred meters away.

What about my flight? I've got to get my bag first, it's got my passport and ticket. Plus, I packed it at home. It's real. It's mine.

The trolley turns off the main concourse. Adm picks up the pace. He hurries around the corner as the trolley putters through a set of security doors.

Adm bolts after it but he's not that quick. It's not action-man speed, it's guy-who-gets-puffed-after-50-metres fast. The front carriage of the baggage trolley disappears. He's not going to make it. The remaining carriages are chugging through. There's no elegance now. As the doors start to close, Adm slide-dives, feet first. It's sporty and ambitious.

The polished airport floor helps him and he slides further than expected. Just as they close Adm gets his foot wedged in. The doors push hard against his ankle. It's a minor win. He's stuck, with one leg jammed in a door and the other bent up and sticking into his chest.

He's gasping for air, like a dog in the summer, tongue out panting. His arse is hurting, his elbow is burning from the lino ripping off his skin, plus his foot is being crushed.

An alarm sounds, triggered by the doors not closing. Adm

leans forward and tries to push himself through the gap. The pain intensifies. Twisting around, trying to get free, Adm lies on his back, and from his upside-down perspective sees two stewards, in crisp blue-and-white uniforms, running towards him. She's on her comms reporting the security breach. He's looking pissed.

Adm gets upright and shoves his shoulder against the door. He forces the door open and having freed his leg, squeezes himself through. Behind him it seals shut.

Fifty metres ahead the baggage trolley is parked alongside a grey conveyor belt. The airport employee is shoving the luggage off the trolley and onto the conveyor belt.

'Hey, mate! Excuse me. Buddy!?'

Oblivious to Adm's attention, the Handler continues his work. He's wearing brown shorts, boots, gloves, and a brown, collared shirt with a cream-coloured singlet underneath. As Adm gets closer, he realises the Handler's standing on a box. He is smaller than three overnight bags stacked upright, plus he's stooped like a hunchback. He looks over sixty and has glorious grey hair that's cut like David Lynch's *Eraserhead* and makes him appear three inches taller.

The Handler seems perfectly happy in his own little world, focusing on the task at hand. He pushes the top bag onto the conveyor belt, then the middle one followed by the bottom two. The moment he's completed one column he kicks his metal box, that's the size of an applecart, along to the next pillar of bags, steps up and repeats.

Adm interrupts. 'Excuse me, mate, but I've lost my bag.'

The Handler looks startled and blinks repeatedly.

'Stop right there.'

The stewards are running to towards them.

'Immediately!'

The Handler returns to his unpacking.

Maybe the little guy's deaf?

'Hey, look…' Adm starts a high-speed game of charades, pointing to the bags and then back at himself. 'I'm trying to find my bag and I think it's here. It's a black overnight one, it's pretty standard-looking and I think it's here.'

The Handler stops shoving bags and turns to Adm. Face to face. Stock still. He blinks twice then resumes his work.

In the commotion, Adm finds this response kind of perfect.

The female steward shouts, 'Sir, this is a restricted area.'

Adm looks at bags tracking along the conveyor belt.

Didn't Kinki tie a green ribbon on it? Or did I rip that off?

'Do you hear me?'

No, she got it in Ireland, for good luck.

Then that's it for sure!

Adm jumps onto the conveyor belt.

The stewards yell, 'Don't do that!' 'It's not safe.' 'Sir!'

Running the same direction as the conveyor belt, Adm finds himself going faster than he expected. He staggers about, tripping over bags as he overtakes them, which ricochet and bounce off the wall as they motor along the conveyor belt towards the black flaps. Adm spots the bag with the green ribbon.

'Stop! You can't go there!'

'It's forbidden!'

Adm crouches down and keeps running.

What if it's a furnace?

His thoughts are scattergun shots.

It'd incinerate everything.

But then the flaps would be metal.

Adm, squatting down, runs through.

Wouldn't they?

The conveyor belt ends abruptly as its black track curves underneath. The bags fall into a steel funnel which feeds into a large chute. Adm's momentum sends him off the edge and down into the funnel.

He hits it feet first. Like a water slide, he spins down, steep and fast. The angle so acute that he's falling as much as he's sliding and within seconds has dropped several storeys.

His yelling empties out into a cavernous space. Adm pushes his feet out to the sides, trying to slow himself down but it's hopeless. The spirals get tighter and tighter and then, whoosh... as he's flung out of the funnel, he makes his body into a ball and crash-lands with an almighty thud. Bags shower down onto him. Adm crawls out of the way as they keep raining down.

Once out of the bag-drop zone, he takes a moment to look around. He's inside an open metal container, perched upon the top of a pyramid of carry-on bags. The container is twice as high as a shipping container and is filled to the brim. It rumbles and shakes, slowly sliding back and forth to evenly distribute the bags falling from above. Adm clambers towards the edge as the luggage keeps pouring down.

Laid out as far as the eye can see are containers. They steeple up around him like stadium seating. In the distance, they appear to be twenty containers high. Nearby, even the mid-level columns look towering. Scattered amongst them are smaller columns only two or three containers high. From Adm's vantage point it's like ocean waves, swelling up and down so dramatically that it's impossible to see the horizon.

And this isn't even the checked luggage, it's just the stuff people want to take on their flight.

Spiral chutes identical to the one Adm fell from are perched on the ceiling like fire-sprinklers in an office, while thin metal pylons from floor to roof serve as the vertical link between the containers and the chutes. Adm feels dwarfed by the enormity of the place.

When he was nineteen, Adm first went to the States and, while on a backpackers' mini-bus tour from LA to Vegas, visited the Grand Canyon. The scale was stupefying. The emptiness was vast. Even the two Kiwis who said they were scientists and that the average human farted twenty-five times a day, so it was inevitable that the minibus would stink, were silenced by the Canyon.

To Adm this feels bigger.

Is it easier up or down?

Adm looks up at the chute hanging over him, then peers down over the edge. Adrenaline from the chase and fall is pulsating through him.

There's no way I can go up. Even if I piled up a million bags, I couldn't reach the chute. And what about my bag?

Adm looks out at the world before him. It's humbling.

A billion bags? More.

I just need to get back up to the concourse. Get to the gate and get on that flight.

Without a passport? Or a ticket?

Adm rubs his face, trying to scrub his thoughts. He leans over the edge. The sides of the containers are straight vertical steel.

Just be smart.

So, why'd I chase it?

'Cause… it was dumb, sure, but it's done, so, I just have to get back…

He scrambles over to the corner that's closest to the pylon and re-arranges the bags into a launch pad.

If I edge out as far I can, then it's just a little jump to try and get my foot wedged into the girder. Okay. And a hand too.

He balances on the edge of the container with his leg stretched out as far as it can go, but can't touch the pylon.

If I just jump and fail, then what? Would the coma end? Would I die twice? Would they still be waiting?

It's just too shitty and fucked…

He shifts back.

The gap from the funnel to the container is about the same as from here to the floor and that took no time to fall, so that's how quick it'd be if I miss.

Adm sits beside the overnight bags raining down.

If I miss and fall, make it into a dive and hit head first.

This idea of him having the presence of mind to reposition himself as he plummets to the ground cracks him up.

Nice one, Darryl.

*

Earlier in the year Ella wrote a list of movies that she was determined to watch. Adm had no idea what her source was, but based on the list, he knew it was definitely not Nina, and so he tried to be a positive influence. For every *Titanic*, *Forrest Gump* or *The Notebook* he'd offer an alternative. *Talk to Me* for when she was older. *Four Weddings and a Funeral* for now, along with *The Castle*.

Not to be confused with *The Last Castle* which was a forgettable late-career Robert Redford prison flick, *The Castle* came out just as Adm had arrived home after two years living in London. Starring a young Eric Bana playing the son-in-law, the dad character was called Darryl Kerrigan, and was the embodiment of his own father. Adm's brother had called it and Adm had agreed 100 per cent. Their dad and Darryl looked practically identical. Long face. Seventies moustache. Plus, they both had a well-intentioned, misplaced heart of gold.

Watching *The Castle* with Louie and Ella almost twenty years later, chilling out with them on the couch, Adm found himself bawling his eyes out. Laugh crying. He wasn't entirely sure why, but it was something among the familiarity of the Aussie characters and the identifying with his dad and Darryl's desire for a family history; for building a home with its convoluted results. Watching it with the kids, he was confronted with wondering if he'd achieved it himself.

Crying in front of them was no big deal. They'd seen him get teary watching moments that ranged from a highlights package of the Wallabies winning the 1991 World Cup, to Will Ferrell's crotch-shot, free throw in *Semi-Pro*. Once, Ella'd even suspected that Adm had gotten choked up over *The Waterboy*.

'Dad, are you crying?'

'No.'

'Over *The Waterboy*?'

Adam shook his head.

'You are!' squealed Ella.

'No, I'm not.'

'Oh my goooooooddddd, Dad.'

'He's just really good at foosball. That's all.'

'I can't believe you're crying over *The Waterboy*!'

From the couch to the house and the neighbourhood at large, Ella announces, 'Dad's crying over *The Waterboy*!'

Louie, who never can hear 'Unpack the dishwasher' when he's sitting at the kitchen table opposite his father, somehow while upstairs with his headphones on playing Minecraft, heard Ella's proclamation and with equal volume, replied, 'Dad! You're such a bot.'

*

Adm sits on the edge of the container.

Am I as good a dad as Dad? What sort of question is that?

His thoughts return to the hospital. Moments repeat. Louie shielding his sister. Ella looking at her mum like she was an alien. Nina's realisation they were terrified by her talking to no one. To air. To him.

Kinki... I really thought we'd worked it out. That it'd end differently... but it never goes how I think it will.

The gnawing anxiety of his family's bedside vigil starts to rise. Adm tries to block it out by focusing on the task at hand. He shifts over to the edge.

What if I chuck out a shit ton of bags, and then I'll jump onto them the same way I landed from the chute?

Adm grabs a couple of bags and throws them over. They hit the concrete floor with a brittle crack. One bag snaps open and clothes spill out. He regrets being so cavalier with someone's stuff. It feels shabby, like he's violated their privacy; plus, his body is infinitely more fragile. In the dumb ideas box, this one's the winner.

He returns to plan A and scrambles over to the bag platform he'd made near the pylon.

If I get my hands in the girder and my foot in the gap and hold on for dear life, then...

He steps back from the edge. Among the din of the machinery crunching around him, Adm whispers, 'Please, God, let me make it.'

Adm's relationship with God is one of timely requests: in high school and uni wanting to get good marks, or, more recently, when Louie was put under a general anaesthetic. He liked Elvis Costello's idea of being agnostic, that atheists shut the door on God, whereas an agnostic leaves it ajar.

Unlike playing Spidey or Bruce, this jump is simple and terrifying.

It's about 50 centimetres. Just line it up and hold the fuck on. Okay. Okay. Okay.

He takes a deep breath.

Don't look down.

He fires himself up, gets ready, and at the very moment when he should commit and go for it, he backs away, too scared to jump.

Come on, mate. There's literally no other option and it's not that far, and it'll be fine.

But if I fuck this up there's no way I'm getting out of that coma.

Well, then don't fuck it up.

Adm steps back up to the edge. He looks down. He sees the broken bag with the clothes out. There's a pair of yellow shorts and something pink. And headphones.

You think they're broken?

Focus.

Adm looks back at the girder and centres all his attention on a single strip of metal.

After all those action flicks you know what to do.

Don't wait.

Adm jumps.

It's further away than he thought. His right-hand whacks into metal, he's missed the gap. As he falls, he lunges with his left. His hand goes through a gap in the metal, wrenches and jams. The weight of his body crushes it as his right-hand grabs onto the girders. The metal rips through his skin. He's kicking. Trying to jam his feet into a gap. His right leg gets wedged in. It takes his weight.

He's across! He's clinging on, but his left hand is so fucked he can't feel his fingers. He wraps his good arm around the girder. The pain is so intense he can't move. He clamps his eyes shut trying to hold on.

*

The burning pain is a trigger. It sends Adm back to the San Fran Airbnb where, stoned off his gourd, entering the bedroom, he clutches at his chest. A metallic taste in his mouth, he collapses to the ground, knocking over the bedside table, and smashing the light. In the dark his heart stops.

He sees the outline of the tall man, trying to resuscitate him.

The nightmare was real.

*

Adm opens his eyes. He's perched on the girder, like a bug on a tree.

Jesus.

Clinging onto the pylon, Adm tries to replay it.

A heart attack. Fuck.

He closes his eyes wanting to see it more clearly.

So, did I collapse and then get saved? And has everything from that night onwards been in my head?

Why can't I remember more?

He fishes around trying to remember the sensation.

That guy, I thought he was death personified, but without him I…

I'm so lucky.

The pain of his wrist intrudes. His legs are struggling to hold his weight. He opens his eyes. Blood drips from his wrist, to leg, to the floor below.

Don't give up now. Legs are good. One arm's good.

Yep. Just get to the bottom.

His movements are clunky as he tries to work out the least painful climbing method.

Slide the good hand down, take the weight then step down. Just do it once. Okay. That's one.

It's slow progress. His heart is thumping. His thighs burn.

A heart attack at my age – how's that lucky?

Well, I'm not dead.

His body is in shock. His muscles twitch.

So, did I ever see the Golden Gate Bridge or was that last day all made up?

He pushes against the girder with his bad arm wrapped around the frame, slides his good hand down, grabs onto the girder then lowers his left leg, followed by his right.

Settle the grip. Right, okay... now repeat... I'm just going to count it down Nina-style, brick by brick. Get back to the concourse. Get on that plane and get home.

That's two. Well, how many to go? Fifty-eight? More like sixty. What else can I remember? Alright, okay, let's think.

Among the shipping containers and the whir of the bags falling down, Adm is perched up high on a thin girder. It's not his slow, awkward movements that stand out, it's the fact that among the automated order and metal, there's something alive and bleeding.

Fifty-eight Victoria Road: our address in the Cross in our early days, Kinki, when all I wanted was for you say that I was amazing, but instead, you said, 'A woman should give her lover the freedom to achieve their dreams, but not expect them to reach any of them.'

How many now, fifty-six to go… so, what now, Kinki? You're heading towards the big five-o and I was supposed to take you to Florence for your fortieth, but because of cash you said, 'Wait a bit', and now that's off, too, and… fuck I wish I was better at everything…

Remember purple velours for my birthday? The kids were at my folks, and you had those Valiums that you'd squirrelled away from Christmas, and we sprinkled them on a birthday joint and I spent the whole time thinking I was thirty-seven because you kept saying you were almost forty. But you were just rounding up your age, so I lost out being thirty-six 'cause you'd decided to skip being thirty nine.

You always miss it before it happened. I always miss it after the fact. Like the kids' end of year concerts; I'm always stressing out about taking heaps of photos, or some work crap, and you just beam, watching them weave their magic.

Adm's jeans are soggy with blood. He takes a deep breath and steadies himself.

We're over halfway, now… so…

Let's go to Florence. Whack it on the credit card. Okay…?

And what about your obsession with Saturn returns and turning thirty?

Or Dad in the early days when I accidentally called you Kinki in front of him and his face lit up, while you acted like it never happened.

Ten… ten to go and Ella these days on the cusp of adolescence. She's all 'No' and 'Nothing.'

Although Adm has his technique, his legs are turning to jelly, and his wrist is in agony.

And seven… little Louie playing cricket and that endless run-less summer when he thought I could do no wrong, and how you'd look at me, Kinki, with that smile of yours, enjoying me falling off the pedestal before I even knew I was on it.

Okay, now is it really just two to go? Thank fuck. Thank you, Kinki. Brick by brick.

Adm's foot touches the floor. He gingerly leans against the girder. The broken bag is in front of him, there are splotches of blood splattered around. Sweating and faint, he nurses his wrist.

I'll just have a minute.

Using the bag as a pillow, Adm lies down.

*

Mechanical beeping, like a fire alarm, wakes him up.

Is that my hospital monitor?

Directly above him the beeping gets louder. It's coming from the chute that flings out the bags, as it tracks overhead from one container to the next.

Ohh... okay... well.

Adm awkwardly gets to his feet, takes a green shirt from the broken bag, and tries to make it into a sling.

Adm checks out the chute above him.

Maybe I can use it like a star to navigate.

But the containers crowd in on him, making it impossible to get any perspective.

It's like a maze, or a desert sequence from one of the Star Wars, *or* Dune, *or... Spies Like Us.*

Boom! Exactly! Chevy and Dan, welcome back! So, let's take it just one step at a time, because if I'm stuck down here it won't matter what's happening in the hospital.

Hobbling along, Adm tries to minimise the jarring pain that, with each step, sears up into his broken wrist.

Hey, Louie, not a bot, I'm hardcore.

This thought immediately sparks Adm's memory of Louie sitting in the back seat of the car, singing along to *Boggis, Bunce and Bean*, a song from *Fantastic Mr Fox*, with his toddler voice so bright and precise as he emphasised every syllable: das-tard-ly, none-the-less and e-qual-ly.

Why is it that I always fixate on when they were, like, pre-school little? Is it just 'cause it's easier?

I don't know; I mean, Ella was nine when we watched Isle of Dogs, *so, maybe, yes.*

It had been an impromptu daddy-daughter movie-night. Louie was having a sleepover and Nina was working late, Robbie Rose was snuggled up, and Ella was resting her head on her father's shoulder, domestic and peaceful.

Then, snap, Ella cracked it, furious because Adm kept leaning forward to the little coffee table to reach out and check his phone.

'You're way more obsessed with your phone than I am.'

'Hang on…'

'Why should I get off it when you never do?'

Drunk on the pleasure of turning the tables, Ella repositioned herself at the other end of the couch with her legs tucked up so not a skerrick of her was touching him as Adm muttered, 'I'm perfectly within my rights to check my phone.'

'Hypocrite.'

He'd been expecting a confirmation email as it would affect whether… whether what? Adm couldn't remember. But her face. Nine and resolute with her Betty Boop haircut, ice-cream cone earrings, and bright freckly face. He remembered that.

And her knowing the meaning of hypocrite.

As the movie reached its happy-sad climax, unlike Adm and *The*

Castle, Ella wasn't going to give him the pleasure of seeing her cry, so she turned away to hide her face. Robbie, sensing her sadness, shifted from her diplomatic doggy post in the middle of them and plumped herself down on Ella's lap, placing her little furry chin on her arm.

Robbie Rose Robinson was patted and embraced while Adm sat in exile at the other end of the couch.

Standing among the containers, Adm imagines wrapping her in his arms.

The frigging dog was smarter than me.

*

Because of the containers' grid layout, Adm loses his sense of time and progression. At first, he tries to keep track of how many grids he's passed, but the numbers start to merge. It's maze-like and confusing. As he wanders, he discovers that one of the pylon's iron mesh columns is larger than the rest and has stairs inside it, like a fire-escape stairwell. With his good hand he gently pushes down on the handle. Click. The door opens.

Outstanding.

He steps inside. Pad. Pad. Pad. Flight after flight. Step after step. Slower and slower. The repetition. Step, step, step. Adm stops to catch his breath. He's as high as the chutes that track over the containers. He leans on the frame and looks out at the stream of carry-on bags pouring out of the chutes and filling up the huge containers. These bags, full of essential items, pile up like drab smarties: blacks, browns and greys. They're interrupted by an occasional dot of colour. Hello Kitty pink. Stormtrooper white. There's so many Adm struggles to make sense of the scale.

Every single bag somebody packed, and speculated over the weather, or if their present would be liked, or…

Do they bring the sexy undies? Or a book?

Periodically the containers are lifted, like Tetris blocks shuffling and reconfiguring into a better, higher, more efficient use of space, moved by automated forklift units that slowly roll along the steel corridors.

What if the bags are peoples' leftovers? Or their souls…? And they leave them here and then they go through the departure gates and that's it. Done.

This idea flattens him. It glugs out of his head and down into his belly.

And somewhere down there is my bag with Nina's ribbon. It's like this whole system's designed to retain the materials but never return them to their owner.

The more he thinks about it the smaller he feels.

It doesn't matter, it's not the point.

Adm pushes himself off from the railing.

Just focus on Nina and the kids.

There's more bags here than people in the terminal.

Just get to the top, and get on a plane.

He takes on the final two flights.

So, how will the plane get me home?

Just get there first.

He arrives at the top. Finally. He puts his ear to the door, but the beeping chutes drown out the sounds on the other side. He takes one last look at the ocean of baggage.

THE WEDDING CRASHER

Adm peeks out into the airport concourse. From his limited view, no stewards are visible. He quickly pushes open the door and slips back into the public-facing world of the airport. No one seems to notice him standing by the thoroughfare wall. Given the stewards' pursuit before he fell down the chute, he's expecting a blare of sirens and a horde of stewards swooping. But there's nothing. Passengers amble about. Congregate at shops. Business as usual.

Find something that's a marker, something I can reference if I need to come back.

I'm opposite Gates 46 and 48. Easy.

Adm looks like a standard airport punter, but without any carry-on bags he feels self-conscious. He needs a prop to help him blend into the crowd and avoid the stewards' attention. He crosses over to a shop and grabs a little duty-free shopping cart. As he starts to push it, he automatically uses both hands and in doing so realises that his wrist feels fine. Much like earlier when he'd crashed as Spider-Man, his wrist has healed in record time. He takes off the makeshift sling, joins the streams of people wandering about wheeling their trolleys and walks towards the signage listing the flights. Among the departures he reads:

QF11 Sydney: Now boarding Gate 36.

Okay, this is it! Fuck yes. Head to the gate, join the queue, slip through, and get on home. Piece of piss.

A cluster of stewards is heading straight towards him.

Shit!

To mask his nerves, he grips the trolley tightly. The stewards approach.

They don't want me. Just be cool. I'm not the point.

He wheels over and sits down alongside Gate 36. He maintains his cool by retrieving his mobile, and, while scrolling through the PFEC app, gets ready to run.

Shouldn't they be here by now?

Sneaking a glance, Adm sees that they've congregated at the little counter in front of Gate 36 and have begun the process of on-boarding people. Adm allows himself a wry smile over his paranoia.

For all the times I say I'm not the story, I still don't seem to buy it.

Two seats away a woman is chuckling to herself. She looks like life's given her some knocks but she's still giving it a red-hot go. She's wearing grey leggings and a matching tight yellow-and-grey striped shirt. Her sandal jiggles as she wiggles her foot with pleasure. She has a mousey brown ponytail, her AirPods in, and is loving watching her phone, so much so, that she looks around trying to grab somebody's attention and share it with them. Adm is caught. He feels like a prick for wanting to leave as fast as possible, but he's trapped, so instead, asks, 'Good show?'

'Yeah, it's amazing, it's my niece's big day.'

Of course she's an Aussie. Why is it our accents always sound more extreme overseas?

'Here.'

The woman shuffles over and hands him her phone. The blokes' guts are girdled by their tucked-in black-tie shirts. They are drinking beer in little function room-sized glasses, alongside women in strapless dresses holding champagne flutes and periodically hoicking up their fronts to keep their frocks in order. Nothing seems to be happening as the wedding crowd flounder and chat in between the ceremony and the speeches.

'It's really special.'

'Yeah, absolutely.'

'She's a sweetheart, you know. I was there in the hospital when she was born. Feels like just the other day. Kayla. She's my brother's little girl. There he is.'

How can she see a live feed of her niece's wedding?

She points at the screen, but her finger blocks most of the picture. 'He's a bit older. Got two kids from his first but she's so happy so…'

'Your brother?'

'No, the groom.'

She moves her hand away to reveal the PFEC app logo. It feels meta, watching people at a party struggle for conversation while Adm's stuck in the same predicament. He hands back her phone, and offers, 'It looks like a great day.'

'Ta,' says the Wedding Woman. She stands up and starts collecting her things in preparation for her departure.

The other passengers are getting themselves sorted too. Looking for a way to sneak on board, Adm studies those at the front of the queue and searches for an angle.

Each person shows the steward their ticket on their mobile. Once the steward has scanned the boarding pass, they keep the phone and usher the passenger through the double swing doors.

Hang on, what? What's with their phones and bags?

It's done very subtly and gently. No one notices, let alone protests. The departing passengers seem content to go empty-handed through the gates.

What the fuck?

Adm's analysis of the stewards is interrupted by the Wedding Woman, 'You a nervous flyer?'

'Sorry?'

'You feeling okay?'

'I'm fine, thanks.'

'You look like you've seen a ghost.'

'Ha, no, I'm good thanks.'

Standing beside him, with all her bags sorted, she sees that Adm's not moved an inch, 'Aren't you on this flight?'

'Yeah.'

'So, don't you wanna get home?'

'You think this'll do it?'

The Wedding Woman looks at him unsure if he's a moron or a smart-arse. 'This is your flight, yeah?'

'Yeah…'

'Well then, yeah, that's what the sign says.'

'I don't know what's past those gates.'

'The plane.'

'Are you sure?'

She laughs.

To minimise his awkwardness Adm says, 'Safe travels.'

'You coming?'

'In a bit.'

'Suit yourself.' She half waves and wanders off.

At the counter the stewards repeat the process, acquiring all departing passengers' phones and bags, and ensuring each person walks through the gates empty-handed.

The rows of people queueing up to return home obstruct Adm's view. Wanting to see what happens next, Adm gets up and heads towards the large windows overlooking the tarmac.

A steward scuttles over. Her hair is pulled back tight. She has pencil-thin eyebrows and a gummy smile. 'Can I help you?' Her neck-tie scarf is at a jaunty angle. 'Sir?'

Adm tries to act casual. 'I was just stretching my legs.'

'Can I be of any assistance?'

'No thanks.' Adm smile-nods, pulls out his mobile and begins toggling. She stands between him and the tarmac windows, gums out, waiting.

Are they checking up on me? Does she know I was chased?

He turns away from her and heads back towards the concourse and the Wedding Woman, who is standing in line, resting her phone on her belly, watching Kayla's wedding on her mobile.

How did she get such an amazing video stream? Unless its PFEC related somehow...

Adm channels Nina's investigative journo mode.

What's through the gates? And why's no one sitting by the windows, looking out at the tarmac?

He wants to see if there are planes taking off, so he slows down, about to change tack and check out the view, but he feels like he's being watched. His suspicion's confirmed. It's the gummy steward. She's locked in on him.

Shit.

Acting like he didn't notice her, Adm spins away from the windows, ignores the urge to see if she's following him and instead observes the LED billboards continually promoting the PFEC app. He checks out other people waiting around for their flights. Everyone's on their phones. Obsessed.

That woman's wedding was on the app so maybe that's what everyone's watching, a live stream of the people they know.

Adm shifts his gaze back to the billboard promoting the app with its stylish montage of everyday people, and the tagline, 'Take your departure to new heights'.

So maybe the home channel doesn't mean what I thought it did. And if that woman can watch her niece's wedding then presumably could I watch Kinki and the kids.

But why did I get immersion mode? Was it the coma? Or Nina playing me movies?

This idea is a mistake. The failure butterflies arrive. The powerlessness of that hospital room sickens him.

Anyways, they're probably back on the couch watching something funny. Kinki's first choice has been shouted down and they're watching something silly and fun like Starsky and Hutch *and Louie's saying, 'Dou it! Dou it!', and they're all lying on top of each other and Nina's pointing out how cute Robbie is.*

But if they're all in San Fran, where's the dog?

His adrenaline starts to rise. The fear that gurgles is both abstract and specific.

This can't all be in my head. There's no way I could make it all up. Plus, I've still got Ella's panda so it's not like before… but if this is real then what does, 'Take your departure to new heights', actually mean? Is this… what…?

Maybe there's no way home.

Adm wants to get the hell of out there. He whips around looking for an exit. Feeling scrutinised by every steward, he looks for something to help calm him down before he does something stupid, but all he sees is punters zoned into their screens, headphones in, watching stuff. It's not age-specific, it's everyone, and they're not bored waiting for the flight, they're straight-out captivated, like it's the world's most gripping global phenomenon.

Cutting through this vision, a four-year-old boy wheeling a Buzz Lightyear mini suitcase blithely walks past him. It's odd to see a young kid flying solo, plus, given Louie was once obsessed with Buzz Lightyear, Adm can't help but notice.

Although the kid doesn't seem lost, Adm wants to confirm he's not alone. He sees a couple nearby and concluding that they're the boy's folks, Adm keeps walking.

But his anxiety is layering upon itself, and walking doesn't help. Among his backlog of agitation, the fear of being caught and questioned by the stewards remains an unsettling constant.

He shifts off the main passageway, seeking to hide among the passengers sitting in the rows outside a departure gate. He spots a gap where he can sit down without affecting anyone.

His mobile buzzes, pinging him a notification. Adm gets out his phone and looks at the interface. The PFEC app pop-up says, 'Home Channel: View now'.

There's nothing stopping me.

Don't.

I could just see what they're doing? See if Robbie Rose is with them. I mean, why not?

In what movie does the hero sit around watching some shitty telemovie of his life?

If I go through the gates, I think that's it. That's why the stewards take people's stuff? 'Cause they can't go back.

But if I stay here, then Kinki and the kids are stuck in that hospital, with their life on hold.

SHIFT WORK

Adm is skittish and distracted. He keeps looping through his two choices and can't stop himself from repeating them over and over.

In an effort to break his mental loop he resolves to return to the Irish Pub, but as soon as he tries to find it, the airport design confounds him. It circles out like a spider's web and just as Adm thinks he's back where he started, he realises it is a similar layout but a different wing. By the time he reaches the pub, he's worn out.

He loiters midway between the tables and the bar, not sure why he bothered coming back or what he wants to do.

'Are you the new guy?'

'I don't think so.'

'Aren't you Ad?'

'Well, yeah, I guess.'

'You guess?'

'I am.'

The Waitress grins. 'They said you did a runner but that you'd be back.' She walks off towards the bar. Ad realises he's expected to follow. To the barman she says, 'Ad's back.'

'Great.'

The Waitress places a round of drinks on her tray and returns to the floor.

The barman hands him a green and black paisley vest and says,

'Welcome to the team.'

'Cheers.'

The barman drops his apron on the swing door and walks out into the thoroughfare of the airport.

'See ya.'

Initially Ad thinks it's a 'See ya' end-of-shift goodbye, but then it dawns on him that he's never coming back.

Ad holds the vest. The bar is unattended.

Perched on a barstool, facing the TV sports channels, is a guy wearing a sky blue collared shirt tucked into crisp khaki chinos. He's a little older than Ad but looks fitter, and seems earnest and can-do. 'How you doing?'

'Yeah, good.'

'You an Aussie?'

'Yeah.'

'G'daaay maaaite.' The Can-Do guy's accent is horrific.

Ad fake-laughs.

As Can-Do finishes his beer he asks, 'You new?'

'Kinda.'

Ad takes the hint. He slips the vest over his black tee, and steps behind the bar. 'What are you drinking?'

'It's the low-carb one.'

Ad looks at the different taps. 'The Skinny Goat?'

'That's the one.'

Ad pours the ale, miraculously with a perfect head.

'Thaeenks maaaite.' The Can-Do guy's attempt at an Aussie accent sounds like a sheep being assaulted. He sips his beer and returns to his mobile.

Ad looks out to the terminal wondering if his assumptions about the barman are correct. From behind the bar, the airport looks completely different.

The first time Ad stood behind the bar, seeing himself as characters from movies and freaking out, he hadn't taken in the grandeur of the concourse. Framed by the dark foreground, the departure terminal now captures his attention. It's stunning, like a modern aeronautical version of Grand Central Station.

The Can-Do guy makes a sharp whistling gasp as though he's just been stung. He's on his mobile watching two teenagers playing tennis. Never taking his eyes off his phone, he reaches out and grabs his beer. Another whistling gasp followed by a long slow sigh. He tugs at the corners of his jaw. 'You just don't want it enough.'

'Want what?' Ad can't help but ask.

'He was up four–two in the first, serving at forty love and now he's lost it in straight sets and you can't tell me he wasn't the better player.'

'Who?'

'Marcus. My son.'

'Ah well, maybe next time.'

'Maybe…'

The Can-Do guy nods over and over, as though Ad's response needs further consideration and each nod is giving the 'maybe' its due.

Can-do finishes his beer.

'Maybe…'

He picks up his bag, and leaves a fiver on the bar. 'Thanks, bud.'

'Take it easy.'

'You too.'

The Can-Do guy tries to step around a quartet of backpackers sprawled out at a nearby table. They do little to assist. Athletic limbs hang over armrests. Each on their own device. As he squeezes past

Ad hears one of the girls say, 'Very wild.'

Her friend laughs, enjoying her response to the clip she's just presented. Ad doesn't know if it was wild or tame but is confident whatever conclusion he draws will be wrong.

Seeking distraction he looks around at the pub's patrons. Just like the punters out on the concourse, everyone is obsessed with the PFEC app. Ad pulls out his phone, but it feels kind of gross, like a shitty drug. So he puts it away and starts wiping down the bar.

He tries to block out all the noises of the lounge and just focus on the wood. He wipes the same spot over and over, in the vague hope that it calms him down, but all his busyness can no longer mask his fear, and the single thought that he'd done so much to ignore refuses to be held at bay. It gurgles and erupts, blasting crap everywhere, a spluttering and spewing shitstorm that's vile and panic-making and crystallises into the statement, 'I'm dead.'

The Waitress steps back.

'Aren't I?'

She takes the glasses off her tray, acting like she's not heard him, but he persists. 'There's no way back. Is there?'

The Waitress says, 'I don't remember when my shift started and—'

'Sorry, forget-about-it.'

'My feet feel hideous—'

He talks over her. 'Please don't... I didn't...'

'I mean, are you actually going to get me to—'

'No! Like, really, no.' Ad sees her weariness and backpedals, suddenly not wanting to know the answer, 'It's cool. Honestly.'

He gets out the container of beer nuts and re-fills the several bowls laid out along the bar. He over pours the nuts. He cleans up the mess and in doing so, he knocks over a bowl, then cleans it up. He tries not to look her but he can't help himself. He flinches when they make eye contact then returns to tidying up the nuts. He hears her take a deep breath and slowly exhale. She taps her purple fingernail on the bar. 'See on the third shelf, the Captain Morgan?'

Ad, following her directions, finds the rum.

'Yeah, that's it. Lots from the Captain and just a splash of Coke.'

Ad starts filling the tumbler with ice.

'Half that. Don't waste the space.'

Ad tips out some ice and starts to pour. His hand is shaking. He has to concentrate to aim straight.

'Right on. Don't skimp.'

Ad does as requested. He makes one for himself too.

'Good for you. First real shift, make it count.'

They cheers. She takes a big sip, places her drink on her coaster and then looking past his expectant face, she focuses on the shiny wall of the spirit bottles and rips it off like a band-aid. 'We all are.'

She finishes her drink.

'Some more than others.'

It's not so much a kick in the guts as an aching, hollow punch.

This'll be the last time I ever feel this because... I'm dead.

And that realisation is another sickening kick.

I'm fucking dead. Fuck.

Ad grabs a plastic cocktail stirrer and twirls his rum and Coke into a whirlpool, then lets go and watches it spin. He feels empty. 'So, what is this place?'

She doesn't answer. She's back on the floor serving tables.

Out past the passenger queues and the stewards monitoring them, Ad stares at the departure gates.

Maybe it's bullshit... or... maybe... what does 'some more than others' mean?

What is that?

A guy in his late twenties arrives. He is tanned, wears a baseball cap, singlet, and board shorts, with his sunnies perched on the brim of his cap. He has an open, straight-up kind of face.

Maybe the coma can save me, Kinki...? Fuck, I'm sorry... but I don't know what to do. What if...

Adam can't finish the thought. There's so many questions and what ifs that he can't complete a single one of them.

The Baseball Cap guy is patient. Not wanting to impose, he starts munching on the nut mix, picking out the cashews and leaving the rest. As he watches his phone, he works his way through two bowls before asking, 'Hey, buddy, can I trouble you for a Corona?'

It takes Ad a moment to realise he's being talked to. The question takes him out of his head. 'Um... yeah, for sure'

Ad places the Corona on the bar, sticks in a slice of lime and hands it over. He glances down at Baseball Cap's phone. Onscreen is a woman in bed with a brand-new baby in her arms.

Fuck.

Ad looks up at the guy, who's chilling at the bar watching his phone, and swigging his beer.

The Waitress returns. Ad looks at her to see if she's clocked it.

She subtly nods at him.

Ad asks Baseball Cap, 'Is that your partner?'

'Yeah man, they're my girls.'

'It's very sweet.'

He grins at Ad and replies, 'Tonight it is.'

'Yeah?'

'Absolutely, bro, she's been having trouble feeding, but it looks like tonight's good. If my flight's not delayed, I should be able to help her out tomorrow. Let her get some rest.'

And with that, he takes his beer and heads to his table.

Ad avoids grappling with his own existence and his bulbous vat of questions and instead focuses on Baseball Cap Dad, by asking the Waitress, 'So, does that guy know where he is? That he's…'

'I don't know.'

'He's acting like he's flying home, but he's—'

'You'd have to ask him.'

'But what's going on?'

'Look. I don't want to… everyone's got their theories. The stayers, that is. And everyone's different.' She clears her tray of empties and as she starts preparing her drinks orders, she speaks rapid fire. 'And I don't like to say what I think because each to their own and the moment you say something then it's more real and who am I to say what's real or not and it doesn't get any easier, no matter how long, so this is only because you asked and you're so…'

'Freaked?'

'A-huh, so, I'm just going to just say what I think and that's it. It's not gospel or anything and don't think that my opinion means anything because who am I to say, you know?' She talks even faster. Rattling it off as she pours beers and mixes spirits, 'But I think folks hang out here when they're not ready to go and they watch their people like it's reality TV, watching their family and friends, and I think the app was introduced by the stewards to cushion people and smooth out the transition, but…'

Trying to not wig out as she keeps ticking boxes on his gut-feel questionnaire, Ad starts making two more Captain and Cokes.

'But maybe it's too effective 'cause there's regulars everywhere and they're all addicted and watch everyone. Everyone they know, every day, everything, all the time, and some stay here and wait for their husbands, wives, kids, lovers whatever, so they can say goodbye again.'

Ad hands over the next round of Captains. She swirls her glass, talking as much to herself as him. 'But it's no guarantee. None at all. And there's plenty who wait and wait, watching out for their loved ones, and then when they pass on, they think they'll find them here but... they don't, and I don't know why and...' She lets out a big sigh, '... that fucks them up real nice.'

She picks up her glass and holds it aloft waiting for him to cheers.

They clink glasses, toasting as much to each other as to those left waiting. She takes a sip.

'But most folks just go straight through the gates and barely watch a thing.'

She swigs the rest. A big gulp. The ice falls and hits her lips. She drains the glass, then plunks it down and fiddles with her coaster, tracing the outline with her long fingernail.

Ad waits, hoping there's more but she's shut up shop. Speech over.

As he watches her fingers play with her coaster, he mumbles, 'I didn't get reality TV, I got movies.'

'Huh?'

'As in I was in them.'

'Get out!' She's shaking her head and seems genuinely surprised. 'I have never heard of such a thing.'

'I was told I was selected for a beta trial of an immersion mode...?'

'A-huh.'

He waits for her to reply but she gives him nothing, so he fishes. 'Is that good?'

'How would I know?'

'I thought maybe if I was different then maybe I'd have more of a chance.'

'Of what?'

'Getting back.'

'Ha!'

Ad wants to add, 'To my wife and kids,' but he doesn't say a word. Her response was a total shut down. Instead, he says nothing, and her little explosion of laughter gives way to a silence that sits among the bar's general noise.

The Waitress finishes off her drink and gets up, 'I'm sorry. I didn't mean it like that.'

'What then?'

She shrugs and takes her tray full of drinks back out to the floor.

Let's say she's right and this is the link between one life and the next.

Ad grabs the Captain and pours a shot.

That means that when I had the heart attack I went straight to the hospital.

He adds a splash of Coke.

But because I'm in a coma the immersion mode links the two worlds…

So, based on that logic, everyone watching stuff on their phone will never see themselves, because they're dead. But if they're in a coma or on life support then they'd have the same view as me.

Feeling buzzed, he takes a swig of his Captain and Coke.

She said 'some more than others.' That's the thing. That's the distinction.

But none of us are getting back.

BEER AND SKITTLES

Laden with the Waitress's theory rattling around in his head, Ad feels like he's watching the world from inside a mirror.

But how long have they been here?

Just be a barman.

But.

Just serve and shut it.

Among the patrons is a sensible-looking woman in her early sixties, with her phone leaning up against her handbag so she can watch hands-free. She has a dyed strawberry blonde bob, and a tight looking face. Her small lips are pursed and covered with a shade of pale peach. She has a half-eaten blueberry muffin and a cold cup of tea. Her arms are crossed, and she clearly doesn't like what she's watching, but nor can she stop. Ad tracks the Waitress to see if she'll disturb her. She does not.

Past the sensible-looking woman, among the people to-ing and fro-ing on the concourse, Ad sees a little boy. It's the kid with the Buzz Lightyear bag. Ad scans for the boy's parents, but it's hard to get a clear line of sight so Ad wanders down to end of the bar, but this results in a trio of college lads asking for some more brewskis. They're watching a game on the telly and are nicely set up, working their way through a bowl of nachos and a plate of ribs. With pouring the Blue Moons, it takes an eternity for Ad to get the head just right, but when he does, it's pretty damn satisfying. They give him a drunken nod of gratitude.

This hospitality caper feels alright.

Ad's thoughts return to the Buzz Lightyear kid and wanting to make sure he is with his parents. Ad steps out from behind the bar, and heads towards the concourse. On the way, an elderly woman sitting with her husband grabs his attention. 'Excuse me?'

'Yes?'

She looks mischievous. 'We're after something sweet.'

'Righto.'

'Which is better? The crème brûlée or the affogato?'

'They're both amazing.'

'But if you had to choose?'

'I'd get both.'

'Done!'

Smiles all 'round.

Ad places their order before checking in with Baseball Cap Dad to see if he wants another Corona. He does. Then as Ad heads out to see where the kid is, he passes by another couple and asks if they're ready to order. They are not.

With the little boy and his family nowhere to be seen, Ad reviews his remaining patrons. There's one table he's not checked in on. A man is near Ad's original table, with his back to the bar, facing out to the airport's main thoroughfare. Ad strolls over.

It's Slick.

No way!

'Would you like another wine?'

El Slicko is startled.

Does he recognise me?

Slick puts his hand over his phone, 'Yes, I would.'

'What are you drinking now?'

'A Napa sav blanc.'

Slick returns to his call.

'And did you see who took my bag?'

Slick says down the line, 'Just hold on a moment, would you,' before asking Ad, 'What did you say?'

'Did you see who took my bag?'

'I don't know what you mean.'

'I was sitting there before and—'

'We've never met.'

'It's cool, it was before my shift. But you never saw my bag?'

'I've never seen you.'

'Oh… okay. Well, um… can I suggest a pinot gris? It's South Australian and I had a cellar door session there once, not at that specific vineyard, but Aussie wine's pretty good.'

Slick reads the menu's description, sizes Ad up, and after a considered pause, says, 'Yes… Thanks.'

It seems genuine.

'My pleasure.'

Regardless of whatever satisfaction he derives from working, throughout his waitering merry-go-round, Ad's insides keep churning. The repeating soundtrack of what the Waitress said casts a shadow over everyone he serves.

How much do they know or deny? Like the Baseball Cap Dad… and what's with the Buzz Lightyear kid?

*

Time passes. People drift in and out. The elderly coupled savoured their desserts, Slick liked his wine, and the Baseball Cap Dad necked a bucket of Corona. Outside, the stewards continued to usher people through the gates.

If the stewards are like shepherds, then what are the staff?

Ad watches the Waitress move between tables, unobtrusive and yet present when needed. Unlike the stewards who treat the passengers like they're tasks, she seems authentic.

And am I staff now?

Shortly after Ad clears away their dessert plates, the elderly couple, Dean and Janet, realising he's an Aussie too, drip-feed Ad their story; Janet as the ball-by-ball commentator, Dean the side-line eye.

Janet kicks off with, 'It had been our first real trip since Dean's retirement, and about half-way through our second week we're on a day tour out on the reef in a glass-bottom boat. Height of the season, so, fantastic weather, but—'

Dean cuts in, 'It was a freak wave.'

'They'd over booked it. There were just too many people on the boat but of course we didn't know until—'

'It was just a terrible business.' Dean fiddles with the inside of his nose, scowling. 'Just terrible.'

Janet, trying to water down her husband, adds, 'But at least we're here together.' She gestures to her mobile. 'Mind you, watching the kids grieve was… I don't know why we did it really.'

A long slow huff from Dean.

She waits to see if he has anything more to add, then picks up their story. 'And he's been ready to go a few times. Seeing the kids make choices we couldn't stop.' Dean nods in agreement. 'They sold our house too cheap, which cut their inheritance cut by—'

'At least half.'

'Dean was ropeable. He stormed out of the bar and I was beside myself but then when he saw those stewards start to hover—'

'Seeing Janet by herself, I couldn't. I wasn't ready.'

'More than 40 years and he's still hanging around.'

'We got married young.'

'But I wouldn't change a thing.'

'Except the tour operator.'

Janet offers an obligatory smile as Dean chuckles at his own joke.

'Plus, you wanted to see Mila.'

'Yes, it's true, I did.'

'Our first granddaughter.' Janet leans over to Ad, touching his arm conspiratorially. 'We would have loved to have met her, helped out with nappies and that sort of thing, and watching on this app thing when Claire told her bub how much we'd have loved her, well… it makes it hard to go really.'

Over the course of several different orders of tea and sweets, and the occasional beer or white wine spritzer, Ad learns more about their history.

They remind Ad of his folks. They were, as his mother would say, 'Very unpretentious.' It was her way of noting that as she'd aged, she preferred the company of genuine people. This inner chat which Ad plays out with his mum connects him to Janet and Dean.

'I mean, they were just muddling through. Wanting a connection, and I was so up my own arse that…'

Dean, with his furrowed brow, mutters, 'I'm sure your folks know how much you love them.'

Janet pops out of her seat like a jackrabbit and hugs him. Ad steps back. It's unexpected, shocking and lovely. Janet's shaking. It takes Ad a moment to realise she's sobbing, big body-shaking sobs.

'It's alright dear.'

He feels like he should be saying that to her, instead of her to him. She squeezes him tight with her grandmotherly arms.

Ad looks over at Dean, seeking some low-key blokey reaction, but he's stock still, blinking furiously, trying not to cry. Ad wants to change it all. Send them back. Get back himself. Just make it all different. He hugs Janet, thinking of his mum hugging Louie and Ella, and thinking of Janet's kids and the fact that Ad could hug their mum, but they never could.

Eventually, they separate. Janet wipes her eyes and nose on a napkin, and gives a self-conscious little laugh, looking almost coquettish. 'Sorry.'

'Not at all.'

From behind, Ad hears Dean say, 'Here mate.' He turns around and before he can say, 'Easy big fella', Dean is in his grill, giving him a bear hug. Ad holds his face together. The old bloke doesn't have the full-body shakes, but he gives Ad a ten-barrel embrace. Ad feels like a son, a loved son, and struggles to keep it together. They separate. The three of them stand in an odd little triangle.

Dean sighs. 'We're going today. We're done.'

'You're kidding?'

'No, mate.' Dean pulls off his wedding ring and hands it to Ad. 'Here.'

Janet hands over hers too. 'We can't take them with us.'

'And we don't want them collected.'

Ad 's speechless as he cups Janet and Dean's wedding rings in his gormless hand: their last connection, and they're giving it to him. It feels enormous. He mumbles, 'Thank you,' which is the right volume because it's too small a word for what they've given him, and Ad knows it.

With nothing more to be said, Dean and Janet head towards the departure gates.

A steward comes to their table to collect their luggage.

'Hang on.'

Tied to Janet's overnight bag is a green silk ribbon. It reminds Ad of Nina's one. He takes the ribbon off, threads the rings through it and holds it tight as the steward takes away their luggage.

As Dean and Janet make their way through the crowd, doubling-down regret rolls over Ad, thick and fast. He thinks of how many times he closed his bedroom door after his folks had driven him around all weekend, or they'd spent a day babysitting his kids, or he'd met them for a weekend brunch and he'd said, 'Thanks,' and, 'Bye,' without bothering to ask them anything.

Ad senses someone's been watching him. The Waitress gives him a little smile. He doesn't know what to make of it. It's doesn't look like pity. But it's not far from it. Perhaps compassion. She gets back to serving. It motivates him.

I'm not going to mope.

Ad clears Janet and Dean's table and returns to the bar. He pulls out two thumbtacks that hold a tattered menu together, threads the ribbon through their wedding rings, and pins it to the spirits shelf. Their rings dangle, lassoed through the silk like a little memorial. It sits well with Ad.

Then he's back serving customers. The backpackers want another round. The soup 'n' salad for table two needs to be dropped off. There's work to be done.

YOU WANT FRIES WITH THAT?

'The beauty of hospitality is the mix of old and new. The actions are repetitive, but the people are fresh.'

'Whatever Ad,' says the Baseball Cap Dad.

'It's true! And the time goes fast.'

'Well, I'm good for now.'

'And I'm not recruiting.'

'Alright then.'

As Ad re-sets his tables, he realises he likes being an Aussie working in a bar and likes folks, in between watching stuff on their PFEC app, talking to him.

'Whatcha watchin'?'

'Oh, yeah, what's he like?'

'A sneaky fucker?'

'Reckon she'll bust his balls?'

'How long were you together?'

'How'd you meet?'

'What a cutie.'

'How's she going at school?'

'Are they any good at… (at this point, Ad inserts a sport based on nationality and gender)?'

'Oh wow, just like your dad/ma/gran/pop/mum/sister/bro/auntie.'

And even though everyone's different, there are patterns to the questions, and it generally drifts back to family.

Ad tries to be attuned, to listen. He uses the same banter that he leveraged when presenting at work, but now it's real. He begins to feel the weight of what they're telling him and appreciate the moments that sit between what they're saying and what they know, but can't articulate. These bits start to stick.

But people don't ask Ad his story and he never volunteers it. Occasionally a notification buzzes on his phone but he refuses to 'View Now' for fear that Nina and the kids are still by his bedside with their life on hold. It compounds his guilt. If they've waited so long and sacrificed so much, he can't give up now and go through the gate.

So, he keeps serving tables, wanting to leave but unable to get home, and the loop continues.

*

After the Janet and Dean farewell, Ad thinks that the goodbyes will get easier but they don't. Each one is so full. Plus, he doesn't want to get immune. The whole point is he's asking the questions because he gives a shit and because of that, he unlocks as much as they do, like Edward Norton in *Fight Club*'s 'Men with Testicular Cancer Workshop', sinking his face into Meatloaf's sweaty bosom and wailing; it's Ad's way to release.

Somewhere in the flow of all this, the rings dangling on the green silk ribbon become a collection. People ask, 'Why are they there?' and Ad tells the tale of Janet and Dean, and when other patrons choose to go, they too want to leave something. The collection becomes an ever-expanding assortment of trinkets, wallet photos and whatnots. Its clutter begins to take over the spirits shelf.

During a quieter moment as they share a drink, the Waitress points out, 'You can barely get to the Captain.'

'That's fine, it's Nina's wall anyway.'

'I'm sorry?'

''Cause of the green ribbon.'

Ad sees the Waitress waiting for more of an explanation but instead he offers, 'And she always preferred rosé.'

'Well, I prefer rum.'

'Hang on…' Adam, thinking out loud, mutters, 'What if you could take it with you?'

'Take what?'

'Something that was yours. What if it gets you back home?'

'What if it fractures your soul like in *Being John Malkovich*?'

'No really…'

The Waitress gives a dissenting grunt, but Adam persists. 'Isn't it worth it, like… isn't there someone you want to get back to? That's why you're staying isn't it? To find out a way—'

'We're so very done.' She spins around and with a flourish returns to her tables.

*

As the routine of the bar drifts along, Ad wonders why the regulars stick around. The woman with the blonde bob haircut and the pursed lips was already there when the backpackers arrived, and she's lasted long past them. The Slick guy too. He's still on his phone talking to someone, about a project that seemingly has no end.

But the one regular that Ad finds increasingly troubling is the boy with the Buzz Lightyear bag. The departure lounge is not kid-friendly and when Ad asks the Waitress for her take on this topic she replies, 'Why are you asking me?'

Recognising that his questions, instead of forging a friendship, are creating a wider gap, Ad enlists the Corona-loving Baseball Cap Dad to be his undercover agent. Firstly, Ad finds out that Baseball Cap Dad is called Tye. Secondly, he asks Tye, 'Will you help me find out the Waitress's name?'

'Why?'

'Don't you think its rude, her not wanting to say?'

'Not if she doesn't want to.'

'But…' Ad, seeking a justification, says, 'We need her to open up. I reckon she's been here the longest and don't you want her take on things?'

'Like what?'

'Like why's there's no kids around.'

'Sure, why not.' Tye acts cool and dismissive, then, 'Fuck…'

Ad has never heard him swear, and immediately realises what's happened. Ad feels sick. He was clumsy dumb and now he's privy to Tye piecing together the PFEC app, his family, and the departure terminal in a *The Usual Suspects* drop the coffee cup, it-all-makes-sense, moment.

'I mean, it's probably nothing…' Ad offers, trying to step away from the crash he's just created.

So, this is why the Waitress plays it the way she does.

Tye stares at his mobile, not bothering to reply.

Say something. Or at least get him beer.

As Ad wedges a lemon slice into the top of the Corona bottle, he sees the PFEC app icon on Tye's home screen. He waits to see if Tye will open it up but instead Tye puts his phone face down on the bar and starts watching the soccer on the pub TV.

Ad sees an opening. 'I never understood this shit… the world game? Please.'

Tye ignores him.

'I mean, it makes no sense and without sound, it looks like human pinball.'

Tye offers an obligatory nod.

Distract him. Like the Waitress did for you.

'Plus, two hours later and it's a nil-all draw, makes cricket look good.'

A middle-aged couple arrives at the bar. As Ad heads towards them he keeps talking. 'And Tye, don't think these newbies will stop me from explaining to you the joys of cricket.'

Tye takes off his cap and runs his hands through his hair. Fidgeting with his cap he quietly takes the bait. 'Now that's a dumb-ass game.'

Clunk. Clunk. The buffers are back in place. Behind the scenes, Ad knows that Tye's processing will play, wrestling the puzzle of what the departure lounge really is, but for now, on the surface, it's a return to the social roadmap of sport and beers.

*

Having served many drinks, cleared lots of tables, and exhausted the topic of baseball versus cricket, Ad asks Tye to be his covert operative in 'Operation Speckled Feather'.

'What's that?'

'You know... I said it before, to find out the Waitress's name.'

'That's right...' Drunk, Tye slurs, 'Why's it called that?'

'The Speckled Feathered Donny Sparrow is a magnificent creature that has eluded birdwatchers for centuries; it's rumoured to have been sighted in Ho Chi Minh City but the reports are unconfirmed.'

'So?'

'So, it's a made-up name for a made-up mission.'

'Ah, dude, how hard can it be?'

'For you, not hard at all—'

'Exactly, bro, you know it.'

Tye raises his bottle and they cheers, 'To Operation Speckled Feather.'

'Hell yes.'

Having learnt of their mission, the Waitress plays along. She enjoys giving clues and it quickly becomes a running gag that seems to get funnier with repetition. She suggests that her name has something to do with Kevin Costner which leads Ad and Tye down a *Bodyguard, Waterworld, Field of Dreams* path. Neither of them has seen *Dances with Wolves*, so they're not sure if that's the connection but if it is, they're okay with it being a dead-end as they'd rather not know her name than admit to having seen that pile of Oscar turd. The Waitress respects this.

Whenever they need something to disperse the muck gurgling away as they watch people grimly immersed in their mobiles, whenever they want a release from the constant repression of the stewards ushering people through the gates, whenever the weight of the keepsakes pinned on Nina's wall starts to overwhelm, Operation Speckled Feather is there.

To stoke the flames, the Waitress alludes to *Baby Driver*. Ad thinks perhaps her name is linked to an actor in *Baby Driver* who has also worked with Costner. This makes no sense. Tye's okay with that, and building on the random *Baby Driver* meets Kevin Costner connection he asks the Waitress, 'Is your name connected to any films by an actor called Kevin?'

'Such as?' she asks, and with rapid-fire, Ad and Tye jump in.

'Spacey.'

'Bacon.'

'Hart.'

'Smith'

'Bacon.'

'You said him already.'

'Did I?'

'Pollak.'

'Isn't he an artist?'

'No, that's Jackson Pollock.'

'No, Kevin Pollak'

'What?'

'Shields.'

The Waitress replies, 'Musos don't count.'

Tye wants clarity, 'Okay, but what about those other Kevins?'

'What about them?'

'Is there a link?'

'Well, they've been in a lot of films…'

'Ad, this is it!'

'Is it? I don't know… I mean, maybe it's a bit too male-skewed?'

Tye, enjoying the irony. 'Yeah, but that's what we need.'

'So true! We need more male stories.'

'White male?' asks the Waitress.

'Absolutely. Not enough of 'em.'

She raises her Captain and Coke, 'To the heteronormative Caucasian underdog.'

'Pale, male and stale.'

'Amen.'

'Long may our impact forever reduce,' Ad adds.

The Waitress clinks glasses, 'To your shrinkage.'

'Cheers!'

Down the hatch goes the Captain. Ad pours more.

'You know, bro, given she's a woman it's possible that—'

'Tye, are you thinking what I'm thinking?'

'For sure.'

'Good.'

'Which is?'

'If we're talking women in film, there's got to be a Jennifer.'

'Hell yes!'

'So many Jennifers.'

'Connolly.'

'Aniston.'

'Lawrence.'

'Garner.'

'Hudson.'

'Coolidge.'

'Love Hewitt.'

'Ad, I can't think of anymore.'

'Dig deep, mate... um... Jason Leigh!'

'Lopez!'

'Hawkins!'

'Who?'

'You cannot tell me you do not know Jennifer Hawkins; for starters, she's an Aussie.'

Tye scoffs. 'There's your first mistake, Aussies don't count.'

'Mate! Aussies count.'

The Waitress weighs in, 'Only Cate or Rose count, and neither's a Jennifer.'

'What about Nicole?'

'Nope.'

'What about Margot?'

Tye chimes in, 'Yeah good call—'

'She's heaps Aussie.'

The Waitress is incredulous, 'Heaps Aussie?'

'Yeah, mate, heaps.'

They're all feeling loose as they keep drinking. During a moment of consolidation, as Ad makes the next round, the Waitress offers a teaser. 'Or maybe my name is inside a movie.'

Ad stops pouring. 'Hang on, as in, like, part of the title?'

'Yep.'

'Tye...'

Theatrical pause.

'Ad...'

Longer and more theatrical pause.

'This... Is... A. Game-changer.'

'Brother, this is huge.'

Ad takes a deep breath, basking in his drinking buddy's look of expectation. He announces, 'Operation Speckled Feather: DEFCON 1 edition, is... Activated.'

'That's a big ten-four, captain.'

The Waitress sinks half her drink, gives a mocking farewell salute, and having rolled out her game-changing grenade of a clue, leaves the party. 'I'm going back to work, boys.' She drains her glass and returns to the floor.

Tye yells out, '*Me, Myself and IRENE*.'

'*Breakfast at TIFFANY'S*.'

'*Along Came POLLY*.'

Standing in the middle of the restaurant, the Waitress clears away the remains of a surf and turf, and a plate of half-finished nachos.

'*HOPE Floats*.'

'*TAR!*'

'Who is called Tar?'

'The chick in the film.'

The Waitress stops what she's doing, 'I didn't actually hear you say that.'

'What...? Chick?'

'Yeah.'

'No.'

'Good.'

Ad, grinning, boozed up and unrepentant, says, 'Unless by "no" I mean "yes", in which case, "yes," I did just call our Cate, the chick in *Tar*.'

She shakes her head, suitably outraged, and heads towards the kitchen.

Ad responds by adding, 'Cate loves being called a chick. I know this as a fellow countryman, we have a connection—'

Not to be outdone, with an absurd accent, Tye yells out, '*La Vie en ROOOOOOOOOOSE.*'

The Waitress pushes open the kitchen doors and goes inside to drop off the cleared plates. Tye gets off his barstool, scampers over, stands just outside. He brings a finger up to his lips and gestures, 'shoosh'. Some of the patrons are staring at him. He flaps his hands at them and whispers loudly, 'Don't look at me! I'm undercover.'

The woman with the pursed lips and blonde bob has an ever-so-slight smile creep across her face. It's the happiest Ad's ever seen her.

Tye readies himself. The suspense builds. People are on tenterhooks and off their phones, in wait. Just as it feels like the pause has taken too long, the Waitress steps out. Tye jumps out singing, JUUUUDY!' with jazz-hands vibrato.

'Jesus fucking Christ!' The Waitress steps back in shock.

Amongst the laughter and clapping of pub patrons, Tye bows to his audience as Ad yells out, 'Bravo, encore!'

The Waitress, smiling, looks to the pursed-lips woman for support. 'You see what I have to work with?'

She replies with a sympathetic, 'Kids…'

'One hundred per cent.'

Returning to the bar, the Waitress is met by Ad channelling his best Richard Gere cheese-ball slime,

'Pretty WOMAN.'

The Waitress is droll in her reply. 'You think my name is Woman?'

Tye jumps in. '*WONDER WOMAN!*'

'Yup… Tye, my name is Wonder.'

'I knew it!'

Ad looks to his Operation Speckled Feather partner. 'I feel like she's not being honest.'

But Tye's on a roll. '*STAR Wars, A Fish called WANDA, A Christmas CAROL… Girl with a PEARL Necklace.*'

'It's earring.'

'You guys are so bad at this.'

'What are you talking about?' Ad hands her another Captain.

'Thanks, but let's do shots.'

'What?'

'Vodka.'

Ad quickly lines up three. The Waitress holds her glass up like an auctioneer's hammer, makes eye contact with each of them, skulls it, slaps it down and rattles off,

'*LOLITA, NIKITA, ERIN BROCKOVICH, JACKIE, ALICE in Wonderland, FRANCIS Ha. Blue JASMINE.* Or just go with Mary: *MARY SHELLEY. MARY Queen of Scots. MARY Poppins—*'

Ad interrupts. 'Holy shit, it's Mary?!'

The Waitress rolls her eyes. 'Not a chance.'

'There's Something About MARY!'

Tye's convinced. 'Shut the fuck up, it's Maaaaaaaaryyyyy!'

The boys are triumphant.

'Do you really think I'd make it that easy?'

Ad toasts her, 'To Mary.'

'To Mary!'

The lads down their shots as the Waitress says, 'And my little lambs.'

*

One afternoon, when there was a lull, and after the three of them had sunk a raft of Coronas and a shipful of Captain Morgan, Ad, drunk and becalmed, and feeling as though all their jokes had been wrung dry, leans over to the Waitress and asks, 'So, like, for real, what's the story?'

'Huh?'

'What's the point in not telling us your name?'

'I'm sorry?'

'We're friends, aren't we?'

'Why do you care, Ad?' She pointedly hits the word 'Ad'.

He knows he's struck a nerve but persists, 'What's the problem with like—?'

'What gives you the right?'

'I just want to know you—'

'Know me? You wanna know me?'

Ad's never seen her mad before. It's very contained, she doesn't raise her voice, but nevertheless a rage flares behind her clipped words.

'What more will you know by knowing my name? You don't want to know me; you want to label and frame me. Fuck you, Ad, you're a child.'

And with that she's gone.

Tye sighs.

A new piece of regret cloth settles over Ad, it feels dank and shitty like all the others.

I just pulled the same shit I do to Nina. Push and push until she bites. Then what?

He looks to Tye for some support, but he's conspicuously focused on his phone.

Surely after all this time talking with people, I'd have gotten better at not being such a dick.

'Do I say sorry?' asks Ad.

Tye raises his eyebrows exasperated, 'Are you really asking me that?'

'I—'

'You just cooked Operation Speckled Feather, bro.'

Ad takes the cue and heads towards the waitress, who is resetting tables at the furthest point from the bar. She sees him approach. Rather than do a fake ignore and act busy, she stares him down. He feels ashamed but maintains eye contact.

Upon arriving, Ad is straight up, plain and simple. 'I am sorry, I really am, I had no right to badger you and pry and...'

In the past, when arguing with Nina, Ad would have provided context and tried to justify his actions, incrementally watering down his apology until it became a springboard for him to self-validate, but now he feels different.

'I'm truly sorry.'

It is the longest he's maintained eye contact with anyone since

Nina in the hospital. The waitress doesn't speak as she evaluates his sincerity. The silence lags, but Ad resists the urge to blurt out something just to break the tension. Finally, she quietly replies, 'Okay.'

'Yeah?'

'Yep.'

'Thanks… Thank you.'

The waitress acknowledges his gratitude with a little nod, and resumes her work. Ad watches her finish a nearby table and then as she moves further away, he heads back to the bar.

Tye asks, 'You okay?'

'Yeah.'

'Is she?'

'I think so, but…' He takes off his vest and unties his apron. 'I'm heading out for a bit, so…' He gestures to his uniform. 'If you want, it's all yours.'

Ad doesn't wait for Tye's response, he steps out from behind the bar and for the first time in a long time finds himself wanting to explore the terminal.

BUZZ LIGHTYEAR

Out on the concourse, **A** isn't sure what he wants to find, or where he wants to look. He wanders around, staring at the airport shopping troupe of magnets, booze, and perfumes, like he is vegging out watching telly.

In the news agency, **A** flicks through the magazines, reading the latest on The Royals, and post-baby bods, and then just as he is about to give up and return to the bar, he sees, tucked away in a corner, surrounded by fluffy owls and other Harry Potter merchandise, the Buzz Lightyear boy on his iPad.

A crouches down.

'Hiya… What ya watchin'?'

The boy shows him.

On screen is a hospital room with curtains drawn. A faint light from the heart monitor is cast across the bed, and laid over the hospital sheets is a *Toy Story* blanket. A woman is lying on the edge of the bed cradling the little boy, who has tubes linking him to the equipment. Sitting beside them is a man looking vacant and drained. The stillness catches **A**. The only movement is the pulse of the monitor, and the intimacy that **A** has stumbled upon leaves him feeling intrusive.

While working at the bar, **A** found it excruciating encountering adults as they realised the world they're viewing on their mobile was the life they've left behind, but nothing compares with the focus of this little boy glued to his iPad.

A sits down next to him. The boy rests his hand on **A**'s knee. **A** is touched by the innocent presumption of this gesture. It serves as a portal back to when Louie and Ella would lie all over **A** on a Sunday morning poking their feet under his hip or waist, searching for a way to instantly freeze him and Nina with their icicle toes.

'You need to go now.'

A steward has arrived, and her quiet, forceful tone intrudes. She looks like Nurse Ratched, her thick dark eyebrows framing shark eyes that pass judgement as she takes the little boy's hand. 'Come with me.'

It feels icky to **A**. 'I'm sorry, but where do you want to him to go?'

'It doesn't concern you.'

'You're not his parent.'

'Sir, I must ask you to calmly please—'

'Absolutely, I understand, and rest assured I am calm, it's just, I offered to give his folks a little time out, but we can go back now to them if that's your preference?'

A's strategy of seeking permission is effective. As far as **A**'s been able to observe, the stewards aren't comfortable with people doing things for them. Their purpose is to serve the passengers and assist them with their departure, so **A**'s offer leaves the steward unsure. She looks puzzled, hesitates, and lets go of the child's hand.

'Very well then.' She gives a measured, 'Good,' turns on her heels and exits the store.

A knows this concession will be brief, that she will inform the other stewards who will want to know more, and with more attention comes the likelihood of trouble.

With this in mind, **A** reverts to pre-schooler parent-mode.

'Righto, buddy, let's get out of here.' He picks up the bag and swings the little boy up onto his hip. He's light-ish, as four-year-olds are, and holds on tight to his iPad.

En route to the bar, **A** notices a handful of passengers stop watching their PFEC app as they are distracted by the unusual sight of a child being carried through the terminal. His passenger wraps his arm tightly around **A**'s neck, while **A**, sensing stewards are observing their every move, walks as fast as he can without appearing guilty. He feels like a well-intentioned smuggler carrying a cute time bomb, and although the stewards scrutinise his every step, **A**'s path is not blocked. As they enter the Irish Pub, **A** sees the stewards circle around the perimeter of the bar.

'Thank you, I'll take him from here.'

A feels the little boy being pulled out of his arms. Nurse Ratched has snuck up from behind and intervened, leaving **A** outmanoeuvred.

What was I thinking... that I'd hide him in the bar, like he's JoJo Rabbit?

As she leads the boy out of the pub, he looks so small and vulnerable.

A shouts out, 'Where are you taking him?' but she keeps forging ahead. 'Oi, Ratched, stop!'

She meets with the other stewards on the edge of the concourse, who gather around her as she leads the child away.

A keeps pushing, 'I know you can hear me!?' and runs out to the middle of concourse. 'Give him back!'

His shouting gains attention. The majority of people in the departure terminal are old enough to be parents, and **A**'s demand coupled with the boy's scared little face awakens them. Plus, Ratched looks cold and mean.

A, sensing their support, ups the ante. 'You have no right to take him!'

This outburst is the kicker. It prompts others to speak up.

'What are you doing?' 'Excuse me?' 'Stop!'

Folks get up from their seats, wanting to see what all the fuss is about, and what follows is a groundswell of raised voices and heckling questions.

'What are you doing?' 'Who the hell are you?' 'Answer me.'

Suddenly the woman with the blonde bob screams, 'Give him back!' It's piercing.

A's little rebellion has unlocked something. She keeps going, 'You heard me, give him back.' Like a primary school teacher, she claps for emphasis as she repeats, 'Give him back.'

The stewards are rattled.

'Give him back. Give him back.' The passengers start chanting. 'Give him back. Give him back.'

Further ahead, provoked by the noise, other passengers get curious and begin walking towards the bar. Momentum is growing. Front and back, Nurse Ratched and her fellow stewards are getting boxed in. To keep the child now would be too bald-faced and aggressive. In the middle of the concourse, Nurse Ratched releases the little boy. He stands planted with his knees shaking. **A** runs up and hugs him, wanting to comfort him before he starts to cry. The crowd cheers.

The stewards slink away. As quickly as it flared up, it cools down. Normal services resume as the crowd returns to the stupor of their devices, hits 'Play', and the PFEC-fog that momentarily lifted swiftly returns.

A's mate doesn't want to let go of him. His arm is locked around **A**'s neck and his iPad is jammed so hard between their bodies it presses into **A**'s chest.

'It's okay. It's all okay.' **A** slowly prises himself free. 'Wanna meet my friends?'

Staring straight down at the floor, the boy shakes his head.

'No? Hmmm, okay… What about ice cream?' **A** sees his little mate's conviction start to waver. 'I think they've got chocolate… how's that sound… in a cone…?'

A hears an almost imperceptible, 'Okay.'

'Righto, deal!'

Carrying the boy on his hip, **A** returns to the bar, looking wild-eyed and pumped. He knows the stewards are tailing him, but for now they're at a non-threatening distance.

He finds the waitress and Tye behind the bar. **A** recognises the apron Tye's wearing. 'So, you got the gig?'

'Looks like it.'

'Just don't stay too long, unless you wanna end up a steward,' offers the waitress.

'What!?'

'It happens all time, staff get immune. That's why I love Nina's wall. Reminds me what's important.'

'I can't believe you're telling me that now—'

A's ignored by the waitress, who kneels down, 'Who's this then?'

A keeps going. 'You don't mind, do you, just rolling out the grenades?'

But she focuses on **A**'s new companion. 'Hello there. Hi… you and that old bloke,' she glances over at **A**, 'put on bit of a show.'

'I've promised him ice cream.'

'You did, did you?'

'Hey, little dude, you want to help me get it, yeah? Great.' Tye heads over to one of the bar fridges taking the boy with him, as **A** askes the waitress, 'See his iPad?'

'Yeah…?'

'Well, he showed me what he's watching, and he's in hospital and his parents are there with him and—'

'Okay—'

'But he's not done, I can tell, he's fighting hard, and he doesn't want to go, not one bit, but if the stewards get him, they'll put him straight through the gates and then—'

'No way man, look!' blurts Tye.

Along the pub's perimeter, where the tables and chairs meet the airport concourse, the stewards are spread out in a single, thin, poisonous line.

Tye hands over the ice cream cone. 'You've brought the whole band.'

'Follow me.' The waitress quickly ushers the fugitives out of the bar, through the kitchen and into a grimy storeroom filled with cases of booze and cleaning products. She tries to hide them by shoving boxes and buckets together in the corner and tucking them behind it, 'I'll be back in a sec.'

Jammed in among the mops, the little boy looks bewildered as the chocolate ice cream dribbles onto his fingers. **A** squats down to his eye-level and talks in unfussy terms, 'Never let 'em touch you, and if they do, scream as loud as you can.'

They hear the waitress shouting, 'What are you doing?' followed by the crack of the shelves and shattering glass. It sounds like the stewards are pulling down Nina's wall.

'You have no right! Get the hell out of here!' yells Tye.

Why would they do that? If you can't take it with you, why does it matter?

Cramped in among the cleaning clutter **A** whispers to his buddy,

'As still as a statue, as quiet as a mouse.'

Yanking the storage door open, the waitress appears, 'Let's go.'

A picks up his little mate as the waitress grabs the Buzz Lightyear bag. She bustles them through the kitchen, past the stovetops and chefs. Outside, Tye's loud and defiant, 'No! Staff only! Get the hell out of here!'

Two hefty male stewards bulldoze their way past the waiters dawdling in the kitchen's entrance carrying food. 'Move!' A kitchen hand using pots to obstruct their chase is bumped aside, and a sous chef who steers her food prep table into the passageway is met with a forceful shove.

The waitress hurries to the dishwashing station at the back of the kitchen. 'Come on.'

She flicks the wheel-locks off a large trolley that's stacked with plates. A helps her heave the crockery table out from the wall. Underneath there is a steel trap door.

She yanks it up and drops the boy's carry-on bag down the hole. 'Go.'

A clambers down the rickety iron ladder, then reaches back to the waitress, who hands him the child, ice cream in one hand, iPad in the other. As A gently lowers him down onto the metal landing, he loses his ice cream.

Standing at the trap door entranceway, the waitress is silhouetted against the kitchen's bright lights, looking magnificent.

'Get to the handler. He'll help you.'

'Okay.'

'Good luck.'

A's 'Thanks' is drowned out by the almighty clang of the trap door slamming shut.

In the shadows A and his little mate stand on a thin metal plank that hangs from the concrete ceiling.

At **A**'s feet is the half-eaten ice cream. 'It's okay, you got most of it...' Seeing how precarious the floor is, **A** adds, 'Man, we're lucky we didn't lose your bag, it could've just gone straight through.'

The gangway floats among the airport's underground innards. Surrounding them are streams of piping and rectangular air-conditioning vents. Bolted into the roof are thin wires which hold it up and provide a handrail. It's lit by a yellow fluoro light, but beyond the tubes and vents they can't see anything.

A's little mate reaches out with his sticky chocolate fingers and takes his hand.

'You ready to get out of here?'

The little boy shakes his head.

'No? Are you kidding... Ha, well, we can't really stay here, hey? We'll be right.'

A scans the hanging walkway but can't see the end. 'I tell you what, I'll carry you over, then come back and get the bag. Actually, no that's nuts have you ever seen *Indiana Jones*? Not yet? Well, anyways, the golden rule when crossing dodgy bridges is never ever split up.'

A gives a reassuring little squeeze, 'Let's do this.' His buddy wraps his arm around **A**'s neck and wedges his iPad up into his chest.

The moment they begin to cross, the gangway starts to sway and squeak. **A** walks slowly, trying to avoid any lateral movement. As they approach the halfway mark, the exit stairs become visible. They're only twenty feet away.

Suddenly there's a harsh scraping sound as the trap door opens. **A** feels the boy's entire body seize up. With a thunderous crash a steward jumps down onto the gangway and charges towards them, yelling, 'Come back here!' The light cast from the kitchen makes him look as big as Kingpin.

A runs away as fast as he can. He's lurching from side to side and barely able to keep his balance as his shit-scared passenger wiggles around. 'Easy, mate, easy.'

There's another crash as a second steward lands on the gangway. Explosive bangs ricochet throughout the cavern as the metal bolts are wrenched out of the roof by the weight of the two stewards. The wires whiplash around, shattering the fluoro light as the gangway unravels. The little boy shrieks as the planks split apart, slicing and ripping through the tubes. In the darkness, A lunges for the exit stairs and grabs hold. He clings on as the screech of the punctured air vents and wail of the stewards falling create a horrific din. His little mate is screaming too.

A climbs up the ladder and pushes open the trapdoor. With his torso partially through the entrance, in one movement he drags the boy over his chest and out of the hole, then he tosses up the Buzz Lightyear bag before dragging himself out.

Rolling onto his back, gasping for breath, A kicks shut the trapdoor. His lungs are burning, his arm feels like it's been ripped out of its socket and his head is ringing from the screaming in his ear. A leans over. There's tears streaming down the boy's face. He's holding onto the iPad like it's the only thing keeping him alive.

A holds him in his arms. 'You're doing so well. You really are. You know that?'

He's in shock.

A keeps talking to him, hoping it's of some comfort. 'You're a little rock star. A super star adventure-ra. Tougher than Gibralt-ar. Who eats ice cream cavi-ar... You ever had that before? No... well, it's pretty good, not as good as Nutell-ar, but still...'

Only once his little mate starts to calm down does **A** take in their surroundings. They're lying on the floor of a long, white corridor. It looks vaguely familiar; then it dawns on him, *This is where the baggage cart took me.*

A feels as fragile as the bridge they just demolished, but acts resolutely positive.

'You ready to explore?'

'No.'

'Why not, it'll be fun.'

The boy shakes his head.

'What if I pop you on my shoulders and we see if you can touch the roof?'

His little mate looks up.

'You reckon you can reach it?'

'A-huh.'

'And what if I carry this, so you can stretch up higher?'

'A-huh.'

A takes the iPad, tucks it under his arm, and then pops the kid up onto his shoulders. One hand paws at **A**'s face. Pudgy chocolate-smelling fingers dig into **A**'s forehead and cheeks as the boy tries to touch the roof with his free hand.

A lowers his passenger's hands and feels them cut deep into his neck.

'Mate, I'd rather be choked than scratched, okay?'

As they hurry down the corridor playing 'Touch the Roof', the rattle of the Buzz Lightyear carry-on bag is drowned out by the hydraulic whir of doors opening and the noise of the terminal bleeding in.

At the end of corridor, **A** sees a baggage cart enter. The handler is sitting behind the wheel, his Eraserhead locks looking splendid as he drives towards them.

A looks past him to see if the stewards are following, but he's alone.

A starts to bring his mate down off his shoulders.

'No.' The little boy squirms around.

'I'm sorry mate, but I think this is the guy.'

As he drives towards them, the handler looks perturbed. A, wanting to make a good impression, steps to the side as the handler pulls up, and says, 'Thank you very much…'

A offers his hand. 'Hi, um, good to meet you.'

The handler ignores A's outstretched hand, and instead picks up the kid, puts him on his lap and resumes driving. A scrambles to keep up, 'Hang on. Are you alright, buddy?'

'A-huh,' says the little boy.

'Well that's good, and thanks for giving us a lift, I'm guessing you're the handler…?' says A, but gets no response.

He must be deaf? Or offended from before?

A trots alongside the baggage trolley. 'Sorry about last time…? I didn't mean to muck things up for you… but is there room for me?'

The handler keeps looking straight ahead.

'Mate? Can you hear me? Are you able to help us? Hide us?'

Nothing.

The baggage cart is a mini train that's pulling along three carriages full of bags. A looks for a gap that he could squeeze between, but it's packed tight, and housed by straps that fence in the luggage.

At the final carriage, A pushes hard up against the bags and creates just enough space to sit himself down. He rests the boy's iPad on his lap and the Buzz Lightyear bag beside him.

The trolley's puttering engine and the squeak of the bags echo down the passageway. These sounds, coupled with the corridor stretching out behind him, with its depth and repetition, are calming.

A zones out, staring at his sneakers hanging off the edge of the trolley floating above the floor like he's sitting at the end of a wharf looking down at the water, and feels his adrenaline start to dissipate.

He remembers learning to fish with his grandfather and his dad, and then teaching Ella and Louie, showing them how to cast and accidentally getting his line stuck in a tree, and how they jumped around thinking it was the funniest thing in the world. 'You caught a tree!' 'Dad's caught a tree!'

He remembers Kinki on his birthday years earlier, when they hired a boat and she was pregnant with Louie, and she wore a pink one piece, her body so curvy and full.

'I'm Max.'

The little boy's voice is bright and singular, like a bell. It reverberates down along the corridor and breaks **A**'s reverie.

Max?

A sits up and waits to hear more but the handler offers no reply and the little boy called Max has nothing more to add.

So, he's Max. I spent all that time hassling the waitress for her name but never asked my little mate... Is that what happened to the waitress? Is that why she wouldn't answer, 'cause she doesn't actually know? I wonder, if the handler asked me, what would I say?

A squirms.

What is my name? Fuck, I know it, I mean... I haven't forgotten it. Well, then...?

Agitated by this train of thought, **A** fidgets with Max's iPad and opens the PFEC app. On the screen **A** is immediately confronted by the image of Max's parents huddled around their son's hospital bed. There are no doctors present, but it's clear that he is very sick. Life support equipment is monitoring his vital signs as his dad sings, '*Galumph went the little green frog one day. Galumph went the little green frog.*'

His mum chimes in with, '*And the ladies on the bus go la-de-da-di-da, la-de-da-di-da, la-de-da-di-da.*'

Max looks so tiny and feeble, wired up to a suite of machines. His parents are trying to stay in control. There's no histrionics, they're just holding his hand and singing his favourite song as their son lies still.

A puts down the iPad.

Hiding him is not going to be enough.

An image of Nina nursing Louie pops into **A**'s head.

Ahh, Kinki singing You've Got a Friend *so gentle and so off-key. I can remember that, but... I can't remember my name...*

To distract himself, **A** pulls over the Buzz Lightyear bag and opens it. It's a treasure chest of Max's most precious items. There's a fluffy blankie, crinkled and green, and a soft, faded tiger with a chewed ear, and trinkets, too: a red, plastic grasshopper; a pair of mini binoculars; lots of superhero badges, some matchbox cars and Toy Story figurines; and scrunched up among the colouring-in books are several versions of the same drawing – a house, the sun and Mum, Dad and Max. Each of them is drawn with a different colour crayon – blue, yellow, orange – and while there are size and colour variations, all drawings have the same cast and are all signed by the artist: 'Max' with the 'm' looking like birds flying.

The stewards were so set on destroying Nina's wall. What are they so afraid of? What if you did take it with you? What if I filled his pockets with his toys, wrapped him up with all his treasures using his blankie as a cloak, and pinned his paintings all over it? What then?

A feels a spark.

If I get him close enough without being spotted, I could send him through the gates with all his treasure before the stewards rip off his stuff.

A strokes the iPad.

His parents are singing to him right now trying to coax him back.

The trolley slows down and pulls up alongside a conveyor belt. The handler turns off the engine as **A** packs up the contents of the Buzz Lightyear bag, and returns to the front.

I can do this.

The handler leaves Max in the driver's seat, and carrying his crate, shuffles past **A** down to the end trolley where he unhitches the side straps, steps up onto his box and begins pushing the top bags onto the conveyor belt.

At the front, **A** tells Max, 'So, mate, I think I've got a plan. It'll be a bit like Hide and Seek, and a bit like Chasings.'

Max looks apprehensive.

A asks, 'Which do you like more, Hide and Seek or Chasings?'

The loud whir of a door sliding open cuts in before Max can answer. Down the corridor and past the handler, **A** sees two stewards stepping through.

Shit!

A immediately darts out of sight, hiding in the gap between the driving cart and the first trolley.

Okay. Okay. Okay. Don't stress. It'll freak him out. And just stick to the plan.

To stay hidden from the stewards, **A** uses the wall of trolley cart bags as a shield. He leans over, picks up Max and turns him around to face the trolley full of carry-on luggage, and with his best non-hectic parent-voice says, 'You see all these bags…? We're going to use them to make a cave to hide you in.' **A** gestures at the bags, 'Right in here.'

Max nods.

'Okay, cool, cool, cool, quiet as a mouse, here we go.' **A** lifts Max over the back of the driver's seat and places him on the edge of the conveyor belt. 'Hold the fort just right there, mate.'

Like a game of speed Jenga, **A** quickly but carefully pulls out a column of bags and carves out an entrance. The handler seeing **A** making the cave, takes the discarded bags and carries them away. Up front, **A** pulls out four more bags to complete the little hole. 'Here we go... as still as a statue.'

Max shakes his head.

'Please, mate.'

A uses his phone as a torch. Max's looking down at the ground, arms folded. He doesn't want a bar of it.

'Look, it's a secret Buzz Lightyear space hideout.'

Max looks super scared. Staring at his feet, he won't look up. **A** knows the stewards are fast approaching.

'Maxie, please...'

A hears their steady clip as they march to towards the cart.

'Look, it's cool. Look.'

A flashes his phone torch into the cave. Max refuses to look. Shaking his head, he is absolutely resolute.

For fuck's sake. Just get in there! What if I just push him in? Hell no. The steady clip of the stewards' approach gets louder and louder.

It's like when Louie wouldn't get in the car? Of course!

'Hey, buddy... here.'

A offers Max his phone.

'So, if I give you this, you'll hop in?'

'A-huh.'

'A-huh indeed! Alright we're in business.'

A puts his mobile on silent mode, opens up the PFEC app, hits 'Play', and hands it over. 'Here.' He doesn't bother to see what Max's watching; he's too preoccupied by the approaching stewards.

A places Max inside the cave.

'Duck down. That's it. You can't touch the sides. Perfect. And be super still and quiet. Two more tiny little steps back… that's the way. Standing as still as statue. Okay?'

Max whispers, 'A-huh,' as he's boxed in by the baggage.

'I'm just going to close it up. Okay? You'll be safe. I promise.'

Max watches **A**'s every move as the bags pile up and he seals the cave. Just before placing the final bag, **A** gives Max a little wink and a thumbs up. Max looks like he's about to cry. **A** kisses his fingers and gently touches Max's forehead, mouthing the words, 'It's okay,' then seals the cave.

The handler is slowly unpacking the second trolley, methodically working his way through the columns of baggage and tossing them onto the conveyor belt. **A** crouches down and looks under the trolley carriage to find out where the stewards are standing.

A can hear them talking to the handler: a man and woman. Their bureaucratic voices snipe at the handler.

'Have you seen anything?'

'He can't understand you.'

'Yes, he can.'

The handler says nothing and continues to unpack the bags, seemingly oblivious.

Every nerve, every fibre in **A** is absolutely wired. He's in full fight or flight mode. He instinctively taps into his action flick know-how and, using the technique of hiding in a bathroom stall by standing on the toilet, puts one foot on the trolley and the other on the edge of the conveyor belt.

Just as he gets into position the male steward looks under the carts, sees nothing, and starts walking up to the front. If the steward inspects the gap between the trolley and the conveyor belt, **A**'s cover is blown, so **A** quietly heads towards the back and hides in the gap between the first and second trolleys. It's cat and mouse. The female steward circles around the end of the train. She sees Max's Buzz Lightyear bag lying separately from the other bags, 'What's this?'

The handler steps down off his crate and wanders down. She scowls at the handler, as he picks up the Buzz Lightyear bag and tosses it onto the conveyor belt.

'You're getting sloppy.'

The handler doesn't react, he simply returns to his crate.

Perched between the two trolleys, **A** sees the Buzz Lightyear bag on the conveyor belt creep past.

No! It can't go down.

A leans forward to peek around the edges.

Where are they?

At the front, the male steward walks past the driver's seat and looks down the side between the trolley and the conveyor belt, **A** lurches back out of sight.

Did he see me? Shit.

A's on high alert, listening intently, waiting for footsteps coming towards him.

I can't save the bag and not get caught.

The steward calls out to his colleague, 'We should see off all the bags, to be certain.'

'Copy that.'

The handler returns to unpacking the second trolley. He slowly completes the penultimate row. There's now only one column hiding **A**. To buy some time, the handler stops his work, gets off his crate, sits down, unties and reties up his boots.

Wedged between the trolleys **A** hears the stewards approaching from each end, closing in on him.

But if Max's bag goes down the chute it's all over. Ugh!

A jumps out onto conveyor belt but stumbles over the luggage, trips and face plants onto the belt. He gets to his feet, chases the Buzz Lightyear bag, dives and misses.

God damnit!

He commando crawls forward and grabs the bag's handle just as it slides under the plastic flaps. With his body sprawled out over the conveyor belt, **A**'s pulled through. There's only a metre of conveyor belt before it drops away and the bags fall down the chute.

A lunges back and grabs one of the plastic flaps. Fighting against the constant roll of the conveyor belt **A** uses his shoulders and hips to snake his way to the side. One hand grips a plastic flap, the other has the Buzz Lightyear bag.

A wedges his feet into the sides of the wall and metal strip. He pulls on the plastic flap like it's a rope, and gradually gets himself upright, bag secure and body secure.

Hell yes!

He leans over and peers through the plastic flaps back into the corridor. The handler standing near the cart is looking freaked.

The male steward suddenly thrusts his body past the flaps and lunges forward, 'Agh!' He starts chopping at **A**'s hand trying to break his grip on the plastic flap.

'Fuck off!'

A retaliates by swinging the Buzz Lightyear bag straight into the steward's face.

Thwack. The steward groans. **A** tries to whack him again, but the steward grabs onto the bag. **A** yanks it back and wrenches it around, making the steward lose his footing and fall onto the belt, dragging **A** down with him.

A kicks his chest and shoulders, but the steward won't let go. Just as they're both about to slide off the edge, the fear of failing Max drives **A** to a new level.

'I said get the fuck off me!' **A** unleashes a barrage of kicks into the steward's face, who defends himself by blocking **A**'s foot. This gives **A** the initiative. He wrestles the bag out of the steward's grip, and rolls to the side, as the steward is sent over the edge and down the chute – 'Ahhhhh!' – **A** swivels around and hurls the Buzz Lightyear bag back through the flaps. It lands in the corridor near the trolley. Safe.

As **A** looks through the flaps, the second steward pops into view. She's kneeling over the belt trying to see what's happening. **A** grabs her by her buttoned-up blouse and yanks her down.

She falls onto the conveyor belt. 'What are you doing?'

A pins her down, like a bug on its back, as she slides head-first past the flaps.

'You can't do this!' She flails her arms about trying to grab him, but **A** stays out of her reach. She rolls off the edge of the conveyor belt – 'Noooo!' – down the chute and into the baggage container below.

With these stewards no longer a threat, **A** gets himself off the conveyor belt and returns to the corridor. The handler is standing hands-on hips by the baggage cart. Seeing **A** clamber through, he gives a relieved nod of approval, returns to the second trolley and resumes pushing off the bags.

'No, wait, we've gotta keep Maximo hidden.'

The handler stops. **A** takes the bags off the belt and returns them to the trolley.

'We need more bags, not less.'

The handler starts copying him.

'I knew it! You can hear.' **A** offers a high five, but the Handler backs away, leaving **A** hanging.

'Righto, mate… sure, act like you're deaf, whatever, but you rock.'

The handler grabs the bags off the belt as **A** returns to the baggage cave. He moves aside the bags to reveal Max, transfixed, watching on **A**'s phone something from the PFEC app.

The light of the corridor pouring into Max's hideout, coupled with **A** asking, 'Are you okay?' breaks the spell. Max hands him back his phone. It's a live stream of a hospital scene.

Reality TV.

A's reality.

A feels light-headed. He reaches out and slumps down. The airport terminal slips away.

LAST CALL

A is locked inside his body. His family crowds around.

It can't be…

He feels their bodies squish up against his.

Fuck, fuck, fuck.

Nina gently kisses the corner of his mouth.

Don't say goodbye, not yet. Please…

He longs to hold them, to bring her coffee, make their beds. He wants it all back, the mornings, the nights, everything.

Louie and Ella look stricken. She mumbles, 'Bye, Daddy.'

Louie can't speak. He opens his mouth but just gulps and then blurts out, 'Don't do it. Mum? Don't let them.'

'Louie… I…'

Trapped in his body, **A**'s never felt so alive. Every emotion is smashing in from every angle.

Ella pleads, 'Just a bit longer. Just until sunrise… We could open the blinds and—'

'Yeah, let Dad see one more.'

The doctor quietly states, 'You know he can't—'

Louie turns on her, 'How do you know? Maybe he can. And what does it matter to you anyway? Why not? Huh? Why not?'

'Nina?' says the doctor.

Louie pursues, 'Just say so, just say yes. Say it.'

The doctor backs away, she's not going to fight a twelve-year-old, she looks to Nina who gives her nothing, so the doctor concedes, 'Yes… okay then.'

It takes a moment for them to absorb it.

'Yes!?' says Louie.

'A-huh'

They are stunned.

A sees his children embrace and Nina join them, then feels his perspective shift. His view is no longer from the hospital bed; instead, he's floating outside his body and looking down at them like a security camera in the corner of a room. He keeps drifting up…

*

A is on his back, his phone inches from his face, surrounded by the overnight luggage that houses him in. He sits up, rubs his face, wanting to feel something, needing to make sure he's back.

Standing outside the cave, the handler shakes his head, his Eraserhead hair casting an impressive shadow over their hidey-hole. 'Finish what you started.'

The handler's voice is deep, rich and resonating. It's a call to arms. Groggy, **A** takes a moment to recalibrate, 'Did you just say that, or—'

'Yes, I did, now hurry up,' replies the handler.

Beside **A**, Max is huddled down. Tentative, he reaches out and puts his hand on **A**'s leg. 'It's alright, little Maximo, I'm alright, I just…' **A** trails off not knowing how to explain. Max waits but instead of going into the details, **A** asks, 'Have you got your bag?'

Max shakes his head.

'Do you know where it is?'

'A-huh'

'Can you get it?'

Max looks pleased to have a job, and quickly jumps off the trolley.

I could watch for just a bit more...

A unlocks his mobile.

Just while Max's finding his bag.

And opens the PFEC app.

Max returns, hitting the handler's arms with the Buzz Lightyear bag as he attempts to lift it up onto the trolley, 'Found it!'

'Wow, that was speedy.'

Come on, let's do this right.

A puts away his phone.

'Okay, great. Now we're going to take all your favourite things and make a cloak. No, actually, it's more like a shield.'

A unzips Max's Buzz Lightyear bag. 'You're going to be able to transform, just like Buzz when he's on a mission. It'll still be you, but you'll have special powers 'cause we're going to wrap you up in this'—he grabs Max's drawings and the green blanket—'And we'll put these little dudes in your pockets.'

He takes out the cars and figurines, 'And we're going to make you Buzz to-the-Max Lightyear!'

'Yeah!'

'And we're going to be super stealthy and both hide out here in our trolley cave and travel in disguise and then we're going to break out and escape through the gates, and I'm going to have you on my back, and I'll be like your horse—'

'No, spaceship.'

'Yes, perfect! So, what's Buzz's spaceship called?'

'What's your name?'

'Um.'

A blanks.

Max gives him a nudge. 'What's your name?'

It's on the tip of **A**'s tongue and a mile away.

A looks to the handler, hoping he'll have an answer, but he's busy, already rearranging the bags to expand the cave.

As though to excuse himself, **A** says, 'I'm spacey...'

Max starts giggling.

A repeats himself, unsure if that's the joke. 'I'm Spacey the Spaceship...?'

Max's giggle builds into a full belly laugh, a bubbling joyous sound. It's been a long time since **A**'s heard such a thing.

'What's going on?' The handler sticks his head in.

Max points at **A**. 'He's Spacey!'

The handler cracks a smile. 'Is that so?'

As **A** creates his shield, Max returns to his iPad. **A** uses Max's superhero badges to fasten the drawings onto his blankie. He tucks the fluffy toy tiger under Max's T-shirt like a bulletproof vest and fills his pockets with figurines and cars. Once it's all in place **A** asks him, 'Hey, mate, can I please have that for a sec? I need to turn down the volume, so it doesn't give away our hiding spot.'

A takes the iPad and is immediately struck by the scene playing out.

Max looks so frail with the machines crowding in on him. His dad rests the toy tiger on his son's chest. 'Is that okay?' he asks the nurse, as his mother, sitting on the edge of the bed, holds Max's hand and whispers, 'Don't stop, just keep breathing, in and out, like a little engine who never stops.'

Sitting on the trolley Max is following his parents' instructions, huffing and puffing and breathing deeply.

A encourages him, 'That's it, Maxie, in and out.'

Outside the cave, the handler slides the last of the bags into place.

Max and **A** are entombed with only slivers of light sneaking through the gaps between the bags. Their faces are illuminated by the iPad.

Max's mother kisses her son. She coaxes, 'Come back to me.'

Max's dad leans over, and murmurs, 'You hang in there. You can do this.'

A looks over at his little mate.

'It's going to be okay. It really is.'

Max doesn't look convinced. He's bug-eyed with fear.

A instinctively seeks out a circuit-breaker to distract Max and stop him from completely freaking out. 'Here.' He takes out Ella's panda puppet. 'It's my good luck charm.'

A pops it on his finger and wiggles it around like a fly in front of Max's face. 'Meet Pandy.' Max tries to grab it, but **A** pulls his hand away. Max lunges a second time, but again **A**'s too fast. 'Don't you want it?'

'I do!'

From outside, the handler grumbles, 'Quiet now.'

A brings his Pandy finger puppet to his lips. 'Shhhh. But if I give it to you, you'll look after him really well, won't you?'

'A-huh.'

Max is fully committed, as only a pre-schooler can be.

A carefully slips two of Max's little pudgy fingers into the puppet. Once it's secure, **A** gives Pandy a little goodbye kiss and feels something in his heart slip away.

Please let this work.

There's a gentle lurch and rumble as the engine picks up and the trolley starts to move. The bags shake as they travel, but the cave is secure.

On the iPad, **A** sees Max in his hospital bed. Medical staff leaning over him. They flit in and out of the scene. There's rushed movement and an escalating flurry.

The baggage trolley swerves and enters the concourse. The sliding doors whirring open unlock the noise of the terminal.

Among the clatter of passengers milling about and the flight announcements, **A** hears the handler from his driver's seat, 'Steady now.'

F-LIGHT

As the baggage train chugs through the terminal concourse, **A** shifts around and finds a marginally larger slot between the bags for him to look out. Flickering past him are rows of people on their phones, sitting with their carry-on luggage awaiting their flight. Some are lying across seats, others have their arms crossed and are resting their head on the shoulder of their companion; all of them are engrossed in the PFEC app.

From **A**'s vantage point, he sees a steward's neat blue slacks, walking alongside keeping pace with the trolley. The steward snipes, 'Why did you come out with it still half full?'

A waits for the handler's answer.

'Did you hear me?'

A imagines the activity outside, the handler's imperious face, staring straight ahead with both hands on the wheel.

The steward continues, 'You're supposed to empty the trolley, so why come out with it half full?'

No response.

A hears another steward join them. It's a woman's voice, but over the noise of the terminal **A** can't make out what she's saying. The trolley starts to slow down… then stops. **A**'s heart is racing.

Is this the drop-off?

A squints through the gap but can't see any departure gates. It looks as though the handler's pulled up outside a café.

Is this the closest he can get?

As the handler shuffles past **A**'s peephole, **A** sees the two stewards walking alongside the handler, invading his space. The male steward has a ratty, pointed chin, while the woman's wide forehead is accentuated by her hair being pulled back in a fierce bun.

The handler collects a couple of abandoned bags as the stewards raise their voices with their badgering questions.

'Why'd you pick those up?' The rat steward snatches the bags out of the handler's grip, 'It's not your job.'

The woman quips, 'You're supposed to drop them off, not pick them up.'

From inside his cave **A** sees the handler blink repeatedly, exposing a staccato nervous twitch.

Is he giving me a cue?

The rat-face steward continues, 'Do not take it upon yourself to pick up bags.'

'Simply collect it from the designated pick-up points. Is that clear?' The handler offers no reply, so she continues to pester, 'Answer the question.'

The handler backs away and returns to his driver's seat, his face set with determination. A moment later **A** hears the engine turn over. The baggage trolley rolls out.

The rat steward scuttles up to the front, 'We will not be ignored.'

The baggage cart's puttering engine shifts up a notch… then another… The rat-faced steward is jogging to keep pace with the trolley. 'Stop this minute! Do you hear me?' The motorised whir becomes more and more high pitched as the handler shifts up gears.

Through his cave peephole, **A** sees the rat steward running, but he's not fast enough. Beyond him, there's a blur of passengers. The

Irish Pub with its fake wood entrance zips past.

Was that the waitress? Please say yes.

The chasing steward is shrill, 'Stop right now!'

The handler is heading towards the departure gates. People ambling along the concourse must hustle to get out of his way. Hitting top speed and fanging it through the airport, the handler honks his baggage cart. It sounds like a road-train horn, thunderous and wildly inappropriate.

The commotion of the stewards chasing the handler's train and the rumpus of his trolley gets people up on their feet. The terminal PA announces, 'For your personal safety and that of those around you, please minimise unnecessary movement and remain at your allocated departure gate.'

But the passengers ignore the warning and start to follow the baggage train. The handler's trolley commotion is gaining momentum.

Inside the cave, **A**'s heart is racing and his body tingling, but then he realises it is in fact his phone.

What the fuck? Why's it buzzing now!?

A pulls it out of his pocket. The PFEC 'View now' notification is blinking at him.

Do I...?

A stares at the screen, unsure what to do. Without hesitation, Max's pudgy little hand reaches over and taps the button.

A's back inside the hospital, trapped in his body. Nina holds his hand as the sunrise seeps through the window.

Oh, fuck no.

Ella's sitting on Nina's lap. Louie is staring intently at something above the bedhead. **A** wants to turn around and find out what it is, but his body is like a brick.

Is it the doctor turning it all off? Please, no. Wait, for fuck's sake. WAIT!

Inside the cave, the loud beep of Max's iPad cuts through. **A** swivels around and sees frantic medical staff orbiting Max's hospital bed. **A** overcomes the urge to watch more of his family by shoving his phone back into his pocket.

I am sending Max through those gates. That's all that matters.

Beeeep...

Max's monitor is flat lining.

It's all happening too soon.

With controlled panic, nurses place defibrillator pads on Max's chest. 'One one thousand...'

A yells out, 'Stop! Stop! I've got to go now!'

The handler hits the breaks. Bags fly off the roof. Light streams in. **A** swings Max up onto his back, like he's throwing a jockey onto a horse, smashes through the luggage and launches them out of the cave.

The trolley is higher off the ground than **A** anticipated. He flies through the air, with bags scattering around him. Everything feels like it's in extreme slow motion. **A**'s going top speed, but each step takes an eon.

As he crashes down to earth, Max's bodyweight throws **A** off kilter, but he bounces off a bag which helps him stay upright, and he hits the ground running.

The departure gates are forty metres away, flanked by rows of people waiting to be processed. Three oafish stewards, who look more like security guards than airport staff, file the passengers through, repeating the ritual of scanning tickets, taking personal items and then ushering them through the swing-doors.

'Step aside ALL of YOU!' The handler sounds like the MGM

lion roaring, as he cuts in front of **A**. Driving his cart like a Chinese New Year dragon, he weaves it through the crowd, and clears a path for **A** to slip-stream behind.

We can do this!

From out of nowhere a stocky, bulldog-looking steward makes a diving tackle on the handler. The impact is so violent that the handler's body looks like it's snapped, as his face smashes against the dashboard. It's brutal. On-lookers are immediately incensed and rush to his defence, pushing and shoving the bulldog steward. Bags are thrown, punches too.

Among the chaos, **A** hears on Max's iPad the clinical charge of the defibrillator and the medical procedural call, 'Two one thousand.'

A avoids the baggage cart battle and runs to the gates.

Swept up in the moment, wearing his Buzz Lightyear space cape, Max shouts, 'To infinity and beyond!'

His high-pitched battle cry pierces through the riot. The lunacy of a middle-aged man carrying a kid with a bunch of drawings pinned to his blanket, running headlong at three enormous guards, inspires the mob. They shift their focus from the trolley cart and join **A** and Max charging forward. A bunch of backpackers hurl themselves at the three gigantic stewards, trying to smash their way through, but the stewards are monolithic and unflinching.

Like a teeming mosh pit, **A**'s stuck a couple of rows from the front.

'So, you found the handler.'

'What?'

A spins around. In the middle of the insanity, is the waitress and Tye. **A**'s stunned, 'Are you kidding me?'

The waitress grins.

Tye locks an arm around **A**'s waist. 'You ready for this?'

'I can't believe—'

'Let's do this!'

Arm in arm they make a three-person wall, with **A** in the centre and Max on his back. The crowd behaves like a wave. It pushes up against the stewards, gets repelled, regroups and surges again. The waitress yells out, 'Go straight down the middle!'

The crowd compresses and stampedes towards the middle steward.

Slicing through the chaos, **A** hears on Max's iPad, 'Clear.' Followed by the pop of the defibrillator.

The sheer weight of numbers is too much for the steward. As he tries to shove them away **A** sees a gap and ducks down.

'Have we got a pulse?' 'No...' 'And again.' 'Copy. One, one thousand.'

Tye gets down on his knees and makes himself into a ball so his back becomes a boulder which the waitress uses as a launch pad. She takes a running jump off and throws herself at the middle guard. Spread-eagled, she yells out, 'Now!!!'

As she crashes into him, **A** commando crawls past with Max still hanging on. The departure gate is within reach.

We can do this!

Beeeeeeeeeep.

A hears his own flat-lining monitor. He grabs his phone out of his pocket and sees Nina gently kiss his lips.

Slow.

Warped.

Time.

A shoves open the departure gates as Max is wrenched off his back. **A** spins around, trying to hold onto him. Max is screaming as the steward rips off his Buzz Lightyear cape and tosses the iPad away.

A lunges after him. 'I'm not letting you go!'

But the guard's too strong, he drags **A** and Max back from the departure gate, knocking **A**'s phone out of his hand in the process.

The waitress runs up from behind and throws herself at the steward as Tye shoulder-charges into his guts. The steward wrestles the waitress away and punches Tye, but in doing so releases **A**.

Off-balance and with Max still clinging on, **A** stumbles towards the departure gates, and falls through.

The ground slips away.

'Fuck YES!!!'

A sees the waitress standing on the edge, with her arms raised, triumphant. Max and **A** are on the other side.

As they fall, Max lets go of **A**.

'No!'

A snatches at Max's hand, 'Come back!' but the momentum of them tumbling down pulls them apart. As they separate, pandy slips off Max's fingers and into **A**'s grasp.

Max is gone. It's terrifying. **A** didn't see his face before they separated and can't hear his monitor. There is no connection left.

High above them, the waitress and Tye are standing on the edge of the doorway as the departure gates swing shut.

*

A can't feel anything beyond the sensation of continuously sinking down which shifts into no sensation at all and becomes an airy stillness that's open and vacant and builds as though the whiteness is folding over itself, and amongst it all **A** can't sense any part of himself. He knows he's in this void but there's nothing to indicate his presence beyond his one repeating thought,

Let Max live.
It sits with **A**. Timeless. Motionless.

Please...

301

Whatever time has passed is impossible to know. And yet, within the blanketing silence, **A** hears a little fragrance of a sound.

He picks up on it immediately.

What was that? A breath? In and out? Yes! A little boy's breath? Definitely!

A hears laughter.

Joyous and indisputable.

He's alive...

Max is alive!

This revelation, like mist rolling in, rests on **A**. He feels himself taking shape and spiralling into form, like water swirling down a drain, and within this motion he feels Nina, Louie and Ella tornado around him as he's pulled down and sucked in, and all he wants is to return to them, but it's unclear how, and as the sensation gains momentum, changing from a sinking feeling to a guttural skydiving plummet, **A** feels as though he could be syphoned into any number of lives.

He shifts around. He doesn't want to fall backwards; he wants to be headfirst. To hit this next life head-on, or better still return to the one he already had.

*

If this is his last sunrise, its only significance is its timing, and now, after all this, Nina is finished. She is done with the whole thing: the hospital, the driving, the tests and questions. Enough. The shutdown has begun, and nothing matters.

But her memories steamroll through, curling in and branching out.

His face when she told him she was pregnant. Opening every

window and door irrespective of the time or the weather. Always giving her the aisle seat. Continually cooking on the highest heat, so everything was burnt and raw. His looseness, maddening and myopic. A defuser and agitator.

Louie is mumbling a little chant, repeating it under his breath, 'Please, Dad, please come home.'

And then it stops. The last machine. The sounds of the devices keeping the air moving and his heart beating, stop.

Nina bottoms out. She can't feel the kids or herself, she just hears the lack of machines.

She takes her cue from Louie and starts whispering, 'Come home.'

Over and over. Her cheek is resting on his brow, so her lips are by his ear. Barely audible, just loud enough for her to hear something other than the silence of the stopped machines, 'Please come home.'

*

Whether I face forward or not doesn't matter, it's like perpetual turbulence, falling and falling and not getting anywhere... How long has it been? How can I tell...? But... is there something underneath? Something inside all this noise. Shut up wind, and let me hear what's going on. Is that a sound? It is. I'm sure it is, it's... it's like a beacon. Maybe that's enough to get me home. I could hear Max and his folks, so maybe all those trinkets worked like Ella's panda... but what is it?

It sounds so guttural and...

Is it Nina...? Or another woman...?

Hang on... am I hearing a mother giving birth? To me!?

'Ahhh!'

Can I yell? Can I change my direction? Does the yelling shift my trajectory?

If I, 'Ahhhhhhhhhhh.'

Did that make me move? Left maybe?

Is it Nina? Or a woman birthing? Or crying? She's saying something, is she talking to me? She's over 'THERE.'

Am I closer? I think yelling helps. There's that groan again; it's definitely closer now and it's raw. I haven't heard that since Nina giving birth and please no, really no. I'm not ready for some new life, I want to go home.

'Ahhhhhhhhhh!'

'Home.'

Did she say that? Home? Did I hear you say home, Kinki? Where are you?

I've got to control this, and maybe… Hang on. If I make my yell more like an,

'Ommmmmmmmmm.'

That's it. The lower the om, the more of a shift…

'Ommmmmmmmmmmmmmmmmmmmmmmmmmmm.'

It's like a plane, like a glider! I think the oms can move me towards that whisper.

It's got to be Nina… There's three-hundred and sixty thousand…

'Ooooooooommmmmmm.'

…babies born every day. I remember Ella telling me that. Was it Ella? Or Louie?

Focus. Stay focused.

'Ommmmmmmmmm.'

I'm going to do this, I am. I'm just going to,

'Ommmmmmmmmmm.'

So, this is meditation? Am I learning now… the timing's a bit late, or perhaps it's perfect, or better still just shut the fuck up, Adam. What!? Adam? Did I just say my name to myself? Wow… Adam.

I'm Adam. I'm,
'Adammmmmmmmmmmmmmmmmmmm.'
To the birthing woman, 'I'm not your child.'
'Ommmmmmmmmmmmmmm.'
Come on, Nina, where are you? Can you hear me? Am I getting closer?
'Ommmmmmmmmmmmmmmmmmmmmmmmmmmmmmmmmm.'
What is that? Is it a colour? The speed of it, it's...? I can't change it, I can't. Fuck!
This is it, whatever's—

*

He cramps in a full-body lock, waiting for impact.

But then he realises he can feel his limbs.

And a weight upon his chest.

He slowly opens his eyes. Everything is vague and blurry. Among the duskiness he sees three figures shift back a fraction, as though they felt him jolt and spark.

Silhouetted against the grey light, they take shape.

Nina.

Louie.

Ella.

Yes...

Shawline Publishing Group Pty Ltd
www.shawlinepublishing.com.au

SHAWLINE
PUBLISHING
GROUP

More great Shawline titles can be found by scanning the QR code below.
New titles also available through Books@Home Pty Ltd.
Subscribe today at www.booksathome.com.au or scan the QR code below.

Ingram Content Group UK Ltd.
Milton Keynes UK
UKHW041105260723
425806UK00004B/66